P9-CFU-154

## Praise for *Second Sunrise*

"*Second Sunrise* is a fantastic blend of reality and the supernatural. Lee Nez makes it easy to suspend doubt and believe in 'skinwalkers' and 'nightwalkers.' My only complaint: having to wait for the next installment."
—*Romantic Times Bookclub*

"An entertaining start to a new mystery series." —*Locus*

## Praise for the Ella Clah novels

"Gripping. A spirited blend of Navajo culture and police procedure." —*Booklist* (starred review) on *Tracking Bear*

"Realistic, fast-paced, and intense. Action scenes keep the plot moving at a quick pace with some surprises along the way, adding to the excitement."
—*School Library Journal* on *Changing Woman*

"*Red Mesa* is an engrossing mystery as intricately woven as a fine Navajo rug. It kept me guessing to the end."
—*New York Times* bestselling author Margaret Coel

"Prime reading for fans of Tony Hillerman and other Southwestern mysteries." —*Library Journal* on *Red Mesa*

WITHDRAWN
Sno-Isle Libraries

## ALSO BY AIMÉE & DAVID THURLO

# Second Sunrise

A LEE NEZ NOVEL

## DAVID & AIMÉE THURLO

A Tom Doherty Associates Book / New York

NOTE: If you purchased this book without a cover, you should be aware that this book is stolen property. It was reported as "unsold and destroyed" to the publisher, and neither the author nor the publisher has received any payment for this "stripped book."

This is a work of fiction. All the characters and events portrayed in this book are either products of the author's imagination or are used fictitiously.

SECOND SUNRISE: A LEE NEZ NOVEL

Copyright © 2002 by David & Aimee Thurlo

All rights reserved, including the right to reproduce this book, or portions thereof, in any form.

A Tor Book
Published by Tom Doherty Associates, LLC
175 Fifth Avenue
New York, NY 10010

www.tor.com

Tor® is a registered trademark of Tom Doherty Associates, LLC.

ISBN 0-765-34367-3
EAN 976-0765-34367-3

First edition: November 2002
First mass market edition: November 2004

Printed in the United States of America

0  9  8  7  6  5  4  3  2

To Harry David Thurlo,
who began his World War II
service to our country handling
the bombs and shells stored at
Fort Wingate, New Mexico

## ACKNOWLEDGMENTS

Beginning with Bram Stoker, writers have been keeping the undead alive in our imaginations by adding their tales to the vampire legend. These stories, plus rumors of skinwalkers that reached the curious mind of a young man growing up on the Navajo Nation, inspired us in our creation of the Lee Nez novels.

## CHAPTER 1

State Policeman Lee Nez shifted into high gear as his shiny black Chevy department cruiser topped the hill preceding Mesa Montañosa thirty-five miles east of Fort Wingate. The army had an ordnance storage facility there, beside the railroad tracks, where bombs and shells were kept in rows of bunkers.

As the war in Europe raged on, the enlistment of regular state police officers into the military had left many vacancies open and had given him the opportunity he'd dreamed of—an appointment as a state patrolman. Trained on the job, he was the first Navajo state policeman.

Of course, it didn't hurt that his mother and father had connections in Albuquerque, where both taught at the Indian School. Lee knew that it was their association with the pueblo governors and politicians in Santa Fe that had made the difference.

Now Lee was training a newly appointed officer, Patrolman Benito Mondragon. Benny was tall and thin, nearly six feet four, a full four inches taller than Lee. Benny, a full year younger than Lee, had a wife and young son and was quiet on the job except when asking a question about work, or occasionally bragging about his boy. From what Lee could tell so far, Benny's greatest asset was that he was a quick study.

It was a cool March evening, and the ground was drying out from a late-winter snowstorm. The worn, rutted narrow asphalt highway was dangerous to drive over forty-five in many stretches now, especially the closer one got to Fort Wingate, which had its share of large army convoys.

"Officer Nez?" Benny's voice was a bit high-pitched, and Lee had advised him to lower it by an octave whenever possible when speaking to the public so he'd sound older and more experienced.

Lee glanced at the rookie. The cap with the shiny black bill was the same as his, but only served to make him appear even taller. His size and build were imposing, something that would serve the patrolman well when he was out on his own.

"Do you think we're ever going to get the authority to stop drivers from going over the posted speed?"

"That all depends on the governor and the state legislature. Right now, all we can do is report them to their local rationing board, which has the authority to keep them from getting any more gas ration cards."

"But if the driver is related to the local head of the board, like that trading-post operator near Gallup, the whole thing falls apart," Officer Mondragon replied.

"What I hate most is investigating cases like a local farmer who had his farm equipment's gasoline siphoned off. You go into it knowing what happened. The gas got stolen so a black-marketeer could sell it, say, in Albuquerque."

"My cousin's neighbor discovered he can make more money selling gas than by planting corn or beans."

The Chevy was running hot tonight. Lee could feel the

heat coming through the thin fire wall. That always seemed to come with being low man on the totem pole—a phrase his *bilagáana* (white) sergeant used to remind Lee why he usually got the worst-maintained equipment.

He thought about the canvas water bag they carried on the front bumper. It provided radiator water almost as much as drinking water lately, and it wasn't even the hot time of year yet.

"Always make sure your vehicle is in good shape and ready for emergencies before you go out onto the open road. In the winter, or during the rainy season where so many low spots are filled with water, it could mean your life," Lee said.

Most state patrolmen were on their own, with backup maybe hours away. Telephones in the scattered communities blessed with phone service were their only method of communication. State police cruisers were going to be equipped with radios after the war, so the rumors went, but that could take another year.

Lee loved his job and the opportunity to get off the Reservation and mix with the *bilagáanas* and his pueblo brothers farther down the Rio Grande River. Navajos and Mexican-Americans were treated like second-class citizens in *bilagáana* areas, but with the war going on, local racial tensions had taken a backseat to other nationalities currently at the top of the hate list, like Krauts and Japs.

A police officer wearing the well-known charcoal black uniform with gray pockets and stripes down the pants, with a .45 Colt revolver on his hip, commanded respect. They were exceptions, of course. Drunk G.I.s on a weekend pass could become belligerent, but most locals, him included, usually gave them the benefit of the doubt, not wanting to appear unpatriotic.

Coming around a sharp curve in the road, Lee slowed to twenty-five.

"Deer-crossing area, right?" Benny asked.

Mule deer crossed here from the thick juniper and piñon forest down to the marsh along the arroyo bottom to his right, the north side of the narrow highway.

"Whoa!" Lee slammed on the brakes just in time as three does bounded down the hill onto the road. The last one darted to the side, narrowly missing the left fender of the cruiser.

"Navajo Ways tell us not to climb a hill or the deer will see us. I think he saw us."

"Saw us? We almost had venison tonight." Benny laughed.

"I'm just grateful I don't have to explain the crumpled fender to Sergeant Burkholder, or worse, scrape meat on the hoof from the seat cushions while picking windshield glass from our foreheads."

Glancing into his rearview mirror, though he knew heading into the curve that no vehicle had been close, Lee shifted down into low gear and picked up speed from the lugging engine.

"Damn bladder. I never should have had that second cup of coffee in Grants." Benny moaned, stretching his legs in agony.

"Rookie," Lee said, chuckling. He waited until he was on a straight and level stretch of highway again, then pulled over. He hadn't wanted to be the first to complain, but the truth was, he had to go himself before he exploded.

"I'll get a flashlight." Benny grabbed the light from the glove compartment, then opened his door and left in a hurry.

Lee took a quick glance around before deciding to step outside. After hours spent staring through the twin cones from his headlights onto the empty road, his night vision was poor, and he waited for his eyes to adjust.

The road looked clear in both directions. Except for the railroad tracks a few miles to his right and one adobe farmhouse several miles back, this section of New Mexico was desolate, occupied only by a few head of cattle, mule deer, and rabbits.

Noting where Benny had gone by the beam of the flashlight, Lee climbed down the road embankment until he was behind a large juniper twenty feet away from the other officer. Nobody could see them from the road, even if they happened to come along at this late hour. It was nearly eleven-thirty, he knew by estimating their travel time from Grants.

When he was done relieving himself, Lee turned and climbed back up the slope to the cruiser where Benny was standing, waiting.

Suddenly there was a loud pop, and the screech of tires somewhere east, coming from the direction of Fort Wingate. Several more loud bangs could be heard, echoing down the low valley from the nearby mesas.

"What the hell was that?" Benny said, looking down the road.

"Gunfire," Lee said, jumping back inside the cruiser. "Hurry up. Let's go." As Benny climbed inside, Lee heard the rattle of automatic weapons fire.

"Hijacking?" Benny asked, his voice higher than before.

Lee shrugged. "Maybe it's black-market hoods. I wish we had a two-way radio or a telephone nearby."

Now that Prohibition had been repealed, Lee had heard that some of the gangsters had taken to stealing government supplies. Instead of selling booze, they stole gasoline and anything else that could turn a profit. But they wouldn't dare hijack an army truck this close to a military post, would they?

As he drove down the highway, Lee decided against using the emergency lights and siren. "We're going for a silent approach because we need an advantage, and I'm keeping our headlights off so we'll keep our night vision. Take your extra ammunition out of your belt loops and put it in your pocket where it'll be handy."

Rolling down the window, Lee drove as fast as he dared, listening for the sounds of gunshots, trying to gauge their distance. They were much louder now, and more than one automatic weapon was being used.

Mentally adding up their combat potential, Lee knew he and Officer Mondragon each had twenty-four rounds for the Colt New Service revolvers, and there were another sixteen rounds in a bandoleer for the twelve-gauge shotgun under the seat.

He'd give Benny the shotgun, and stick to his own unofficial .30-30 Winchester lever action that he kept rolled up in a blanket in the trunk. He was a crack shot, and that would help their odds.

What Lee feared most was that by the time they arrived, only the bad guys would still be standing.

Lee knew they were close when he heard shouts as clearly as the bursts of gunfire. Lee had been in a gunfight before, but it was with a drunk miner who'd just shot his wife and her boyfriend. The sum total of Benny's on-duty experience with violence was being roughed up in a bar melee his first week on the job.

Lee killed the engine, put the car out of gear, and

coasted to a narrow cut in the road flanked by high ground covered with junipers.

Lee held up his hand, signaling the rookie to remain quiet. The shooting had stopped for the moment and stealth would be their greatest asset. Both of them checked their jacket pockets again for extra pistol rounds and the rookie hooked a flashlight into his Sam Browne belt.

Lee reached down to the floorboard and unfastened the shotgun and its belt of extra rounds, being careful not to bump the barrel and make a metallic clank, then handed it to Benny butt end first. Then, coordinating the opening of their doors, they slipped out in unison.

Lee moved quickly to the rear of the Chevy, unlocked the trunk, and lifted out the blanket containing his rifle and ammunition. He unwrapped the blanket quickly, catching the hammer on the cloth for a moment in his haste.

"*Ch'i'idii!*" he muttered, and Benny laughed silently, though Lee could see he was shaking like a leaf.

Suddenly there was a flurry of shots just over the crest of the hill, followed by shouts. The words had sounded like German, but he couldn't be sure. Lee suddenly remembered a recent briefing by his captain. The state police had been warned that some kind of top-secret military operation was going on northwest of Santa Fe. This operation was so big that convoys would just disappear into the mountains. The entire area was off-limits and under constant military patrols.

"Germans?" Benny mouthed.

Lee shook his head, dismissing the notion of German spies as a movie plot from the matinee at Albuquerque's Kimo theater. He lowered the trunk lid, but didn't risk the noise of closing it. Then Lee motioned for Benny to follow as he moved into the tree line to his right. His heart was pounding so loud Lee felt as if it could be heard a mile away.

Benny, ten feet behind him, stepped on a branch and it crackled loudly. Lee froze, turned around, and scowled at the rookie. Benny mouthed a silent "Sorry," then fell into step behind Lee once more.

Just before reaching the crest of the low hill, Lee lowered himself slowly to the ground and crawled on his belly the last several feet.

He turned halfway and signaled for Benny, who was also prone, to hold his position.

A yellow flare was lying on the road, burning brightly enough to reveal what lay below. On the highway, blocking the entire road, was an overturned flatbed truck, its cargo of firewood scattered around like a giant box of kitchen matches. An olive-drab Jeep, probably the lead vehicle in the small convoy, had its canvas overhead cover riddled with bullets, and was skewed sideways among the firewood. The driver wasn't moving, and Lee could see a dark, bloody splotch below his throat.

The second vehicle in the column was a Dodge weapons carrier. Its windshield was riddled with bullet holes. About ten feet away was a General Motors deuce and a half cargo truck.

A second Jeep, closest to Lee, was on its side in the ditch, the body of a soldier pinned underneath. Another German-sounding word was shouted from somewhere across the road. Lee spotted a tall, lean man with a cap standing beside the trunk of a juniper, aiming a bolt-action hunting rifle at someone below.

The rifleman fired a shot at the weapons carrier and Lee

saw someone move inside the rear of the vehicle. A pistol appeared and two shots were fired in rapid succession toward the tree line.

At least one of the soldiers was still alive, but seeing the man wearing the cap reloading, Lee brought up his rifle.

As Lee placed the rifleman's head in his sights, he heard a low scraping sound, and turned his head to look. Benny had worked his way up to the crest of the hill.

Lee looked back, and saw the rifleman looking right at them. Benny fired. The double-aught buckshot struck the tree beside the German and bark exploded from the trunk.

Lee snapped off a quick shot, but the German was already moving and he missed. Lee rolled to his left, glancing over at his trainee. Benny rose up slightly to feed another round into the shotgun, and an ugly hole appeared just beside his nose. He trembled slightly for a second, then his head dropped, the shotgun tumbling down the slope.

"Benny!" Lee fired three rounds as quickly as he could, aiming instinctively at the rifleman, who was crouched down, apparently trying to clear a jammed cartridge. The rifleman's head quivered as at least one bullet struck him squarely, and he crumpled forward onto his face, dropping the rifle.

"Yeehaw! Got that bastard," a soldier in the weapons carrier yelled in a West Texas accent. He poked his head out from behind cover and fired a burst from a submachine gun at a spot just to the right of the overturned Jeep.

Lee heard a man groan, then saw a body fall onto the highway. The rifle the wounded man was holding clattered onto the gravel beside the road.

Lee crawled a few more feet and glanced at what was left of his partner. Benny had died instantly, at least that was a blessing. Sudden anger for the ones who'd done this left a bitter taste in his mouth. Benny's boy would grow up without his father.

At that instant, he heard footsteps behind him, and he rolled right. A bullet impacted six inches from his head, cutting his face with sand and shattered rock. Rolling back to his left, he drew his Colt and fired twice at the figure, who was feeding another round into his lever-action weapon.

The man dropped forward, striking the ground right at Lee's feet.

Rolling back to his right, Lee picked up his rifle, jammed his Colt back into the holster, and sprinted to some boulders about fifteen yards away. There was good cover there on three sides.

As Lee drew close, he discovered the spot was already occupied. A man whirled just as Lee raised his rifle, and fired a shotgun blast at the same time Lee pulled the trigger.

Lee was spun around as if struck by the horn of a charging bull. The pain was instantaneous and hotter than a branding iron. Lee was surprised he could still see and think as he lay there on the ground, but one glance told him the man with the shotgun was out of action for good.

"Hey, buddy, you still there?" the soldier in the weapons carrier called out. His voice sounded faint now, and Lee realized that the G.I. was probably wounded as well.

Lee managed to sit up. His side was wet with blood and ached like sin, but at least he could move. Getting to his knees, he found his rifle and levered in another round.

Swallowing hard, he pulled himself together, loading more cartridges into the rifle while he had the chance. He wanted to answer the soldier, but to do so now would reveal his position. His side screamed out in pain, worse than the time the mustang had broken three of his ribs.

"We were ambushed. I've been hit, but I'll cover you," the Texas boy yelled, his voice giving way to a wet-sounding cough at the end. "Check across the road."

Lee remained hidden, searching back and forth for signs of movement, or someone else with more patience waiting him out. But the soldier down in the Dodge was sounding pretty rough now, and Lee knew he needed medical attention.

Inching forward a few steps at a time, then stopping behind cover to watch, Lee checked out his side of the road carefully. He found another attacker's body riddled with bullets. As his angle of view changed, Lee spotted another soldier crumpled alongside the cargo truck, a carbine on the road beside his body. This soldier was probably lucky enough to take someone with him when he died.

Lee was numb now, not so afraid of dying anymore. If he was going to face death, it was going to be as a warrior, not in his sleep or in a head-on collision.

He moved in a crouch down the slope and onto the road, keeping his Winchester at his shoulder, ready to react and fire if he heard a sound. As he approached the wounded soldier, he called out softly. "I'm a New Mexico state patrolman, soldier. I'll get some help for us."

## CHAPTER 2

Lee climbed up the slope on the far side, found another dead attacker, and saw two more dead G.I.s who'd tried to get off the road and apparently encountered this man. The first man Lee had shot, the sniper with the bolt-action rifle who'd killed Benny, was lying there, motionless. Nobody could survive a bullet to the brain.

"Don't shoot. I'm coming over," Lee yelled, then stumbled back down onto the road. Up close he could see that the weapons carrier was riddled with bullet holes and reeked of gasoline. At least the flare, which had died down now, was fifty feet away and a slight breeze was dispersing the fumes.

The olive-drab canvas top was holed like Swiss cheese. A prone, light-haired young man with a bloody streak across his face peeked over the punctured side-mounted spare tire. Lee could see the stubby barrel of the weapon he'd heard others call a grease gun. "Lucky you have that black uniform on. The first bastard you hit was a crack shot." He coughed and a trace of foamy blood leaked from the side of his mouth.

Lee leaned his Winchester against the side of the spare

tire, and took a step closer. The solider had two silver bars on his shoulder and that made him an officer, but he wasn't more than twenty years old, if that.

"Captain, do you have a first-aid kit?"

"First Lieutenant Billy Ray Barnett, from Amarillo, Texas. I'm way past first aid." His accent was less noticeable with his voice just a whisper now. He coughed again, then wiped his mouth with a sleeve. "Any G.I.s make it?"

"I don't think so." Lee hadn't heard or seen movement from any of them. "I'll take a closer look as soon as we fix you up."

"Our cargo . . . in the six-by. It can't fall into their hands. Take it away and bury it. Germans tried to get us to surrender. Said they had reinforcements on the way." Lieutenant Barnett gasped, coughing again, spitting up blood.

"These weren't hijackers, were they?" Lee looked down the road in both directions. No headlights were visible.

"German spies . . . after what we've got in the truck. New secret weapon. Very dangerous. Up to you, now. What's your name, Officer?"

"Patrolman Lee Nez, Lieutenant. You said your attackers were expecting reinforcements?"

"Could have been a lie, but they must have a vehicle nearby, and maybe a driver. Can't let them take our cargo."

Barnett coughed, his body shaking, and Lee thought he was going to die right then. Finally the lieutenant looked up again, his eyes tired. "Must be a traitor, or somebody talked. They knew to hit us tonight. Hide the gray metal box where it can't be found. Bury it to keep it safe. Don't open the box. Too dangerous."

"You come with me, sir. I can't leave you." Lee reached for Barnett.

"No. I'll stay here with my men. If more Germans show up, I'll keep them busy. Just go . . ."

The lieutenant gasped once, and the light in his eyes faded.

"Barnett?" Lee recognized the glazed look, he'd seen it in accident victims. As a Navajo, he'd always been taught that when people died, they left their *chindi*, the evil part of them behind, and that ghostlike presence was dangerous no matter how good the person had been when alive. Even Benny Mondragon . . .

Standing, he looked around once more, knowing that if there really were *chindis*, he was standing in a whole crowd of evil beings. Reaching into his pocket, he touched his medicine pouch. The corn pollen and special stones within had always protected him, and he assumed that would be true now as well. But it was better not to put it to the test. He had to go, and unless he completed the task the dying officer had given him, he knew there was one *chindi* that was going to be out to kick his ass. These G.I.s, and Officer Benito Mondragon, weren't going to die for nothing.

Holding his side, Lee walked over to the cab of the GMC.

Ten minutes later, Lee was driving west in the big deuce and a half, as the two-and-a-half-ton ten-wheeled cargo truck was nicknamed. Dizzy now from loss of blood, he was going as fast as he dared with the lights out, hoping that he'd bypass and outrun the rest of the Germans even if they'd been hiding farther west.

He'd found a first-aid pouch with dressings in the cab of the truck and bound up his wounds as best he could, but there were six or seven angry buckshot holes, and they continued to bleed. He knew there were some small caves off the road beyond Thoreau, a small community mostly north of the highway. If he could find a hole, he'd hide the secret weapon . . . if he could hang on.

Lee woke with a start when the truck hit a rock, and realized within the haze that he'd drifted off again. He vaguely remembered having hidden the box in a small cave or animal den beneath an overhanging cliff somewhere back there, and filling the hole with rocks and dirt. But right now he was exhausted, too weak to sit up without leaning into the steering wheel.

He tapped the brakes, and the truck slowed nearly to a stop, still in low gear. The highway was just ahead, clear in both directions. He turned west onto the asphalt, managing to find the next gear. It would be at least an hour before he reached Fort Wingate.

Soon he lost track of time again, his eyes opening and closing and his arms so weak he was barely hanging on to the steering wheel. Lee knew he wouldn't make it. He might as well just pull over to the side of the road. At least nobody else would run into him or, worse, get hit by the heavy truck.

Then Lee remembered that a member of his clan, a Navajo medicine man or *hataalii* everyone called Bowlegs, lived just off the highway somewhere near here. He pulled off the road, trying to think of where he was now. Noting the width of the valley to his right, he decided that Bowlegs lived in the other direction.

Bowlegs could be trusted to tend his wounds, and might even be able to hide the truck. Even in his hazy present condition, Lee still knew the road between Grants and Gallup like the back of his hand, and the hogan of Bowlegs was just five minutes back east. He'd passed it a while ago. If he'd been thinking clearly, he would have headed there before and saved himself some time.

Struggling to stay conscious, Lee turned the truck around, then shifted into low to urge the powerful vehicle up the steep hill. Beyond was the medicine man. He served many Navajos in the Fort Wingate area, and not only healed the spirits of the *Dineh*, the Navajo people, but also their bodies.

The truck was finally gaining speed again as it reached the crest of the hill, and Lee was looking ahead when he suddenly noticed a car in the middle of the road. Lights started flashing, and Lee realized it was some kind of policeman.

Lee slammed on the brakes, and the truck skidded another fifteen feet before stopping just an arm's length from the black car. It had to be a cop from Gallup.

Breathing a sigh of relief for the first time in what seemed like hours, Lee leaned out the window. "Military convoy was ambushed. My partner is dead. I need your help."

Then he recognized the black Chevrolet. It was his own patrol car.

Lee fumbled for his Colt. Someone leaped out of the dark like a mountain lion and grabbed him by the neck, pulling him out the open truck window as if he were a rag doll, then tossing him to the pavement. As Lee gasped for breath, trying to sit up, the man searched the back of the truck, then returned.

"What did you do with the big gray box that was in that truck, policeman?" The man gripped Lee by the collar and shook him roughly.

The man was tall and slender, and the clothes looked familiar, especially the cap. A dark stain ran down the man's nose, and was smeared along his chin. The man's eyes were so light they nearly glowed in the moonlight. Then Lee's heart nearly stopped. "*Chindi!* You're dead. You killed Benny." His voice strained as he struggled to speak past the iron grip of the supernatural being now holding him.

"You're Indian, aren't you, cop? Afraid of ghosts?"

The voice was mocking, just as he'd expected from a ghost. He'd never believed much in the stories about evil spirits of the dead, but now one was staring him right in the eye. He tried to break loose, but he couldn't even get his arms free. The *chindi* had supernatural strength.

"You *are* dead. *Chindi*, get away from me! I have strong protection. Flint!" Lee groped around for his medicine pouch.

"I'm much more than a ghost, Indian, and I can pull your arms off if I decide. And I just might do that if you don't tell me where you took the cargo from that truck."

Lee couldn't draw in a full breath. His side was on fire and everything around him seemed to be fading away. He would pass out soon, then he'd die. The German *chindi* wouldn't get a thing from him. "Go fuck yourself," he said, and as the darkness began to close in on him, he waited for oblivion.

## CHAPTER 3

Y ou're not dying on me yet," the *chindi* said, shaking him. "What in the hell did you do with the cargo the G.I.s were transporting?"

Lee opened his eyes, and the German *chindi* was less than a foot from his face. He could smell coffee on the creature's breath, for some reason, but his other senses were about to leave him. His whole body felt numb and cold. He *was* going to die. Accepting it became freeing. If he was going to die, at least he was going out honorably as a Navajo warrior.

"I shot you in the forehead. You can't be human." Lee knew the being was supernatural, and his strength and speed were unbelievable.

"Okay, I'm a shindy, if that makes you happy. And I will pull you apart like a rag doll unless you tell me what you did with that box! Where in the hell did you go in that truck?"

The evil one grabbed Lee's arm, and squeezed it like a vise. Lee bit his lip, refusing to scream. "What does it take to kill you?"

The evil one spoke softly. "You'll never know. Now tell

me, you pathetic weakling, before I start removing your fingers, one by one. Where did you put the box?" He moved so quickly, his arm was a blur as he grabbed Lee's hand. There was a crack, and Lee passed out.

Someone was shaking him roughly, and Lee awoke from the fog again, his hand numb and his head throbbing. It was like a nightmare that wouldn't end. Through the slits his eyes had become, he looked down. His fingers were still there, but two were at a strange angle. He barely remembered where he was, and couldn't really believe what was happening. The *chindi* was still there, holding his sides in an iron grip. "I'll die before I tell you anything. Get it over with."

"Stubborn ass. Where is the box? Tell me, and I'll let you live."

Lee was drifting and the *chindi*'s words seemed distant. He couldn't remember exactly where he'd buried the box even if he wanted to, he'd been half conscious at the time. "I'm going to die anyway. Screw yourself."

"Tell me where you hid the box, and I can do more than save your life. I can make you immortal. But we're running out of time. Somebody will be coming down this road soon, and I'll have to kill them too. What if it's a family, with little children? Maybe even a baby?"

"What if it's a company of G.I.s armed with automatic weapons and hand grenades? That's more likely after what you did." Lee smiled. "That kind of firepower might even kill a master-race *chindi*."

The *chindi* cursed, and lifted Lee off the ground by his belt with one hand. It was clear that the evil one was incredibly strong. "If you don't tell me where you hid that box, I'll squash you against the side of that truck like a mosquito."

"Go to hell," Lee uttered softly. The darkness was upon him now, and he closed his eyes, releasing his spirit.

Lee awoke feeling as if he'd been on a weekend bender. His mouth had a funny taste and his head was spinning—the kind of dizziness that wouldn't stop until he had one foot planted on solid ground. The little trick, nothing more than a psychological anchor, was surprisingly effective.

He was on his back. When he opened his eyes, everything had a gray cast, something like on a cloudy day. But he couldn't see any clouds in the sky and the moon was still out. There were even stars, and they seemed bright and clear. He looked around and noticed a cottontail by the road fifty feet away, eating some tall grass nourished by the run-off.

He'd been moved away from the highway to a more secluded spot. His car was there and so was the truck, both parked out of view from the highway. The German—was he really a *chindi*—was standing some distance away, looking toward the east anxiously, holding a pistol in his hand. *His* pistol, probably.

Lee looked down at his wrist, and saw he'd been sliced open like a melon. But there was no blood coming out, and the cut seemed to be closing, the edges of his skin knitting back together right before his eyes. If he was dead, at least he felt better now. He felt great, actually, and was getting stronger by the second. It was as if he'd gone to sleep a boy and woken up as a man.

If he was a *chindi* now, it seemed like a good trade over the slow death he'd been experiencing. He checked his wrist again, and it was nearly healed, with only a small scar. He wiggled his fingers. They didn't look or feel broken now, and his side no longer throbbed with pain.

Since he was in pretty good shape for a dead man, maybe it was time to turn the tables on the German. There was no way he was going to hand anything over to a German agent—*chindi* or not. Even ghosts were at war. He remembered the Texas soldier telling him that gray box contained some kind of powerful weapon.

He still couldn't remember exactly where he'd hidden the heavy thing, but he knew he could probably find it by backtracking. He wasn't about to do that for the German, though, even if he was a *chindi* too.

The puzzling thing was, if the German was the evil part of a man who'd died, then he should be evil too, and he didn't feel that way at all. What he did feel was anger toward whatever it was that had killed Benny, and himself as well, apparently.

Lee pretended to struggle a bit as he sat up, hiding his strength. The *chindi* was extremely powerful, like a bear, so he figured the only strategy that might work against him was a surprise attack. The German noticed his movement immediately. The speed and grace of the creature's approach was surprising, like that of a big cougar.

"You're alive again," the evil one said. "You died, so I brought you back by mixing my blood with yours. But I can kill you again, a dozen times or more, each time after hours of torture. Tell me where you hid the weapon in that box, and I might let you keep living."

"If I'm really alive, I'm not a *chindi*. So what am I? What are you?" Lee wanted to stall as long as he could, building his strength.

The German creature smiled grimly. "Just take me to that box you hid. Maybe I'll tell you on the way."

Lee tried to clear the cobwebs from his brain. The *chindi* belonged to the Navajo culture. This man or creature was from Europe. He tried to think of any folklore that might explain how the German could do this, and all that came to mind was the story of vampires. Was that just in books and movies? Maybe the teachings of his people *could* help now. The *Dineh* believed that to know a person's name was to have power over him.

"What's your name?"

"I've been a hundred people but, for now, my name is Hans Gruber." He drew Lee's .45 Colt revolver out of his big jacket pocket. "You already know that bullets don't normally kill men like me—but they hurt like hell and can incapacitate you for a while. You won't die, but you may wish you could." He trained the weapon on Lee. "Take me to the place where you hid the plutonium, the radioactive material in that gray box."

"Maybe we should wait until daylight." Lee wanted to see his reaction.

"Ah, now you're catching on." Gruber's eyes seemed to light up, and his sneer was close to a smile. "But your stalling is over. Get behind the wheel of the truck and let's get going. I'll ride 'shotgun.'"

A few minutes later, Lee was driving west down the highway, knowing that Hans had seen him coming from that direction earlier. He had a plan now that might give him a chance to survive.

After several minutes, he spotted the dirt road he had in mind and slowed to take the turn off the highway. He knew there had been trucks up here, because the army was planning on placing a radio tower at this location. It was important that the German see recent tracks.

The truck was a lot easier to handle now, and Lee figured that was all part of his new strength. Being a vampire, or whatever he was, did have some advantages. He didn't need headlights to drive at night because night was almost as clear as day. "It's just two miles up this trail."

The German nodded, wiggling the Colt slightly. "Don't even think of trying to escape."

Lee had to put the truck in its lowest gear, what some old-timers called "granny," to inch the big GMC up to the top of the tall sandstone mesa, which overlooked the valley to the left. Below was the highway, and beyond that, the railroad tracks.

Lee stopped the truck and set the brake. "This is the place," he mumbled, opening the door and climbing down from the cab. With his newly acquired night vision, Lee could see clearly for miles.

"Where's the box? I didn't come up here for the view." The German, who had appeared at his side within a few seconds after leaving the truck, poked Lee in his side with the pistol barrel.

"Take five, will ya? There's a ledge about ten feet down the side of the cliff, and a shallow cave where eagles nest. I moved the box in there, and hid it behind some brush." Lee walked toward the side of the mesa slowly, dragging his feet and pretending to be weary. It was difficult, actually, because he felt as strong as an ox at the moment, and amazingly light on his feet.

"Where are your footprints, and the truck tire tracks? I don't see them." Hans appeared beside him again, moving swiftly, faster than any human Lee had ever seen, yet in a flowing motion that seemed effortless.

"I'm a Navajo warrior. I brushed out the tracks." Lee kept walking, moving closer to the rim.

He stopped close to the edge, and looked down at the

boulders and rubble below. Hans was beside him, just out of reach. "The ledge is just a little farther in that direction." Lee pointed past Hans to a spot along the cliff side. "See it?"

Hans turned to look, and Lee leaped forward like an offensive guard on a football team, hitting the vampire in the lower back with a full body block. "Can you turn into a bat?" he yelled.

Hans's arms and legs flayed out, grabbing for handholds that weren't there, but at least he had the courage not to scream.

Lee watched him fall. The man struck a rock on the way down before slamming into the ground with a thump he could hear even from this distance. The body rolled and slid another ten feet or so, then stopped. Lee could see a pool of blood begin to form beneath the body. "I guess not."

Lee watched the motionless figure below. He looked dead, but then he'd looked dead before. This time he wouldn't take any chances. Climbing into the back of the truck, he gathered up a can of gasoline and a container of heating fuel from a G.I.'s cooking gear, along with a box of strike-anywhere matches.

Opening the gasoline can, he threw the entire container down the cliff. It struck a rock above the body, and broke open, splattering gasoline all around.

He opened the container of fuel, used to heat individual rations, lit the container, then dropped the flaming material down toward the gasoline.

The container landed right in the middle of the gasoline-soaked ground, and ignited with a flash of red flame that quickly spread. Black smoke billowed into a cloud. Nothing could survive that heat.

By the time Lee reached the highway again, he'd decided

that whatever he was now, vampire or *chindi*, it wasn't really a good career move for a New Mexico state policeman. He'd better try and put a stop to it before it was too late.

He turned east again, gave the truck all the gas it could handle, and built up speed. Lee was going to find that medicine man. If anyone could treat him for something supernatural, it was a Navajo *hataalii*.

Lee arrived a short time later at the large, eight-sided log hogan that belonged to Bowlegs. On the way, he'd barely avoided an encounter with two police cars who'd been heading the other way, emergency lights flashing. He'd seen them coming and pulled off the highway just before they passed. As they went by, he recognized one of the men—State Police Sergeant Ben McAllister. Some motorist must have come upon the bodies and wreckage at the ambush site and gone on to Grants or Gallup to report it. If things went well with the medicine man, Lee would be able to do his part to unsnarl the mystery of what happened there . . . and maybe return that military cargo—if he could find it again.

He stepped down from the truck, knowing that Navajo custom required him to wait until he was invited in. For the first time he was impatient with that tradition. At this hour, Bowlegs had been asleep, almost certainly, but the noise of that truck would have woken a deaf man.

As he waited, Lee wondered if he'd done the right thing in coming here. Would Bowlegs know what he'd become and be afraid? He *had* come back to life, like Hans Gruber before him. And that made him some sort of *chindi*, according to the Navajo Way. But Lee didn't feel evil, or want to hurt anyone . . . well, except for throwing the German off the cliff and torching his body.

"What are you?" An old, shaking voice came from behind the heavy blanket covering the opening of the hogan. Lee, with his vampire vision, could see Bowlegs's wrinkled and wind-burned face squinting at his unexpected visitor from the interior of the hogan through the narrow slit where the blanket was being held open. "What do you want with me?"

"Recognize my voice, uncle," Lee said in Navajo, using the title out of respect, not kinship. "I'm the state police officer the Anglos call Lee Nez. We've spoken several times, and you did the Blessingway for my mother—the teacher—when she had that trouble breathing. We belong to the same clan."

The medicine man said nothing, and Lee could see he was holding a knife in his hand.

"Something bad happened to me, uncle. I got into a gun battle, and was shot. One of the men I killed came back to life, and took my gun away. I was afraid of him because of the stories I know as a Navajo. But he didn't seem like a phantom or an evil one. He could move like the wind, and had the strength of a bear. I grew weak, and died from loss of blood. I woke up later able to see in the dark like an owl. There was a big slit on my wrist where the man mixed his blood with mine. The cut has already disappeared, and I'm as strong as an ox and fast as a deer. But I don't like what I may become. Can you do a Sing that will heal me? I swear I mean you no harm."

Lee tried to express what had happened in terms an old Navajo would understand. Unfortunately, he knew that what had happened to him didn't make much sense no matter how it was explained.

"Please, uncle. I have no one else, and I'm *Dineh* like you."

There was a long pause, but finally the *hataalii* came outside, holding an old kerosene lantern and a medicine pouch. The light blinded Lee for a second, then his vision adapted and he was able to see clearly again.

"Hold out your wrists," the medicine man ordered. Lee did as he was asked. The man looked him over carefully.

"I see what has happened to you, nephew. If all the blood on your uniform is yours, you *should* be dead. Your wrist shows only a faint scar, and your eyes glowed strangely under my light. Only a few of our healers have even heard of the magic you have encountered, and even fewer know the way to influence such power. Come inside with me. My herbs might still be able to help you, but we have to hurry. They'll be useless if too much time has already passed."

Lee entered and sat down on an offered sheep pelt upon the hard earth floor on the north side of the hogan, the side that belonged to the men, traditionally, and was to the left of the east-facing entrance. The *hataalii* followed him inside and began to work quickly, choosing among several pouches, gathering pinches and handfuls of sweet- and foul-smelling ingredients. Lee thought he recognized some of the dried herbs. From the smell of some of the others, he didn't want to think about what they could be.

When the *hataalii* had gathered all the items in a small clay bowl, Bowlegs blessed them with a short song, then mixed the ingredients together with a carved stick. He then placed the contents in a larger fired-clay pot, and sat it on the small wood stove in the center of the hogan below a sturdy-looking metal pipe that led outside through the smoke hole in the roof. It was obvious that Bowlegs was prosperous, many Navajos still depended upon a wood fire in a pit rather that a stove of any kind.

"Do you carry a medicine pouch?" Bowlegs asked.

"Yes. It's in my pocket."

"Take it out, place it in your hands, then close your eyes, nephew, and follow my instructions exactly. In order for you to be cured, the gods must accept the ceremony. Speak no more until we are done."

It was nearly dawn when the healer sat back on his heels, blessed Lee and himself with a short finishing song, and stood. Sweat dripped from his brow, and Lee felt exhausted, as if he'd been chopping wood all night. He was hungry . . . but for what? Hopefully, not blood.

"Now the test, nephew. Stand by the entrance and wait for Sun. When the first rays of light come over the mesas, hold your hand outside so that the light touches your skin."

Lee waited just inside the entrance to the hogan. The door faced east, traditionally, to greet the morning sun. It was getting lighter now inside as well, and the medicine man had blown out his kerosene lantern. Lee felt unsettled and more than a little afraid. If the *hataalii* had failed, what he was doing would feel no different than holding his hand over an open flame.

He tasted the bitterness in his mouth and swallowed it back. Dread filled him as he pushed his hand out into the sun. Would it only burn his hand, or would his entire body burst into flames?

Inching his left hand outside, and looking through the opening created by his arm pushing against the blanket, he saw the first rays of the sun reach his skin. It was warm, and he could sense the heat, but it wasn't unpleasant. He waited a few minutes, then brought his hand back inside.

"Well, I didn't catch fire or anything," Lee said to Bow-legs.

"Let me have a look, nephew." The old man looked closely at Lee's hand. "Put your other hand beside it."

Lee did, and noticed the hand that had been outside was darker, though his skin was already tanned from years in the sun. It wasn't a big difference, but it was there. "I'm going to be getting one hell of a tan, if this is any indication."

"If you hadn't come to me, your skin would have burned to a crisp with that much sunlight. My teacher would have called the one who did this to you a 'walker of the night.' He taught me that Sun would kill night walkers immediately, and their death would be accompanied by unbearable pain. You didn't come to me in time for a complete cure, but at least now you'll be able to go outside during the day for short periods of time. Now let's see what else remains of the curse on you."

Bowlegs handed him a sharp piece of flint, a mineral known to defeat evil. "Run the edge of this across the palm of your hand. We need to see if you can heal yourself like other night walkers."

Lee had to think about it first. Taking a deep breath, Lee acknowledged the need for this test and drew the razor-sharp flake of chipped flint across his left hand, slicing his palm open. Blood flowed from the wound, pooling in the center of his palm.

Fear touched the edges of his mind. He didn't want to be a vampire, but he'd miss the powers he had already experienced. He wasn't sure if that was evil's way of controlling him, or if it just showed his humanity. But he held his breath as he waited to see what would happen next.

## CHAPTER 4

Look! The wound is closing already," Bowlegs said.

Sure enough, the shallow cut was sealing along the line of the injury. Within thirty seconds, only a thin scar remained.

"How is this possible, uncle?" Lee shook his head slowly. "I'm still a vampire, what you call a walker of the night?"

"As I said, you've only been partially healed, but this is as far as my skills can take you. You'll have to be very careful now not to tell anyone what you are. Most won't understand and you'll be called a demon, or worse, especially by the *Dineh*, the Navajo people."

"That means I'll have to avoid sunlight and make sure I don't get injured in front of others who might notice how quickly I heal. I guess my time as a state policeman has ended. What else did your mentor teach you about night walkers?"

"You've already discovered that you are stronger and faster than any human, and can see well in total darkness. The ritual we performed preserved some of these traits as well as your ability to heal. But those you call vampires still remain stronger and faster than you. You will age, though the process will be very slow."

"Will the mixing of my blood with someone else's turn them into someone like me?"

"I don't know. And I don't know if you'll be able to father a child in the human way either. The one who taught me said that walkers of the night are sterile. If that wasn't the case, they would rule the world instead of living in secrecy."

"Am I going to become evil, and develop a taste for the blood of other humans?" Lee asked, remembering the vampires he'd seen in the movies.

"Walkers of the night have the same character as they did before the change. You might like to undercook your mutton and beef, but I don't expect you'll experience anything more drastic than that," Bowlegs said, smiling. "I think your appetite will increase for what you enjoy eating already too. You're going to need more fuel. Do you feel hungry now?"

Lee nodded. "Is that because I healed my wounded side, and now my palm?"

Bowlegs shrugged. "That would seem reasonable, but I have few certainties to offer you. I only know the legends and rituals I was taught. I guess we'll learn together. But, nephew, one thing I do know. Your life will be a lonely one now, because you'll outlive all those you meet, and if you consider taking a wife, remember that she will grow old while you remain young and strong. Whatever magic is inside the blood of a night walker will keep you healthy. People will notice, so you can't stay in one place for too many years. Your life will never be the same again."

"I have a lot to think about." Lee nodded.

"There is another danger you'll face that I have to warn

you about. There's another living creature, one which is always evil and capable of merciless violence toward the *Dineh*. Your power will draw them to you. Listen carefully, because what I'm going to tell you now may save your life." Bowlegs was whispering now, and took a long look outside before speaking again. "I don't say their name because it might call them to us. In the years you were on the Reservation, how much did you learn about the evil ones?"

"Skin . . ." Lee almost said skinwalkers, the English language name used for Navajo witches said to use dark magic and have special powers, especially the rumor that they could change form into animals such as coyotes and wolves. "I've heard of evil Navajos who attempt to harm others through magic. They are said to carry out many crimes and to use the dead in their perverted rites. But other cultures have their sick people. The war has shown us this."

"I'm not talking only about those with disturbed minds, but about those who actually have great power, such as the shape-shifting you mentioned. These people are real, not the spirits of those who have died. They crave power more than anything, and they will want what you have. In animal form, they have the abilities of the creature they become. They will recognize you as a night walker, and they will want your blood to make themselves even stronger. You'll have to be very careful at night. That's the only time they can change their form." Bowlegs paused. "You'll be in great danger from them as long as you remain among the *Dineh*."

"But I'm stronger now, and at night I can see as well as any animal. Can they be killed, these skin . . . evil ones?" Lee lowered his voice as he spoke.

"Yes. They're only as strong as the creature whose form they take. But they often run in packs and there's strength in numbers. Until you know more about yourself, you should get as far away from the *Dinetah*, our land, as possible." Bowlegs gave Lee a small pouch.

"A medicine bundle? But I have my own," Lee said, reaching into his pocket.

"This is a hunting charm, a flint arrowhead bound to the figure of a bear that I was given by my teacher many years ago to protect me from the evil ones. As you can see, so far, it's worked." Bowlegs's voice was light, but his eyes were deadly serious.

"And I'm going to need this now?"

"More than any man on earth."

In the afternoon, Bowlegs slept, and Lee kept watch, listening around the hogan but only venturing outside briefly to relieve himself, which was just another indication that he wasn't a *chindi*. Ghosts or spirits didn't get full bladders, at least not that he'd ever heard. He washed his uniform, cleaned up, and waited for it to dry.

Later, he kept to the shadows beneath the junipers as much as possible, and didn't feel uncomfortable at all. With long sleeves, and the state police cap he'd somehow managed to keep on his head during last night's chaos, the light didn't bother him that much, though he did show a tan on his exposed skin by the end of the day.

Not daring to risk full, prolonged exposure to the sun, he waited for darkness to come, and hoped he wouldn't have to deal with skinwalkers right away.

When night came, Lee knew he had to leave. It wasn't easy. He knew he might never see the *hataalii* again or find someone who could help or understand him. He gave the man half of the money he had in his wallet, twenty dollars, which would keep Bowlegs in groceries for several weeks if he was frugal. From the looks of the walls of the hogan where a few shelves had been attached to the logs, Bowlegs was good at living off the bare essentials. Metal drums containing flour, cornmeal, beans, lard, and a few cans of food were all he had.

When Lee thanked Bowlegs again, the man simply nodded, then sang a short blessing and gave Lee a small piece of turquoise, something believed to be effective against Navajo skinwalkers and monsters, to add to his medicine pouch. There were no words of good-bye, and none were expected. Lee simply turned and walked away.

Lee went to the deuce and a half, quickly removed the canvas cover on the GMC, rolled it up, then tossed the bundle into the bed of the truck. It would appear somewhat different, at least, with just the framework showing. As additional insurance, he poured water in the dirt and splashed mud on the vehicle markings in the front and back so they would be obscured as naturally as possible.

He then looked over the contents, thought about leaving some of the tools or one of the cans of gasoline behind for Bowlegs, then realized that anyone finding the military-issue items would think the old man had stolen them.

There were two cases of C rations, however, and Lee put one and most of the other down by a tree for Bowlegs to find later. The food was something he could hide and consume as needed. Each ration included soluble coffee, premixed cereal, hard candies, canned meat, and several other items, including cigarettes, chewing gum, and even water-purification tablets. All would be very useful for the old man.

Lee started the truck up and drove to the highway. Smoothing out the tire tracks where they reached the road with a trenching tool, he did what he could to keep Bowlegs from being investigated.

Although he had no need for headlights, he decided to use them anyway to avoid attracting suspicion.

The more he thought about it, the more Lee realized he should check the body of the German vampire, Hans, to confirm he really had died. After shooting him in the head and having him recover completely within an hour or so, nothing seemed impossible anymore.

Running low on fuel, and knowing he didn't dare stop to try to borrow or steal some, he arrived at the mesa where he'd thrown his enemy over the ledge. Lee stepped down from the cab of the truck and walked to the edge. He moved quickly and seemingly without effort, and felt like a cougar on the prowl.

The night was nearly daylight to him, and he realized he could be spotted by another vampire as easily as an owl tracked a mouse. Stepping just close enough to the edge to look over without exposing himself, he took a look down at the spot where the body had been.

The area below was blackened by fire, but Hans was gone. He'd seen the remains of livestock killed in the wild many times and even the largest predators left some evidence behind. Even the fire would have left traces of his skeleton. The German had disappeared without a trace and Lee was forced to conclude he'd moved away from the fire before it could consume him.

Lee thought about his next move. Should he assume his enemy was down there somewhere, maybe watching for him? Or perhaps he'd moved on, searching for the hidden weapon or trying to contact others who were part of his raid—the second squad, as Lieutenant Barnett had believed existed.

Lee looked around carefully, taking his time to check for motion or any human shape, listening for the slightest movement. Lee realized that he had the upper hand now. The German couldn't ignore the possibility that Lee could have managed to deliver a message to the military and told them where to find the weapon. There were probably hundreds of men looking for whoever had ambushed that military convoy.

But Lee also knew he was in danger from the German vampire, who had powers that would allow him to hide and survive. Who knew how old the vampire was or what skills he'd learned? And if he was near and saw Lee with the truck, he might reasonably conclude that Lee hadn't paid the military a visit yet.

On the other hand, this was Navajo country, and if Bowlegs was right, skinwalkers would eventually sense the German's presence. If they could track Lee, who was only half vampire, Hans might be even easier to detect. Between the military searchers and the skinwalkers, the vampire had enemies everywhere, and he was thousands of miles from his own country.

Lee considered the situation. In his heart, he knew what he had to do. He'd never run from responsibility, and inside he was still a police officer. Cursing himself for wasting time, he jumped into the truck.

Before he could build a new life, he was going to track the man responsible for the murder of Patrolman Mondragon and the death of all those soldiers. No one else could fight Hans better than he could, so that duty fell to him.

Turning around, he drove to the base of the mesa. From there he'd try to pick up his enemy's trail before it grew any colder.

Leonard Hawk, the name Lee Nez was using in his most recent identity, glanced at the gray cuff of his New Mexico state policeman's charcoal-black uniform, then unclipped his gold shield and placed it in the small wooden box he used to store the symbol of his profession when he was off-duty. After more than fifty years, it was good to be back in uniform.

For over a decade, he'd dedicated himself to finding Hans Gruber, but the German had eluded him despite his best efforts. He'd simply disappeared after their last encounter, and Lee had never seen him again.

Months turned into years, and years into decades. During that time, Lee had learned about himself—his own nature, his capabilities and limitations. Yet, as it often was, the more life changed, the more things stayed the same.

Stripping off his uniform shirt and pants, he hung them on a wooden hanger and placed them on the brass hook he'd attached to the inside of his closet door. He had a small apartment in Las Cruces, which was the city he called home for his current duty assignment.

The light was intense here, and especially so this time

of year in May. He figured he wasn't the only vampire to consider sunblock the greatest invention of the twentieth century.

These days he knew a lot about sun protection. It was the ultraviolet rays, the part of the sun's spectrum that caused sunburn in humans, that killed vampires. The best sunblock, covering every square inch of skin, protected full vampires for several minutes at a time, assuming they had excellent wraparound sunglasses to protect their eyes, covered their heads, and wore long sleeves and pants.

Lee guessed that for the first time in history, a sunblock-protected vampire could actually survive outdoors in the sun for a few minutes at a time. And, with his half-vampire status, he barely got a tan nowadays, even when he was out in the sun for a half hour. The light hurt his eyes, but he'd found it didn't actually damage them.

Just in case, however, he always wore sunglasses and used sunblock literally all over his body. Many times he'd seen an accident victim have their clothes cut away by the EMTs, and he wasn't about to risk adding burns to his injuries if he was ever involved in a major collision.

Removing his underwear and socks, Lee stepped into the shower and washed away the perspiration from his ten-hour shift, plus his protective oils. The lotion would be reapplied as soon as he'd dried himself off and before he dressed in civilian clothes. It was a ritual he'd followed for years and one of the things that would make him appear "different" to anyone getting to know him well.

Such "differences" were why Lee rarely allowed himself to make close friends. He'd done so just once since 1945 and experienced the best years of his life—followed by the darkest times he'd ever known. Falling in love was something he'd sworn never to let happen again. Someone had once said that dying was easy—living was hard. He agreed with that sentiment completely.

Lee took several minutes to apply the sunblock, then dressed in the dark blue slacks he normally wore off-duty. Anyone glancing into his closet would find tightly woven black, brown, and dark gray clothes, and boots. He had several caps, and usually wore them outside at night as well as day just in case he didn't get a chance to reapply sunblock when it wore off.

Picking up his deerskin medicine pouch—he still carried one in his pocket, even on duty—Lee attached it to his belt via a leather strap he'd added. It carried the same items the old *hataalii* had given him: flint, corn pollen, turquoise, and quartz crystal, plus a flattened plastic bottle of emergency sunblock.

For less esoteric dangers, he carried a small .45 backup auto in his front pocket in a special holster, even when at home. He'd found that locks meant nothing to vampires who'd been threatened by his nearly equal abilities and his dedication to destroying evil. Vampires, good or bad, had learned to get around obstacles. If they couldn't pick a lock, they had the strength to force just about anything open but a safe. It was a survival trait for those who had a desperate need to get out of the sun.

The skinwalkers he'd met were a mixed bag as well. Bowlegs had been right to warn him about them. If they came at him out from behind cover or through a door or window in the form of a two-hundred-pound wolf or cougar, he needed stopping power right then. He'd learned that the hard way. He forced himself to put those memories out of his mind for now as he prepared dinner.

He quickly cooked and ate two nearly raw hamburgers

with everything, a skillet full of french fries, a pound of bloody calves liver, and a quarter of a thick chocolate ice-cream cake.

After all that, plus two cups of coffee, no sugar and strong enough to stand the spoon up straight, he was ready for tonight's hunt. He quickly cleared the table and loaded the dishwasher. When he returned, he didn't want a mess to clean up. He might be gone all night, or even for several days.

He checked the razor-sharp commando dagger, then placed it back into the custom-made boot sheath. With his off-duty Beretta nine-millimeter clipped to his belt inside his Levi's jacket, he sang a quick blessing, as was his custom, and touched his hunting fetish and sacred turquoise before returning them to his pocket.

Turning off the light, he left the apartment, locking the dead bolt before he walked down the hall and left the building.

Lee stood for a while in the dark under the porch, looking up and down the sidewalk, and at the doors and windows of the apartments in the surrounding buildings of the large complex. Then he studied the cars and pickups in their parking spaces underneath the long carport. Somebody's overweight cat lurked beside the tire of a white Dodge pickup, but at barely ten pounds, it was way too small to be a skinwalker.

Around the Xeriscaped buildings, with their sparse drought-tolerant plants surrounded by a lot of gravel, footprints were hard to spot, but he'd recently noticed some enormous tracks from what looked like a wolf in several places, including one spot beneath his window where the drip watering system had been repaired and the gravel not completely replaced.

Casually walking beside the building, he saw another track, this one less than twelve hours old. The animal had been there early this morning, before dawn, probably looking for him. This complex only allowed small dogs and cats, so these were definitely not prints from the pet of a resident. His finely honed hunting instincts told Lee this was no stray domestic dog or a Mexican gray wolf either. The only real wolves still in the wild were those that had been reintroduced, and all of them were monitored. It was a skinwalker seeking him out and waiting for the opportunity to strike.

He'd learned that even though they had the ability to shape-shift into a specific animal, the form couldn't change its mass, so if one attempted to assume the shape of a bird, it would weigh the same as its human form. A 150-pound hawk would have a hard time flying unless it had the wing-span of a Cessna. It wouldn't be subtle and certainly not very sneaky—both traits skinwalkers favored—and probably not possible. Besides, he'd never seen a skinwalker except as a wolf or wild cat, and didn't know if they could become a hawk or, say, a giant catfish.

He'd learned that any animal under eighty or so pounds wasn't likely to present a danger to him unless there were a lot of them working together, and skinwalkers had no self-healing abilities that he'd been able to observe.

A rifle would have been better but impossible to conceal easily. His pistol would serve him when the time came to act. But he'd have to wait for the animal to strike. Killing a citizen's malamute, then claiming you thought it was a shape-shifter, was a lousy alibi. A cop couldn't afford to get the reputation for having an itchy trigger finger.

Though he had his night-walker abilities and sufficient firepower, Lee knew skinwalkers had advantages too. Navajo witches could smell a vampire at a considerable distance, for one, even when they were in human form. Maybe their animal side remembered the scent or they had some kind of instinct or intuition that enabled them to sense a vampire's power. But whatever it was, when it came to initial detection, vampires were at a disadvantage. The fact that he was only half vampire didn't seem to make Navajo skinwalkers incapable of tracking him, and he'd never had a vampire around for comparison tests.

Lee strolled casually over to the mailboxes noting that there was a woman sitting in a small green sedan three slots down from his parked police cruiser, apparently waiting for someone. Perhaps she was waiting for a boyfriend to get home, or maybe it was a process server waiting for a tenant so she could serve papers.

He took out his key, opened mailbox C-8, and looked inside. All he found was a flyer addressed to occupant from a local supermarket, and one of those "have you seen this child" cards. As a responsible cop, Lee looked at the image carefully, reading the name of the father who'd taken the child and noticing his photo as well. He had a good memory for faces and if he ever came across the man or child, he'd remember. By now, tracking down people was second nature for him as well as his job. There was only one person who'd ever evaded him completely. But that would change someday soon.

The woman opened the door of her sedan, but the dome light didn't come on. This wasn't typical and sent off warning signals in his head. The police officers and law-enforcement personnel he knew never set their interior lights to come on when the door was opened, preferring not to make themselves a target at night when entering or exiting their units. Perhaps the woman was a cop or a skinwalker in human form. He waited, pretending to be absorbed in his mail, and watched her approaching, out of the corner of his eye.

Lee noted that she was a natural beauty—an attractive, light-haired Hispanic woman with subtle red lipstick and little other makeup. Her eyes were a beautiful shade of brown—amber—but they didn't conceal her alertness as she drew near. Her arms remained by her sides but as she moved, her black leather jacket opened and Lee caught a glimpse of the pancake holster and semiauto pistol attached to her belt.

He'd seen several of the local PD officers in the course of his patrols, and she wasn't one of the ones he'd met. This woman carried herself like an experienced officer, and she had brought backup, a man in a suit who was walking slowly along the sidewalk behind Lee. He had to hand it to them, they were playing it cool. Her partner even had a dog with him, and was doing his level best to look like a tenant walking his pet.

Lee decided to preempt her. He went up and greeted her, keeping his hands well away from his handgun. "Hello, Detective, or is it Special Agent? I'm a state police officer, off-duty, in case you noticed my handgun—as I did yours," Lee said, deciding to neutralize the superior attitude many federal cops wore instead of a uniform. "Oh, and by the way, you might remind your partner that he needs to clean up after the dog. Complex rules."

The woman gave him a half smile, then reached into her jacket pocket. "FBI Special Agent Lopez, Officer Hawk." She held up her badge. "You're very observant, or were you expecting me?"

"I've been a police officer long enough to spot 'feebees' from five hundred yards on a stormy night. This isn't your usual hunting ground, is it, Agent Lopez? Somebody still looking for a motive for that incident up on the Rez several months ago?"

Lee knew that the Bureau hadn't come up with a credible motive, much less a perpetrator, for the attack on him that had taken place along Highway 666. They weren't going to get the real answer about that from the locals or the Navajo police either.

Of course Lee had been forced to lie about that attack from the very beginning. The truth was too difficult to swallow without the X-Files explanation—that skinwalkers with supernatural powers were out to get him—and that was something he was never going to admit.

"The Bureau is still working that case . . . and none of the local residents are talking," Special Agent Lopez said with a shrug. "You mind if we go somewhere and discuss this?"

"How about one of the picnic tables over by the clubhouse? I've been cooped up in my unit for most of the day, and would like to breathe a little fresh air. Your partner can let the dog run loose on the grass. I won't tell."

The woman agent gestured to her partner, who nodded back, then followed them at a discreet distance to the brightly lit clubhouse in the center of the complex. The large outdoor pool was being used by several serious swimmers doing laps, but it was quiet outside, even here.

Selecting the table farthest from the clubhouse, Lee sat across from the agent on the wooden bench. "Want me to start from the beginning?" he offered.

"Not necessary. Just stop me if I get something wrong or you need to add something new you just remembered. I've read your written report," Agent Lopez responded. Her voice was pleasant and casual, which probably disarmed less experienced suspects, but her eyes were strictly business, analyzing his every reaction.

Lee knew he was still under suspicion, not because he had killed the skinwalkers who'd attacked him, but because the events surrounding the shooting would never make sense to anyone except vampires and skinwalkers. "Okay, Special Agent Lopez." Lee nodded.

"Just Diane, please."

Lee could see how someone with her natural charisma could lead a suspect to provide more information than they'd planned. He'd have to work hard to stay immune. "Call me Lee or Leo, Diane. Unlike most of my tribe, I don't mind you using my Anglo name."

He'd always tried to keep his current name close to his real identity in case he ever slipped up and responded incorrectly. It would do more than raise a few eyebrows if anyone realized he was Lee Nez, and since he hadn't aged physically more than a year or so since 1945, he'd been forced to assume new identities from time to time. Those years had been hard ones, with skinwalkers constantly on his trail. But he'd learned about his powers and how to survive. In the world of night walkers, by and large, it had been kill or be killed. That was another reason why he never remained in one place for long.

"Okay, Lee." Agent Lopez smiled and this time it was a real smile—or as close as he could expect since she was questioning a suspect she didn't know she could trust. "You were on routine patrol, moving north on Highway 666 between mile markers forty and forty-one when you came upon a rollover accident involving a Honda Accord and a Ford pickup."

Lee nodded. He remembered the license numbers, the years of the vehicles, and a wealth of other information too, but didn't want to show off his nearly photographic memory. "The vehicle on its side was the Honda. The pickup was parked adjacent to the sedan, as if the driver had stopped to render assistance.

"A Navajo man was standing beside the driver's door of the sedan, looking inside the vehicle. When you slowed and turned on your emergency lights, the man turned, waved, and yelled for your help. You put in a call to the Navajo police dispatcher at Shiprock, then exited your unit and went to investigate." Agent Lopez caught his eye, and waited in silence until Lee nodded.

"You walked to within ten feet of the overturned Honda, saw that there was no one inside, then heard an unusual noise to your right. Two large, wolflike canines emerged from concealment on the far side of the pickup, and leaped toward you. You realized you were being attacked, dodged away quickly enough to avoid all but a grazing cut on your forearm from the teeth of one of the animals. You then drew your weapon and shot each animal three times at close range."

"I fired eight shots. Only six actually struck the animals."

"At the same time, you were also evading the man, who was slashing at you with a long-bladed hunting knife. When he saw the animals had been stopped, he ran off the road into the brush and you gave pursuit. Did you have a flashlight?"

"Yes." Lee nodded. He still carried one to create the impression he needed light to see in the dark. It was one of the first lessons he'd learned about concealing his powers.

Diane nodded, then continued. "When you caught up to him several minutes later, he lunged at you. The man, raging about you having killed his animals, stabbed at your heart.

His blow failed to penetrate your protective vest, and only ripped your uniform shirt." Diane Lopez looked him in the eyes again, searching for a response.

If she was watching for one of those large pupil, small pupil reactions, the woman agent was going to be disappointed. Lee had learned to lie convincingly decades ago, not because he was immoral, but because he'd gotten so much practice as he'd created new identities and sought out his enemies.

"That's basically it. I staggered back, managed to swing my service weapon around, and fired twice more." Lee remembered his attacker's curses. The man had been a Navajo skinwalker and so had the enormous wolves that had attacked him, both females. Naturally, the man's girlfriend and her sister hadn't been seen since the attack. He'd seen the two wolves approaching in the dark and realized it was an ambush. When he'd taken out both the females, the man had run into the brush, hiding and trying to shape-shift into a mountain lion.

Lee had caught up to him and shot him during the transformation. It hadn't been complete, so the man had reverted back to human form before he died, retaining the wounds. Since the females had been transformed into wolves when they'd died, there was no way to be absolutely certain of their identities.

"And you still have no idea why the Navajo man, later identified as Johnny Tanner, decided to ambush you?" Diane never took her eyes off him.

He held her gaze while answering. "I think Tanner was probably planning on carjacking the next vehicle that came along. It just happened to be me. The Honda didn't even have an engine under the hood and the investigating tribal police officers were able to determine from tool marks that he'd used the winch on his pickup to overturn the car in the road to simulate an accident."

"So, where do those vicious wolf-dogs fit into the picture? The investigating Bureau agent told me that none of Tanner's neighbors had ever seen them before, yet they were apparently trained to attack humans at his command."

That's because they were his female companions, shape-shifted into a more lethal species for an unarmed attack, Lee thought. But of course he couldn't say that. "He'd have had to have kept them somewhere, but nobody seems to have discovered the kennel. Maybe he only got them recently from someone else." It was the most convincing story he'd been able to come up with and he was sticking to it.

"Those were the biggest wolf-cross dogs I've ever seen. But because it was an officer shooting, I didn't participate in the remainder of the investigation, so I don't know what steps were taken to find the pen," Lee added.

Special Agent Lopez nodded, looking around the grounds until she spotted her partner leaning against a tree, watching her.

"According to the Navajo police, there wasn't a trace of dog kibble within five miles of his house, nor any sign of dog droppings either. And there's something else I can't figure out, either," Lopez said.

Lee already knew what was coming. He kept quiet, letting her say it.

"What happened to Tanner's live-in girlfriend and her sister, Nora Jane and Belinda James? Officers checking out Tanner's house found evidence that they'd all had dinner together that night. Why did they leave? Where did they go? And where are they now?"

Lee knew the answer to all that, but he couldn't share

it so he simply shrugged. "They probably took off after he failed to return that night. Or maybe they were in on his plan, hiding nearby, and chickened out when they saw Johnny was taking on a cop. They may have hitchhiked to Arizona and are hiding with some relatives."

"Or maybe they're out looking for you, planning revenge. Is that why you're so careful when you go out at night, Officer Hawk? I'm still not convinced you were a random target. Johnny Tanner could have backed off when he saw you were a police officer, but he didn't. I think you were set up, and he knew that you were coming."

"I *was* working that area at that time, and I made my patrols more or less on schedule. I understand the officers found binoculars in the pickup. I suppose he could have been waiting for me and ready with a story about trying to haul the car with the pickup and having had an accident if someone came by who wasn't the target. Do you think his roommates *are* trying to get even?" Lee asked, trying to sound surprised by the thought.

Then he added, "Or does Tanner have a relative who hates cops? What do you know that I don't?" He looked into the beautiful federal agent's eyes, wondering if she knew how to lie without detection.

She couldn't do it yet, he noticed as she answered, "Just trying to dot all the i's and cross all the t's, Lee. The special agent serving the Four Corners area asked me to come down and interview you one more time. He hasn't gotten a lot of cooperation from the locals on this case. You being Navajo, you probably understand. It's not just because he's FBI either, is it?"

"The *Dineh*, the Navajo people, don't like to talk about the dead. When something like this happens, the entire community is upset. Medicine men are called to perform

Sings, ceremonies for protection and to restore balance, and people move out of the area where the spirits of the dead are said to hang out. Nobody wants to talk about it for fear of stirring up trouble. Has the house of the dead man been abandoned?"

"I think so. And the relatives of the missing women are behaving as if they've lost their kin as well." Diane looked away, having apparently realized that the old eye detector wasn't going to work with him anyway and deciding that it might just be working all too well for her interview subject.

"So now what, Special Agent Lopez? Is there anything else I can say or do to help?" Lee noticed that the agent with the dog was now walking in their direction. Apparently she'd given him some sign that the interview was over. Either that or more likely, she was wearing a wire and the cover agent had been listening all along.

"I'm probably going to have more questions in the next few days, Officer Hawk. Will you still be available?" Diane asked, reaching into her pocket for her inevitable business card.

Lee took the card, looked at the number, then shrugged. "I'm just starting a week's vacation. I might be taking a drive here and there. If you need to reach me, I have a cell phone." Lee gave her the number, which she wrote in a small notebook that had magically appeared.

"Is that it?" Lee smiled, nodding at the agent with the dog, a tall, clean-cut man in white shirt and tie and nice wool-blend suit pants.

"Just watch your back, Officer Hawk. Agent Thomas and I will be available if you find yourself in a difficult situation. I'm still not convinced that you don't have another enemy or two out there gunning for you." Diane Lopez shook his hand, then turned and walked off with her partner.

Lee considered what she'd said. Her instincts were on target. He had plenty of enemies and they hadn't stopped coming at him since 1945. But the answers she was searching for would remain out of her reach . . . and understanding.

In the meantime, he had special plans for his vacation. He had to find the skinwalker tracking him.

## CHAPTER 6

Lee went for the walk he'd intended to take, but now was alert for Agent Lopez and her partner. He knew they wouldn't be far, and that he hadn't heard the entire story tonight. Either he was still being investigated in Johnny Tanner's death, or the FBI now had reason to suspect more was going on that he wasn't telling them.

Of course, they were right. The skinwalker he suspected was on his trail—the one who'd left the animal footprint near his window—was probably connected to Tanner's pack. There were no other skinwalkers Lee knew about who were still alive; every time he encountered any, he'd killed them all.

He'd learned from experience that skinwalkers, Navajo witches, seemed by nature evil—even before their change. Maybe that was why they were singled out by other skinwalkers who saw them as worthy successors. The change always took place after one of the *Dineh* sustained a bite from a skinwalker in animal form. But like genetically linked diseases, in his experience only a Navajo could become a skinwalker. Maybe the stories about werewolves were factual, and other races elsewhere had their own versions of shape-shifters. It was something he just didn't know.

He suspected that Navajo witches might attack or defend themselves against a non-Navajo, but they were so secretive and localized in the Four Corners states that it was hard to tell for sure if this was true.

Bowlegs had been right about the fact that skinwalkers seemed to be especially attracted to him, and could detect his night-walker affliction at some distance. In all the years he'd dedicated to tracking down and killing skinwalkers, he'd learned a lot about how to find and kill the creatures. Someday, he knew he'd run out of luck, and he'd be outmatched, not merely outnumbered.

His only chance then would depend on his ability to heal himself. If they cut off his head or damaged his heart so it wouldn't function, he'd be finished. Otherwise, within a half hour or less, he'd be healed and back in action. They couldn't turn him into one of them with a bite either. He'd found that out the hard way. And, because he'd always managed to kill all those in the skinwalker packs he'd encountered, his vulnerabilities had remained hidden.

His mind wandering, Lee found himself in a particularly dark section of his apartment complex, where an intersection met empty lots on three sides. There was a fence that enclosed the entire three-block area, a narrow metal rail construction with fleur-de-lis at the top of each rail, making climbing dangerous and difficult for ordinary people. Here there were few lights and it was especially dark for anyone who didn't have exceptional night vision, like Lee.

Three teenaged boys were sitting underneath the low branches of a nearby pine tree, drinking Coors beer from a six-pack they'd managed to get somewhere. He recognized the boys as residents of the complex. At least they probably weren't going to be driving anywhere tonight and endangering someone else as well as themselves.

Going around the long way to avoid them, he escaped their notice, and kept walking toward a central cluster of apartment buildings arranged like carefully balanced blocks in a sandbox.

Remaining on the sidewalk to avoid crunching the gravel and disturbing residents, Lee strolled along, hoping to appear relaxed and unconcerned, occasionally stopping to look up at the stars. He was listening carefully, hoping for a sign that would signal the approach of the skinwalker.

He was setting himself up as bait, of course, counting on his keen senses, lightning speed, and strength to counter the attack he suspected was coming. If skinwalkers knew about the superior night vision and hearing vampires had, he'd never noticed them using that knowledge sensibly. They invariably stalked him in animal form. That meant they attacked in the dark, but it was as bright as daylight to his eyes, so the darkness gave them no real advantage.

Most of the decorative trees in the complex weren't suitable for animals to climb except for the squirrels and house cats, but a few had sturdy enough branches to hold a cougar or other wildcat. Those, Lee avoided like the plague. He went around an enormous pine in the center of the cluster of buildings, then walked toward what was to him the most dangerous section of the complex, a narrow covered bridge between two buildings that crossed an irrigation ditch disguised as a stream and lined in textured brown concrete.

He stopped and looked down the passageway. There were large bushes at both ends of the structure and he couldn't tell if a human, much less a morphed wolf, was lying in wait unless it happened to move. Because it was out of the sight of witnesses, Lee realized that it was a perfect place for an ambush. To go in was like walking through a bad part of town at midnight with fifty-dollar bills hanging out of his pockets, but it was a risk he had to take.

Looking around once more, then listening for the slightest sound, he stepped onto the redwood passage and moved briskly forward, his boots thumping noisily on the wooden floor. He could have run through it at a world-record speed, of course, but that would only risk revealing his capabilities to any stranger who happened to be looking out his window at the wrong time and noted his swift entrance and exit.

Nearly at the end of the bridge, Lee turned. He'd heard a small thump—as if someone, or something, had hit the side of the structure. Realizing it could be a diversion, he picked up the pace. As he emerged from beneath the covered bridge, he turned to see if anything was following him. Just then something struck him in the sternum with a loud thwack. It was a small, thick arrow.

Lee was wearing his bullet-resistant vest that he'd donned especially for this hunt, but the impact was still hard enough to make his eyes water.

Leaping forward, Lee hit the sidewalk and rolled, coming up behind a startled Navajo man holding a crossbow, which made the first arrow technically a bolt. The weapon was loaded and cocked, and the man was swinging the short crossbow around. Before Lee could close the gap between them, his attacker fired a second bolt.

Lee turned to avoid an impact above his heart, protecting one of his few vulnerable spots, and the powerful bow sent the short, metal-tipped bolt into his right bicep. It passed through the muscle, the bloody metal point emerging just on the other side of his arm.

Ignoring the pain, he reached across his midsection for his handgun with his left hand. It was awkward, though he'd practiced such a move before, and slow for him, though it was still quick for someone without vampire-level agility.

The Navajo who'd attacked him dropped the crossbow and pulled a big revolver out of his jacket pocket. Lee was faster, but he would have to change his grip to fire the pistol once he pulled it from the holster.

He heard gunfire from somewhere across the lawn, and a bullet buzzed by with a whine, striking the bridge post near Lee's assailant. Out of the corner of his eye, Lee could see FBI Agent Lopez standing fifty yards away, her pistol aimed in his direction.

His attacker turned his head, snapped a shot at Lee that went wide, then jumped into the irrigation ditch, diving beneath the covered walkway and disappearing from sight before Lee had a good shot.

Lee thought about going after the skinwalker, but first, he reached down and broke off the metal tip, then pulled the shaft out with a grunt. Hopefully the wound would heal and he wouldn't have to try explaining being shot to Diane. He sat the pieces down on the grass.

The woman agent ran up to Lee, barely catching his eye as she instantly tried to assess his condition.

"Do you need medical help?"

"No, it just grazed me. I'm fine. I'll search the upstream side, Agent Lopez. He's probably headed downstream underwater, but he'll have to come up for air. Watch out for his revolver."

"Let's don't waste any more time, then."

She ran down along the side of the ditch, pistol ready, watching for signs of movement in the fast-flowing stream. Farther down, about a hundred yards from the covered bridge, the ditch widened and became quite shallow. The center of the ditch contained a sandbar, and the area was filled with cattails and other water-loving plants.

Lee looked down at the wound in his arm through the tear in his sleeve. It was sealing up already. Watching for signs of motion in the water and the shrubs along both sides of the ditch, he walked upstream. The Navajo witch had to surface somewhere, and Lee doubted the skinwalker would try to change into a two-hundred-pound alligator—if that was possible anyway.

He'd had a good look at the man, and would recognize him again immediately. The facial resemblance between his attacker and Johnny Tanner was close enough to make Lee suspect the man was a relative, which made sense. He was undoubtedly one of Tanner's pack, hopefully the last one still alive. He definitely hadn't been around when Tanner attacked Lee on the highway.

When he saw wet, pressed-down grass above the concrete banks of the "stream," Lee waved, catching Diana Lopez's attention, and motioned for her to come over. She ran up to him.

"He came out here, then took off toward the parking lot, I think," Lee said, pointing at the wet spot where the man had emerged from the water. He turned and looked back toward the covered bridge. "You can't see this spot from where we were standing, and he took advantage of the blind zone to slip out and run off."

She nodded, then looked at the holes in his sleeve and the bloodstains. "Are you sure you don't need to go to a hospital?"

"No, it just grazed the skin."

He went back to the covered walkway with her. The perp had left his two crossbows there. Tracking the sale of those might give him some idea of where to find the skinwalker—unless they were homemade. They located the weapons immediately, and she examined both arrows without touching them. "Strange-looking things."

"They're called bolts. He used two crossbows so he'd have a quick follow-up shot instead of having to wait to reload."

"I placed a call on my cell phone for backup to search the neighborhood while I was checking the downstream ditch. Agent Thomas should be joining us soon."

"You decided to stake me out, huh?" Lee usually avoided the word "stake," for obvious reasons. He preferred surveillance.

"Lucky for you. You move very quickly, but I think he'd have nailed you if I hadn't seen what was going on from across the grounds." Diane paused, then added, "If I hadn't qualified as a marksman, I probably wouldn't have even attempted the shot."

He watched for a moment. She was confident and beautiful, a combination he liked. She was the kind of woman who made him regret his necessary, self-imposed isolation. Although he hadn't dated in a long time, not since his wife died, his hormones still functioned. Lee knew she could get under his skin if he let down his guard.

"Thanks, Agent Lopez, if I didn't say so already. It looks like someone from the Rez *is* trying to punish me for surviving that attack on the highway. And he took the time to select a nearly silent weapon to avoid drawing attention when he attacked."

He'd deliberately paced himself to arrive back at the bridge a few steps ahead of her so he could ensure a good look at the crossbows. Lee knew there was another reason why the crossbow was used. This skinwalker knew what he was, and apparently had intended on trying the old stake-in-the-heart trick. The man probably watched Buffy back on the Rez, or that spin-off. They were good television. He watched them himself sometimes, but that crumbling-to-dust thing was a bit over the top.

Looking down without need of a flashlight, he noted that both crossbows were handmade out of old rifle stocks, cut down into a pistol grip. The bows were of spring steel, and the bowstring was steel cable. Crude, but effective.

Diane pointed her flashlight at the weapons and bent down to examine them. "They were handmade—crude but functional, and not traceable. Something for the FBI weapons museum."

Diane stepped up to him, standing so close he nearly blushed, and touched the hole in the center of his sweater with her fingertip. "Always wear a protective vest when you go for a walk?"

"Got in the habit when I joined the state police. They're never too hot or uncomfortable when you consider that the alternative is so . . . negative."

"I hear you. I have one on myself most of the time." She shrugged, then reached into her pocket and brought out a pair of thin latex gloves. Looking around the grass, she failed in her quick search to find anything new.

Seeing flashing red lights in the direction of the parking lot, she waved at them, then went up to her approaching partner, Agent Thomas, to make arrangements to have the scene cordoned off and searched. When she was finished, she turned back to him.

"Did you get a good look at your assailant?" she asked, tilting her head slightly, mixing charm with business.

"From his facial features, I think he might be related to

the late Johnny Tanner. I'll work with your FBI imaging software, or make a sketch, if you like. I'm a wanna-be artist."

She nearly laughed. "Sounds like a plan."

A Las Cruces police department squad car pulled up in the parking lot across the grounds, and in the distance, Lee could see their portable crime unit turning a corner and heading in the same direction. He took out his cell phone.

"Guess I'd better let my lieutenant know what's going on too. This was supposed to be vacation time for me." Lee hit the speed-dial number. As he waited for a response, he looked over at Diane Lopez. He knew she would be listening to whatever he said to his boss. As he studied her expression, he wondered what she was thinking now.

"Good evening, Iris, this is Lee Hawk. I need to speak to Lieutenant Richmond." Lee was speaking to the radio dispatcher, who also answered the phone after the day shift was gone.

There was a short pause, then Richmond got on the line. "Hey, Hawk. There's a lot of radio traffic concerning a disturbance at your apartment complex. Is there a connection between that and your call?"

Richmond had the knack for getting to the point. "Exactly, Lieutenant. Someone who looks like he could be a relative of Johnny Tanner, that carjacker from Shiprock, just tried to nail me with a crossbow, then a revolver. Apparently he didn't know I was off-duty tonight."

"Smart-ass. You okay, Hawk?"

"He nicked me, that's all, and I took a good thump on my vest. But the perp got away, at least for the moment. Here's what went down . . ."

Lee proceeded to give a quick sketch of what had happened, got the usual party line about cooperating with the local police and watching his back, then was finally able to end the call.

"Okay, now let's go down to the station. I want to get you started on that sketch as soon as possible," Agent Lopez said.

"Ready when you are."

The next morning, the phone rang early in Lee's apartment. Looking at the caller ID in the darkened bedroom, he noted that the source of the call was blocked, not revealing who it was that had just woken him up. It was probably one of his superiors with a truckload full of questions about last night.

"Hello," Lee grumbled.

"Hawk? Is that you?"

"Oh, hello again, Lieutenant Richmond. Guess I'm still half asleep. You must be calling about last night."

"That's right, Officer Hawk. I just got the opportunity to read your detailed report on the incident and have a conversation with the FBI."

"You need me to come in?" Lee doubted it was really necessary, but once the FBI got involved, officers in other agencies tended to begin covering their asses and doing everything by the book. Jealousy and envy were sometimes factors in the power struggle as well, with locals usually underpaid and often ill-trained.

"Not necessary at the moment, but let me know where you'll be. I'm just calling to advise you that you're being put on administrative leave until the FBI and our Las Cruces area plainclothes agents have a chance to evaluate the threat against you. Continue to cooperate with any investigating officers who have jurisdiction, including the FBI, and keep a low profile. Is that clear, Officer Hawk?" Richmond added.

"Sure, Lieutenant. But make sure the department doesn't dock me any vacation time if I'm on mandatory administrative leave instead. Okay? Remember, you're not the only one who's tight with the governor," Lee joked. The lieutenant had been a bodyguard for a New Mexico governor years ago, and was constantly boring the other officers with stories about the assignment and his association with the politician.

Richmond grumbled an affirmative and hung up the phone.

Halfway into his shower, Lee heard a knock. Reaching for his backup .45, he wrapped a towel around his waist and went to the door, standing to the side as much as he could and still look out the peephole.

It was Special Agent Diana Lopez, and she had two cups of coffee in her hands. Things were looking up. He decided to go with the flow.

He set his .45 down on the room divider that separated the living room from the kitchen, turned the dead bolt, then opened the door. Lopez nearly dropped the coffee.

"Special Agent Lopez . . . Diane. Come inside, and bring that coffee with you. Sorry for the out-of-uniform look. I was in the shower." He waved his hand toward the kitchen table, and nearly lost his towel.

"Nothing I haven't seen before, Officer Hawk—Lee. Go ahead and finish your shower. I'll make myself at home. Afterward, I'd like you to come down to the local office and look at some photos."

"*Mi casa es tu casa,*" he said, smiling, then picked up the .45 from the divider. She looked away from his towel long enough to notice the handgun.

"Good to see you're being careful."

"Oh, this little thing. I carved it from a bar of soap." She smiled and he walked back into the bathroom, shut the door, then placed the backup weapon back between two hand towels beside the shower stall.

Less than ten minutes later, he emerged from the bedroom, fully dressed, with his off-duty Beretta handgun in place. He'd hurried with the sunblock, too, though it meant skipping some areas normally covered by clothes.

Lee had figured Agent Lopez would be showing up again soon, but underestimated her. He hadn't expected her this early. It was barely eight in the morning, and when he was off-duty, he usually spent the daylight hours sleeping. Despite his ability to cope with limited sunlight, he was a walker of the night, and didn't like pushing that terminal sunburn thing.

"Want something to go with that coffee, Agent Lopez?" Lee said, walking over to the refrigerator. He took out a carton of eggs, some bread and milk, and the butter dish. The bottle of calves' blood, concealed in a tomato juice container, was a special treat he'd avoid this morning now that he had a guest.

"I had a glass of juice and a breakfast burrito at a fast-food place, but I hate those chain eateries with laminated menus. Back home in Albuquerque, I'd be powering down some *huevos rancheros*, green chile, and a big pot of coffee right now. You go right ahead, Lee."

"Sure you won't have some french toast and maple syrup?"

She thought about it for a moment. "Maybe two pieces. Do you have any jam or jelly, and some margarine?"

He had peach jam, which turned out to be fine with his guest. By the time she was helping him load the dishwasher, he'd managed to feed her four pieces of french toast with jam and another cup of coffee.

On the way to FBI headquarters, in her sedan, Diane talked about having to diet the rest of the weekend to make up for this morning's indulgence. He told her she didn't need to worry about it, which was the right thing to say, though she didn't act like she believed him.

The FBI offices were downtown in an office building close to the city government facility. There, they looked at some photos Diane had the Navajo police in Shiprock fax them. It didn't take long for Lee to identify his attacker, a cousin of Johnny Tanner's named Darvon Blackhorse.

The revolver Blackhorse had used was recovered from the ditch, and had fingerprints all over it. The weapon had been stolen from a Farmington home a month ago.

The special agent in charge of the Four Corners area planned to use Navajo cops to help him search Blackhorse's residence in the Shiprock area on the Rez, and maybe pick up his trail from that end. Meanwhile, Las Cruces area enforcement agencies would be put on the lookout for Blackhorse, beginning with a search of the local motels.

After an hour, Lee managed to get a ride back to his apartment while Agent Lopez met with other officers to discuss the case. Lee had been asked to remain at home and inside—no problem for a vampire during daytime anyway—and was told that police officers would be patrolling the area, keeping watch, though they couldn't spare a bodyguard.

Finally alone again, Lee sat down on the sofa beside a small stack of local newspapers. He sifted through several current issues until he found the one he'd been keeping for months, sandwiched in between the others for safekeeping.

Turning to the "around the state" section, Lee looked at

the photo of the German Air Force pilots scheduled to come to Holloman Air Force Base for weapons training in their Tornado attack aircraft. The photo had been taken in a large hangar at some NATO airbase. In the center of the front row of pilots and support crew was a tall, slender German major with wraparound sunglasses and dirty blond hair.

Even without seeing the major's eyes, Lee easily recognized Hans Gruber, the German agent who'd ambushed the army convoy that March evening in 1945, killed officer Benny Mondragon, and changed Lee's life forever.

After years of fruitless efforts trying to track down his enemy, including working as a clerk for a private Jewish-led group gathering information on former German officers, especially SS and SA thugs, Lee had gotten lucky. The vampire who had killed his partner had come back to New Mexico. Was Major Wolfgang Muller, as Gruber called himself now, here to finish up old business?

Lee wasn't sure of anything—except that they'd meet. The time had finally come to settle the past once and for all.

Lee had never given up his search for Hans Gruber over the decades, but he'd been unable to keep the vampire from leaving the country, and in the chaos that came at the end of World War II, the vampire had just disappeared. And he didn't know if Gruber was the only enemy he had to worry about. Someone here in the U.S. must have provided Gruber with the intelligence information needed to locate and ambush the convoy with the gray box back in March of 1945.

The U.S. military, meanwhile, had made sure the ambush of the soldiers had been concealed by a cover story of an accident, and the death of Lee and his trainee officer, Benito Mondragon, had been listed as accidental as well.

Because Lee knew that someone in the program or security had betrayed the convoy, perhaps someone in what he later learned was called the Manhattan Project, Lee had never tried to retrieve the gray box all these years, as the dying lieutenant had advised.

He had gone back to the area a month later, but by then, rains had washed away the tracks, and he couldn't be certain exactly where it was. But he had returned as often as he could to check, making sure no one else was digging for it either. He felt responsible for that box, even now. Still, it would be nice to someday be able to shed that responsibility. Maybe someday soon, as a matter of fact.

But now his elusive quarry had come to him. When Lee discovered Gruber's presence and location, he worked to get a transfer to the Las Cruces district—close enough but not in plain sight.

When Lee made his move to take on Gruber for what he hoped would be the last time, he wanted it to be quick and clean. It would be during daylight hours if possible, when Lee's tolerance for daylight would give him at least one advantage. Gruber was stronger, more experienced, and capable of taking a lot of damage, but Lee would try to take him by surprise and use what little he'd learned about vampires in the past fifty years to finish things once and for all.

Now, with the complications brought about by the skin-walker attacks, and the travel restrictions Diane Lopez had requested, Lee was forced to be even more subtle in his movements and plans. He still hadn't decided whether to change his identity again before this was over. It would mean resigning from the state police department. True, Gruber—now Muller—might recognize him more quickly as a state police officer—the uniform was nearly identical today to what it had been then—but as a state cop, Lee had access to weapons, information, and other resources he wouldn't have most other professions. Posing as a member of the U.S. Air Force was a possibility, only Lee knew next to nothing of the role. He'd be discovered by any airman as a fraud almost immediately after he went on base.

The phone rang and Lee answered it. "Hello."

"This is Diane, Special Agent Lopez. I'm just checking in. Have you noticed any strangers around your apartment today?"

"Just one ornery-looking lady with a gun who stopped by earlier," Lee joked, wondering if her call was being recorded. Probably.

She ignored his comment, though he could hear the amusement in her voice. "Just follow the standard drill for a protected witness. Keep a low profile, stay alert, keep the curtains drawn, and try not to place yourself in a situation where someone can get close enough to take you out. We haven't been able to turn up the suspect, Darvon Black-horse, at any local motels, and the Navajo police have determined he's not at home."

"Coming from the Rez, he's probably short of money and may be sleeping in his vehicle, or at a relative's place, if one happens to live in the area. You might see if he has a younger relative or a former neighbor or friend going to NMSU who lives in a dorm or other university housing. Have you searched DMV records for a vehicle registered to Darvon Blackhorse?"

"We've already checked all that out. His vehicle was located in a shopping center parking lot about a mile from your apartment. We have it under surveillance. Evidence inside the vehicle suggests Blackhorse didn't come down here alone," Diane answered, strictly business and obviously very on top of her job. But she would have to be more than just competent in order to be running an investigation out of Albuquerque. New millennium or not, women still had to work twice as hard as men to be cops. His late wife had . . .

Lee checked himself, putting a stop to that kind of thinking. Emotional baggage would just be in the way now, and he had the biggest job of his life to complete. Nothing could be allowed to get in the way.

He tuned back in to what Diane was saying just in time.

"Any other suggestions, Officer Hawk? Your command officers say you've got the investigative skills of a career officer already." Agent Lopez was smart, covering all the bases in order to be on record as cooperating with all agencies involved. She seemed very career-oriented, like most of the FBI agents he'd met or heard about.

"He may have had someone waiting nearby as a wheel-man to pick him up after taking me out. My guess is that Blackhorse is going to need a replacement weapon if he intends to make any more attempts on my life. I'd check for any burglaries last night where weapons were reported missing, and monitor all the service vehicles that enter my apartment complex—everything from delivery people to gardening crews," Lee suggested.

"We're already on that, but you have a point about the weapons situation. With you armed and alert, he won't want to get close unless he can counter your handgun. I will have someone assigned to coordinate with the local burglary detail and patrol officers."

"Who is keeping an eye on my place? You or your partner, Agent Lopez?"

"My partner, Burt Thomas, for today. Las Cruces PD has increased patrols in the area, too, but that's all they can do. I'll take over from Burt tonight. Meanwhile, I'm going to grab some sack time. You might consider doing the same. I hear from your state police associates that you're a night owl anyway."

"Something like that," Lee said. "Would you like me to contact you directly, or go through the local Bureau switchboard if I come up with something?" The question wasn't an idle one. Lee wanted to know just how much she trusted him.

"Call me direct, but if you wake me up for nothing, I'm

going to kick your ass real good." She hung up.

From her response, he still couldn't tell if she trusted him or not. He'd have to assume she didn't. Trust wasn't something he could really afford, because that would put her closer to him. And right now, that was the last thing he needed with a skinwalker on his tail and someone who might be the most dangerous person in the world as his next target.

The FBI and local cops had the best chance of finding Darvon Blackhorse in the daytime, when skinwalkers couldn't shape-shift and conceal their human identities. But being in human form didn't mean they weren't dangerous. They could use weapons, place bombs, push someone in front of a bus, and mix in a crowded mall or an elevator. And they could track him by scent before they saw him, or he saw them. Darvon had attacked him as a human, like Johnny Tanner.

Lee preferred to hunt at night, when his superior vision gave him an edge and he could use his strength and speed with less chance of detection. If he was attacked by a pack of wolves or a pair of mountain lions, he just had to make sure he was well armed. Lee was an expert shot with all the practice he'd been getting and his unique vision. And being a law-enforcement officer, especially a state policeman, he could wear a weapon virtually anywhere, anytime.

Walking over to his closed-up roll-top desk, Lee unlocked the sliding cover and activated his powerful laptop computer, which was on sleep mode. One of the reasons he had selected this particular apartment complex was because they offered cable hookup that included speedy access to the Internet.

Within a minute he was logged on to the state police server, checking on inquiries he'd made concerning Major

Wolfgang Muller, the German pilot he believed to be Hans Gruber. The background check, which he'd begun after getting Muller's vehicle tag number at Alamogordo, where the pilot lived off base, had required him to bend a few rules and imply that Muller had been involved in espionage or drug dealing, which had, of course, sent him to FBI channels.

Muller's background had to have been forged, stolen, or assumed, like Lee's, and he was hoping it would lead to a confirmation, in Lee's mind at least, that he was after the right man. If Muller had a twin or brother who was also a vampire and had survived all these years, or maybe somehow had fathered a son, this could lead things in another direction entirely.

Lee would not take the risk of killing an innocent man. Now that he was a night walker, an investigation that took decades was no burden except to his conscience. He was willing to take time to make sure he'd found the right vampire.

Wondering just how many bells and whistles he'd set off with his inquiries, Lee read the information made available to him, copied the file onto a floppy, then broke the connection.

His system had a firewall to prevent intrusions, but he recalled hearing of an FBI program used to read people's E-mails that could penetrate his protection. He wondered if he was being monitored now and, if so, whether it was because of his inquiries into a foreign national's background, especially one who was a military officer and a NATO ally? Or would it be because of the incident with Johnny Tanner? Diane Lopez was a go-getter, and sounded as tough as nails. He doubted she'd get such mileage over the Tanner shooting, but she might have thought to tap his computer.

Lee decided it didn't really matter much now, because he was finally convinced he'd found the vampire who had haunted his memories for nearly sixty years. The man calling himself Wolfgang Muller wore a cap, a long-sleeved airshow-style jumpsuit some military pilots called shit-hots (the assumption being that they looked like hot shit in them), and wraparound sunglasses. Leather driving gloves, boots, and probably a ton of sunblock rounded out the sun protection the vampire needed.

The key factor in what he'd read that had convinced Lee he had the right man was a medical notation that Major Muller had a skin condition that was aggravated by intense sunlight.

As long as Muller wasn't tipped that someone was checking up on him—and especially that the someone was a Navajo state policeman—Lee was going to be able to make a hopefully lethal surprise move against the German pilot.

World War II was long past, but neither he nor Muller were old, and their memories were nearly perfect because time didn't seem to erode their minds at all. The vampire had killed those soldiers, murdered a shop owner in Albuquerque during his escape, and he'd killed Benny Mondragon, a rookie police officer with a teenaged bride and an infant son. Yes, it was during a time of war, but it was hardly honorable combat. And Muller had also condemned Lee to a life of loneliness and deception, forcing him to remain the perpetual prey of Navajo skinwalkers. Lee owed him, and collection time was near.

Deciding that he needed some food and rest, Lee downed a mug of calves' blood, followed by butter-pecan ice cream, then he stretched out on the sofa in his clothes. He was asleep within minutes.

The sound of footsteps outside his apartment door woke Lee up. He relaxed a bit when he heard a light knock on the door. Looking at his watch, he noted it was nearly seven and the sun was setting. Scooping up his pistol from beneath the sofa cushion, Lee slipped across the room and took a quick look out the peephole. Because of his size, easily six feet six, Lee knew the identity of the visitor immediately. He was Lieutenant Richmond, his local supervisor, in uniform. The lieutenant was carrying a small envelope.

Lee opened the door, and was forced to look up to acknowledge the blue-eyed, freckle-faced officer in his midforties. "Hey, Lieutenant. What brings you here tonight? Any news on Darvon Blackhorse?"

"No, I was just bringing over some papers I need you to sign regarding the administrative-leave situation you're facing," Richmond said matter-of-factly, but the look in his eyes revealed something else was on his mind, and the ex-college basketball star for the University of New Mexico motioned for Lee to remain silent and follow him down the hall. "But I left some of the papers in my unit. Just walk on out with me so I won't have to make two trips."

Lee slipped the small .45 into his pocket, locked his apartment door, and followed Richmond, who held his enormous hand up, a signal that Lee not speak yet. They continued down the hall, into a small foyer, and out the front door of the building.

"My unit is over here, Officer Hawk."

As they walked across the gravel, which crunched under their boots, Richmond began to speak in a low voice. "My guess is that the feds are monitoring your apartment with a parabolic mike, or one of those laser jobs that picks up conversations off the glass."

Lee now knew why Richmond had picked the gravel to walk upon. Hopefully, it would confuse any listening devices. "It sounds like they're after *me* instead of the nut who tried to skewer me with those crossbow bolts."

"What are you doing conducting a background check on some German Air Force major stationed at Holloman? The FBI is expressing concern, and they've been asking a lot of questions about you. I didn't have an answer. Do you?"

Lee was glad he'd thought to come up with a cover story. "I was trying to stay low profile on this. I noticed a man who looked military pushing the speed limit in his Porsche going through the mountains near Cloudcroft. A lot of the hotrod pilots like to race up and down those roads, testing their limits and placing civilians in danger. After running his tags through the DMV, and learning he was a German national named Muller, I decided to pull him over and give him a warning."

Richmond nodded, and Lee continued.

"I'd just reached over to switch on my emergency lights when he pulled to the shoulder and stopped behind another vehicle parked off the road near a picnic ground. I pulled over immediately, and kept watch from a distance. He was acting squirrelly, checking up and down the road before handing the other driver a package or large envelope. The driver gave him something back, then took off. Rather than follow the second vehicle and have to pass the German pilot, tipping my hand that I might have seen something, I turned around and went back down the mountain ahead of him."

"I don't remember reading anything like that in your reports," Richmond grumbled. "Why not?"

"I didn't want to put something down on paper that might get the pilot or myself or the department in hot water if I was misinterpreting the incident. So I decided to see what I could find out about Major Muller before I made any moves. If he turned out to be a former East German or had a shaky background, I would have let the Bureau and you know about it." Lee hoped his lie sounded reasonable.

"From your point of view, I can understand. But now that the attempt was made on your life, the Bureau is looking for a connection between your background request on the German and this attack. Is there one?" Lieutenant Richmond had parked all the way at the other end of the parking lot, probably on purpose to give them longer to talk.

"Not that I can think of." He paused. "You think Agent Lopez also bugged my apartment?" Lee looked around casually, realizing that his hunch about Diane Lopez was on the money.

"I don't know if it was her, or someone else in the FBI, but they're behind it. I trust you, Officer Hawk, but make sure you don't get yourself involved in any FBI entanglements with espionage and the German unit training at Holloman. It could set back international relationships an entire generation and destroy all our careers."

They reached the lieutenant's vehicle, and he unlocked the door, reaching inside to pick up an envelope from the seat cushion. "Here's the paper you need to sign." He wrote something down on a sheet of paper, then handed it to Lee along with the envelope.

Lee read the note. "You're getting twenty-four/seven surveillance. Northwest corner of Building G. They have a nightscope, too, I think. But I only had a quick look. I drove through the complex, then checked the windows across the grounds with binoculars."

"Stay safe," the lieutenant said.

"Thanks, Lieutenant." Lee shook Richmond's hand, a sign of gratitude, in particular coming from a Navajo. The

*Dineh* generally avoided touching strangers, though they did shake hands occasionally with relatives and friends.

"Stay out from under the lights," Richmond warned, looking up at the lampposts, which were just coming on with the gathering darkness. The officer nodded a good-bye, then got into his unit and drove away.

Lee walked back quickly to his building, jamming the wadded-up note into a half-full trash can just inside the lobby by the mailboxes. He was nearly to his own apartment when he heard someone behind him call his name. It was Special Agent Lopez . . . Diane, hurrying up the hall in his direction.

"Hi, Officer Hawk." Agent Lopez smiled a little stiffly. "That was your lieutenant, wasn't it? I noticed him driving away as I arrived. Didn't he used to play basketball for the Lobos?"

"Yes, Lieutenant Richmond made all-conference his senior year. He had papers for me." Lee wasn't going to volunteer any more information than that. Agent Lopez wasn't showing all her cards, so he didn't feel obligated to do so either.

"Come on inside. Have you eaten dinner yet?" Lee offered. He was nearly always hungry, a small price to pay for being basically immortal and self-healing.

She accepted his invitation and he prepared two thick steaks, broiling them on his portable electric grill as Agent Lopez prepared salad from greens in the refrigerator. Despite her congeniality, Diane seemed to be watching him when he was turned away and avoiding his gaze whenever he looked back.

Something was different now, and he tried to recall anything he'd done that might have changed her opinion of him. He doubted that the skinwalkers had been caught and informed the authorities that he was a vampire. It wasn't the kind of story that could be believed without being seen, and even then, you might have to see it three or four times to be convinced.

But there were other secrets in his life, and because he'd spent most of the past century in the Southwest, it was possible that one of his past identities was catching up to him. The curse of computers was that they could make connections it might take years, or forever, for an investigator to discover on his own. He'd been photographed several times since 1945, though he had always tried to avoid it without being conspicuous, and there were a few photos that had been taken when he was young and in school. Vampires could be caught on film, not like in the movies.

Finally, halfway through his steak, he decided he'd had enough of her strange behavior. "I know that you suspect me of something—you're keeping close tabs on me for a reason. But let's put our cards on the table, shall we? What's this really about? Does your interest in me have to do with that German Air Force pilot I checked up on through the Bureau? I'm not a spy or a terrorist."

"Then why did you run the check on him? And what are you hiding from *me*? Is there a connection between the attempt on your life and your interest in that foreign national? I find it hard to believe that you just happened to be following him when he passed secrets to some spy or made a drug deal."

So she'd heard that much. It was time to rattle her a bit. "The listening device you have over in the upstairs apartment of Building G must be pretty good. I guess it filtered out the crunch of the gravel despite the lieutenant's big feet?"

She stared at him for a moment. "How did you . . . Never mind. Just answer my question."

"Can your partner hear us now?"

She shook her head. "The device doesn't work when the curtains are closed. Some technical reason I don't care to know. Go ahead, talk, if you have something to say." Diane poured herself another cup of coffee. "You're not a spy, are you, like that poor Marine at the embassy in Moscow several years ago?"

"Put your tape recorder on the table."

She stared at him, then pulled it out.

"You can keep it running if you want."

She nodded once. "Okay. Now talk to me."

"I'm not a spy. What could I possibly know that would serve our country's enemies? A few Navajo cultural secrets? My war name? The perfect fry bread recipe? The governor's defense plans in case Utah attacks? Even as a state police officer, I haven't done any undercover work. Sorry if you've been wasting your time searching for a leak that isn't there. That German pilot is probably innocent, too."

Lee took a sip of coffee, added a spoonful of sugar, then stirred it before taking another sip. "Or maybe he was looking to get high outside of his airplane. That's my guess."

Diane sat there for a few minutes, taking sips from her coffee, looking around the room, but never at his face. Finally she looked him in the eye. "I have several questions, but I'm not interested in verbal sparring. Will you tell me the truth, or are you going to make jokes about it or change the subject?"

"I guess that all depends—are they personal questions, or do they have to do with any of the cases I was involved with, like the Johnny Tanner shooting?"

He started to walk across the room toward the sofa, thinking of possible answers to her possible questions, stalling for time.

"Stay away from there. The microphone might pick up sounds close to the window, curtain or not. This is between you and me now." Diane started to sit back down again, then changed her mind, turned off the tape recording, then leaned against the kitchen counter, facing him. He stood right across from her, less than four feet away.

"Well?" He believed she was the type to play things close to her chest, so laying her cards on the table wouldn't come naturally to her. Her abrupt change of tactics intrigued him.

"First of all, I want to know what happened with that arrow—what you called a bolt. It hit you in the chest and should have left a hell of a bruise and a sore spot, in spite of the vest. Yet, when I touched your chest, not ten minutes after it happened, you didn't even flinch, though I think I embarrassed you. And don't tell me it misfired. One of the lab people tested both crossbows, and they each shot a similar test bolt all the way through a one-inch piece of oak."

"I'm an alpha male. We don't recognize pain."

"Right. But I'm an alpha bitch, and I'm not convinced. From the holes in your sweater, I could swear that second bolt passed right through your upper arm. And you lost a bunch of blood, based upon what I saw on your sleeve. A scratch? I don't think so. I saw you pull the damn thing out as I was running up. You really had to yank at it. Can I see your arm and your chest?"

"Right now? This is only our second date."

"Don't be an asshole. This is serious. I also have another question and I might as well get everything out in the open now. When you were attacked, you were quicker than anyone I've ever seen in my life, like one of those movie fight scenes with everything speeded up. Can you explain what I saw?"

Diane held his gaze. Lee didn't look away but he was

worried now. She was getting closer to the truth every second. He decided to wait her out in silence.

"Okay, and here's the kicker," she said after a brief pause. "I read the background report on the German pilot, then took things further through the German government and Interpol. He's odd. Do you know he never takes off his cap and glasses outside and he has a rare skin condition that makes him hypersensitive to sunlight? I've noticed you wear your sunglasses outside all the time as well, even at night."

"My eyes are sensitive to light. It's not that unusual. I still test out twenty-twenty."

"I also found out that Interpol keeps their own photo archive gathered from all major European newspapers. When asked specifically for information on the German pilot, their computer matched up two photos—one was the pilot visiting at Holloman. The other was a German glider pilot who was around in 1939. Both men looked identical."

"How come they had photos dating back to 1939?"

"Access to old German military records and photo archives, I assume. It was from a photo exhibit hosted by a veterans' group. Interpol also has access to most WW II-era photos of German men, donated by a Holocaust organization that is still tracking possible war criminals."

Lee wondered if that was the same group he'd worked for years ago. "Coincidence? Screwup? They say everybody has a twin somewhere. That doesn't mean they had to live in the same time frame."

Diane took a step closer, and reached out to grab him in the right bicep. Without thinking, he instantly reached up and grabbed her hand.

"Ow! You have a grip like a vise."

"Sorry." He let go of her hand, and started to step back, but realized he was up against the counter. In other circumstances, he would have welcomed this aggressive woman, but she was too close to the truth and he wasn't ready to share.

"There's an even bigger coincidence I have a hard time accepting. I decided to check with the state newspaper's electronic photo archive. It goes back over seventy years, and it seems that you have a twin too, a twenty-five-year-old New Mexico state police officer who disappeared in March of 1945. Supposedly he drowned when he drove a motorcycle into an irrigation canal chasing after a fugitive, though they didn't find the body. His first name was Lee, just like yours. And another photo came up in 1963 that looks remarkably like that same officer—like you—except for the hairstyle and the fact that he looked the same age as the man eighteen years earlier. It's a wedding photo. Then, several years later, the woman in that photo was apparently killed by a wild animal—a wolf, the reporter suggests." She looked him in the eye, and he had a hard time not showing any emotion.

He took a while to respond. "Okay, I understand that a computer looking for similarities can link photos of people who look alike. That's their purpose. But you've got to know that they couldn't all be the same person—me. People age, right?"

Diane's cell phone rang, and she reluctantly flipped it open. She listened for a few moments, then walked over toward the window. "My partner knows about Johnny Tanner and the attack on you near Shiprock, so he's wondering about something. He's noticed a pack of big dogs roaming around outside the building, and he says they look just like . . ."

"Wolves? Get away from the window!" Lee grabbed his .45, and in two steps was between her and the heavy curtain.

## CHAPTER 8

The window exploded inward and the curtain was torn away from the wall along with the rod as a massive brown-and-gold furry blur crashed into the room with a vicious snarl.

Lee already had his backup .45 out. He fired twice, the noise like a bomb in the enclosed space, striking the animal in the midsection. It howled, and slid halfway across the room, knocking over a chair.

Two more wolves, one a black animal and the other a massive beast with silvery gray fur, leaped through the opening the first wolf had made, landing right in front of Diane. She shot the black one at point-blank range.

Lee's attention went back to the first wolf. The animal tried to stand up on its back legs. The yellow eyes glowed with hatred, razor-sharp teeth snapping at the air. Lee shot it a third time, making sure the hellish beast would stay down this time.

Lee snapped a shot at the silver-colored animal before it could reach Diane but, in a breath, the black one she'd shot once already was upon her again. She fired, but the beast kept coming, and her pistol was knocked out of her hands as she tried to ward the animal off.

Diane grabbed the black wolf by the throat with both hands, forcing it away from her face, but unable to let go to recover her weapon.

In one quick, fluid motion that utilized all his night walker's speed, Lee grabbed the animal by the back legs and jerked it away from Diane. Still holding it by the legs, he swung the one-hundred-pound beast around, launching it into the bedroom where it bounced off the dresser with a yelp.

Diane scooped up her weapon and fired again, striking the silver wolf in the upper body as it launched itself at Lee.

He stood his ground and stopped the wounded wolf's charge with his forearms, giving ground slightly from the impact. The animal howled and raked Lee's right arm with its fangs, then fell to the carpet. The large male beast tried to crawl away, then suddenly sagged and lay still.

"Are they all dead?" Lee spun around, his small backup .45 sweeping the area in front of him. Blood dripped down his arm and the wound hurt like hell. He peeked into the bedroom, and the animal he'd thrown into there was very still.

"I don't know. But they're not moving." Diane stared at Lee, then looked at the two dead wolves before them.

"What's going on? And how in the hell do you move so fast?"

"We don't have time for questions. Where's your partner?" Lee gathered up another weapon, the nine-millimeter Beretta from the holster on the kitchen counter.

Diane flipped open her phone and dialed. "Agent Thomas, what's your status?" Suddenly the sound of gunshots

echoed from across the complex. "Oh, my God! Him too."
She ran to the door.

"I'll go. I'm faster. Make sure the ones here are dead,
and if they aren't, shoot them until they are."

"What? Just go."

Lee nearly flew down the hall. He was capable of running a hundred yards in under five seconds. He'd timed it
once. He planned to beat that record now.

Once outside, he could see the apartment Diane and
her partner had used to stake out his place. A long, sleek
black panther or jaguar jumped out of the window effort-
lessly, spun around, and took three long strides, leaping over
the seven-foot-high fence. Lee thought about taking a shot,
but houses and businesses lay within the sight line, and he
couldn't risk hitting a civilian. By the time Lee got to the
fence, the beautiful, deadly animal had disappeared among
the cars in an adjacent strip mall parking lot.

"Damn. I'll never catch him now." Lee sprinted over to
the FBI's apartment, and peeked into the window. Agent
Thomas was lying faceup on the carpet, a pool of blood
around his right arm, and a virtual lake around his upper
body. It appeared that the man's throat had been ripped
open. The red-haired agent's pale blue eyes were already
glazing over with death.

"What's going on? Were those gunshots?" a middle-aged
woman asked, poking her head out her apartment door.

"Call 911. A man's been attacked by a wild animal.
Don't go outside until the police arrive," Lee yelled.

Then he heard a flurry of shots coming from his building.

He raced back the way he'd come. The door to his apartment was closed, just like he'd left it.

"Diane. It's Lee. I'm coming in now." He opened the door and stepped inside. Diane was standing in the doorway to the bedroom, her pistol in her hand, but now down by her side, the action open, indicating the weapon was empty.

"They weren't all dead—and they've . . . gone?" She looked at him, utterly confused and shaking badly. In front of her on the living-room carpet was a naked Navajo man in his early forties or so, still clutching a long sliver of plate glass like a knife. He had at least three bullet wounds, one in his stomach, one in his leg, and another in his left side. He was bleeding badly, and if not already dead, almost certainly beyond help. "He came at me with the glass. It was him or me. What the hell is happening?"

A small Navajo woman, not much older than a teenager, was also there naked, lying on the floor against the dresser, cut up badly from the glass that had come from the shattered mirror. She was as limp as a rag doll, and her head hung at an impossible angle. The impact of Lee throwing her across the room had probably broken her neck.

"How did they get in there? And where are the other two wolves? What happened to Burt . . . Agent Thomas? Is he okay?" Diane asked, her voice still shaky. Instinctively, she ejected the magazine on her pistol and inserted a fresh one.

"I'll tell you as we go. We still have one to track down." Lee looked around the room, grabbed his jacket and a bandoleer of extra ammunition, then looked back at the bodies. The skinwalkers were dead, but two had lived long enough after their initial wounds to shift back into human form. The big brown-and-gold wolf had died in animal form, and would not change back, this he knew. It would only add to the confusion when more officers arrived. He stepped around the blood and opened the closet door, retrieving his duty weapon, a .45 Smith & Wesson, then left the bedroom and shut the door.

"One got away?" She looked over at the wolf, then holstered her pistol and grabbed her purse and jacket. Still confused, she followed him into the hall. He reached back and pulled the apartment door shut.

They ran down the hall, hearing sounds of excited voices in the apartments they passed. "I'll explain, but we need to track down another animal, a large black panther or jaguar that attacked your partner. We'll take my patrol unit. If we wait around and answer questions from the local cops, the killer will get away." Lee pulled her out the back door of the apartment building, and they jogged toward his police cruiser.

"Killer? Burt Thomas is dead?" Diane stopped. "No! I should have been there." It was obvious she was considering going to the apartment where Thomas's body lay.

"Come on, we can't help him now except to catch his killer. You saw what we encountered. Thomas was alone, and what came after him was in the form of a two-hundred-pound panther. I was too late to stop it, and couldn't risk a shot after the animal leaped the fence. I'm sorry for what happened to Agent Thomas, but do you want the creature to get away now?" Lee grabbed her hand and pulled, urging her forward.

She resisted for a moment, then must have realized what he was saying might be true. "What happened to Burt?"

"The big cat came through the window, like what happened to us. Your partner must have hesitated, or just been a second too slow. You heard the shots. He pulled his weapon, but the cat got to his throat before he could bring the pistol up. If we move fast and get lucky, we can catch the killer while he's still a cat. I saw the creature loping toward the strip mall across the complex."

They jumped into his black patrol unit, and Lee was out on the street in seconds. Circling around to the alley behind the strip mall, he cruised slowly down the narrow path behind an insurance office, pizza parlor, and laundry, working the searchlight with his left hand.

"What do you mean, if he's still a cat? You're bullshitting me."

"You think? Just keep watching. If you see anything move, man or beast, let me know." Lee muttered, his gaze following the beam of the light as he inched the vehicle forward. He really didn't need the damned light, but it would help her see better, and he needed Diane's eyes as well right now.

Diane was silent, and still frightened, but she was helping him search as he drove. She had courage, overcoming her fear when it really had counted. And now that she wasn't operating on automatic anymore, Diane was probably analyzing the situation again. He wondered how much she'd figured out already, and had she tried to make sense of it all? Or did she just think he'd slipped some peyote into her coffee?

"The man and woman in your apartment. What were they? We shot three wolves when they attacked. I turn my back to look outside, and the next thing I know, there's a man trying to stab me . . ." she admitted, her voice steady, but strangely hollow now.

"You saw what happened with your own eyes. You don't need to ask me." Lee pulled out onto the street at the end of the alley, and turned left, intending to turn down the next street.

"But that's fantasy, make-believe, TV-fucking nonsense, Lee. We're not living in a fairy-tale world."

Lee noted approvingly that her attitude was back full strength, and she was keeping her eyes on their surroundings.

"I understand your skepticism. But look at the facts, and feel the ache in your arms and the blood and sweat on your clothes before you dismiss this as some kind of Candid Camera stunt. You saw their fangs, smelled their foul breath, and kept one at bay with your bare hands for a moment. Did they look like fairies to you?" Lee asked.

He saw the disbelief lingering, so he continued. "They've been in the Southwest since the first human walked the land, just hidden from most eyes. It's a Navajo thing, probably has to do with a combination of genetics and some viruslike infection that's remained unidentified. The *Dineh*, the Navajo people, call them skinwalkers—at least that's the Anglo translation."

She looked at him, still shaking her head, so he continued, never taking his eyes off his search. "They are Navajo witches, humans that can take the form of animals, changing to the beasts like some real-life Lon Chaney Jr. character. The ones we shot may have killed a dozen or more Navajos since they were turned. They aren't the nose-twitching, spell-casting demon hunters in designer clothes you've seen on TV either. These people are evil in every form they take."

Lee's police radio suddenly came to life, and he started to reach for the mike, then changed his mind. It was a call for him, asking for his location and information about the situation around his apartment. After several requests, the calls stopped.

"You're going to get a call too, soon, Diane. We're going

to have to hunt down these creatures by ourselves, especially the one who killed Agent Thomas. They'll probably hole up for the night now. Try and buy us some time."

"What can I say? Nobody will believe what really happened." She shook her head. "I don't believe it either, and I was there. Something tells me there's a lot more shit going on than what you're saying."

"That's true enough. For now, just tell them that some Indian cult using trained wolves decided to attack some law-enforcement officers that were investigating a shooting that took place on the Navajo Nation. At least one human and one of the animals, a black panther, got away, and for some reason known only to them, the humans were naked. You're trying to track them now. They attacked your partner and they're after you, too. You're working with me because it's connected to that incident with Johnny Tanner. You're going to maintain radio silence to avoid being an easy target, but you'll keep in touch and update them at every opportunity. Emphasize this is the best way to catch those who killed Agent Thomas." Lee looked over, hoping it would sink in.

"How much of that crap is really true?" Her phone buzzed, and she flipped it open, but didn't answer immediately.

"About half, give or take. They *were* naked." He stopped the cruiser, turned off the searchlight, and waited. "If you can't deal with it, tell me now and I'll let you out at a safe location. Go have a drug test done on yourself if you think this has just been a psychedelic experience. Or find a shrink. I can hunt down these skinwalkers by myself. It's pretty much my goal in life anyway."

Diane looked at him for a moment, cursed once, then pushed the receive button. After answering some questions, she basically repeated what he'd suggested, argued for a few moments with a superior who obviously wanted to see her, then hung up abruptly.

"I'm sticking with you, for now, but only if you'll tell me the complete truth about yourself, and what's really going on. Otherwise, I'll do what I have to, and you'll be on your own."

Anger in her eyes, Diane looked out the window, glancing inside parked cars and into people's yards as he drove up and down through the neighborhood. They searched for another half hour in a slowly expanding box pattern, then Diane spoke again. "Lots of cops, a few civilians, but nobody naked and no animals other than a few dogs and one cat. We aren't going to find a damn thing doing this."

"Let's get out of here, then." Lee turned north, catching I-25 and heading northwest out of Las Cruces. "We'll take up the hunt tomorrow night. They don't go into animal form in the daylight, and we'd have a hell of a time trying to guess what the human looks like."

Diane sat up in her seat, checking out the side mirror from time to time, then glancing back at him. Lee could tell she was still trying to come up with a logical explanation for this. Unfortunately, he knew that the logical explanation left no alternative but the truth, and she wasn't going to like that at all. Agent Lopez was one stubborn lady.

"We won't be on the Interstate for long. I have a place just south of one eighty-five, close to the river. We'll be there in fifteen minutes." Lee looked over at Diane again, trying to decide if he should risk telling her any more about himself. He'd been alone for such a long time now, ever since they'd killed Annie, and the life he'd been living was finally starting to get to him.

Could he take a chance and try to find an ally? Diane had already been through a lot with him and seen more than he could hope to cover up, and he'd only known her a few days. It was obvious she was intelligent and motivated, but was she just interested in advancing her career?

It couldn't be just that. She was still sticking with him and certainly what happened tonight was *not* a career maker. There were too many things about this case that could never become public, not without destroying her credibility completely. There was, however, one thing that might keep her playing along with him, at least for a while . . .

The safe house he'd had ready for several weeks was only a mile farther down the road, which ran parallel to the Rio Grande to the west. The dry, harsh Robledo Mountains were across the river, and he could see Cerro Robledo, the highest point, as if it were daylight outside. His night vision was about the only special ability Diane hadn't noticed already.

Just how ready was she to hear about real-life vampires, he wondered, and what would she do if he laid it all out for her? Perhaps the best strategy would be to let her discover it on her own, a bit at a time, so she wouldn't freak out entirely.

Turning off his headlights, he continued another half mile, driving slowly and watching for traffic ahead and behind the vehicle.

"How can you see?" Diane asked, leaning forward and trying to see beyond the hood of the car.

"Trust me a little longer."

Just past a curve in the road, Lee slowed and quickly wheeled into a narrow graveled lane past a solitary mailbox on a post. Tall brush on both sides intermingled with cottonwoods and other bosque vegetation he didn't know by name. The road made a ninety-degree turn and ran alongside a wide levee for another hundred yards, then turned back to the right and crossed a large irrigation ditch over an old timber bridge with split-log railings.

Hidden beneath and within the cottonwoods was a low adobe-style home with a two-car attached garage. Reaching under the seat, Lee brought out a garage-door opener. They entered the garage next to a several-years-old dusty black Ford pickup, and Lee turned off the engine as the door closed behind him. It was pitch-black in the garage, no overhead light had come on.

"Here we are. Unless we've all of a sudden run out of luck, we can stay here as long as necessary. Not even the Bureau can find us here unless we want them to. I've leased this house through an assumed name and the truck is registered under that identity as well." Lee reached past Diane and opened the glove compartment, grabbing a flashlight and switching it on.

"Use this to find your way until I get to the light switch." He handed it to her, then got out, walking over to the door leading into the house, and turning on a light switch. A fluorescent fixture over a workbench came on.

She looked around the inside of the garage. Except for the pickup truck and the police cruiser, the room was empty and there were no windows. The air was dusty, stirred up by the opening of the garage door. "You don't get out here very often, do you?" Diane said, walking toward the door he'd just opened.

"I stop by while patrolling this direction at least once a week to empty the mailbox and check the house. Always at night. Nobody has ever seen me here, that I know of, at least as a state patrolman." Lee unlocked the door and stepped into the house, a modern structure probably less than ten years old, and they passed through a small laundry room into a hallway that led to the interior of the house.

A light was on in the living room, and a radio was playing country music. There was an old sofa and a TV, and a small kitchen table with two chairs. All the appliances looked relatively new. The curtains were floor length, and lined so that little if any light could be seen outside. The illumination came from a table lamp on a timer. Diane looked, noting that the radio was also on the timer.

"You have it set up to look like somebody's here in the evenings. When does the radio shut off? Ten P.M.?" Diane looked around and noted a thin layer of dust on everything. "This is some kind of safe house you've put together, isn't it? I think it's time you answered the rest of my questions."

He turned off the radio. "Let's have some coffee. While I'm brewing a pot, you might want to reload your spare magazine. There is plenty of ammunition hidden inside the broiler. Get out the .45 ammo for me, for my backup pistol, if you don't mind."

"You're always ready for a war, it seems, Lee. Is that your real name anyway? Just who or what are you, and why am I risking everything, not just my career, by coming with you?" She looked in the broiler of the gas oven, and sure enough, there were two boxes of nine-millimeter ammunition and one of .45 cartridges inside a larger plastic storage box.

"Coffee first. And from now on, whether you decide to stick with me on this or not, make sure you always have plenty of ammunition. There are some other things you might need, also. I have another one of these hidden here. You can take it." He reached into his boot, pulling out a slender, razor-sharp double-edged commando dagger.

"That's not a knife, it's a sword, and I carry a backup

pistol anyway. Quit jerking me around. Every time I ask you a critical question, you change the subject. The coffee is brewing now, let's have some answers along with it. Just who are you, really, besides State Police Officer Leonard Hawk, born April 29, 1976?"

Lee looked at the attractive young woman leaning against the kitchen counter, pistol at her waist, and knew that one way or the other, he'd have to tell her something. For the first time since Annie came into his life, someone knew a hell of a lot about him. He could lie, but with all the evidence she's quoted to him before the attack, it would have to take a really credible story. She'd never believe a lie, and unfortunately, the truth sounded even stranger.

"What the hell. I'm going to tell you the truth now, even if I'm screwed. Just remember what you've seen already tonight before you decide I've gone off the deep end, and brought you along for company."

"Don't expect me to believe a word of it. I still don't accept the skinwalker crap; not really. But try me anyway." Diane was using her bad-cop tone now.

"Well, believe it or not, I am State Police Officer Lee Nez, and I'm not really missing and presumed dead. Have you ever worked with a really older man?"

Special Agent Diane Lopez sat there, her coffee getting cold, as Lee told her about that March night in 1945, about encountering the ambush of the army convoy, losing his trainee, killing the attackers, and burying the box containing the secret weapon, then encountering the "dead" Hans Gruber again.

She was still listening, though her jaw had dropped a little, so Lee told her about being near death, his blood being mixed with Gruber's, then being turned into a vampire and healing within minutes. He described how he'd tricked Gruber. By then, her eyes were wide open, and she sipped her coffee absently, shaking her head.

"It still sounds like a movie-of-the-week plot to me, but maybe I've stepped into the Twilight Zone for real. Okay, *if* I believe this load of crap you've been telling me, and you knocked the guy over the edge of the cliff, why didn't this so-called vampire die from the fall?"

"I didn't know it then, but unless key fatal injuries take place, it takes a lot more than a fall off a cliff to kill a vampire. Since I didn't want to remain a night walker, I left what I thought was a dead body and hurried to find a Navajo medicine man. The next evening, when I could safely go outside, I decided to double-check and make sure Gruber was really dead. That's when I realized what a dumb-ass mistake I'd made. He was gone, under his own power." Lee went back to get himself another cup of coffee.

"Got anything stronger to go into that coffee?" Diane looked hopefully toward the cupboard.

Lee nodded. "Above the sink."

Diane retrieved an unopened bottle of cognac from an upper cabinet, and poured an inch of the fiery liquid into her coffee. Lee came over, set down his cup, and she added the same to his.

"I'm still having a hard time swallowing this, and I'm not talking about the coffee. When did you tell the army about that secret weapon? Was this supposed to be part of the atomic bomb set off at Trinity Site a few months later—if I remember my New Mexico history correctly," Diane said.

"That's where things get complicated, and what leads me—us—into the situation that we're in now. I was trying to track down Gruber, and I ran into him the next evening. Actually, he shot me while I was chasing him on a motorcycle, and I ended up in an irrigation ditch north of Socorro. He got away, and I have no idea where he went after that.

"I was assumed to be dead, and had trouble establishing a new identity until the war ended. I kept looking for Gruber, but ran out of time and money," Lee continued. "I couldn't remain Lee Nez, there were too many questions I couldn't answer, and it was hazardous for me to be outside for any length of time during the daytime—though admittedly I can stay out in the sun a lot longer than a vampire."

"What about the missing plutonium or uranium or whatever it was?"

"It was all hushed up with a cover story. The dead soldiers were explained away as having died in a vehicle accident, along with my rookie partner. The bodies of the German agents, well, they never existed officially or unofficially as far as I could learn. They were buried and forgotten. My police cruiser was found and returned to the department, and I was listed as missing, presumed drowned. I never did find out who told the Germans about the nuclear material and the timetable for the convoy, but it had to be a traitor working behind the scenes."

"So what eventually happened to the box all those men died for?" Diane poured herself another finger of cognac without the coffee.

"The military scoured the area under the cover of a war game, but they never found it, and I sure didn't know who to trust. It might have been a decoy to mislead the German agents, or the real thing, but whatever the case, the military still had enough plutonium and enriched uranium to make three bombs. They set the first A-bomb off at Trinity Site, as I found out after the war. It wasn't until then that I knew why Gruber and his men had been willing to take so many risks."

Diane got up and started pacing, obviously trying to decide what to believe. She walked from the kitchen into the living room, back and forth through the archway. In a wastebasket she could see the junk mail he'd received as occupant or postal patron. Finally she returned to the kitchen. Lee hadn't moved, he'd been watching, gauging her reaction to all this.

"The photo of that woman, Annie something, that I saw in the newspaper article. Was that your wife?"

Lee nodded.

"Was she a vampire too?"

Lee shook his head.

"But she knew what you were—are?" Diane realized she was whispering at this point. She sat down at the kitchen table and poured herself more cognac.

Lee put the dagger back into his boot scabbard. "I told her just before I asked her to marry me, though she'd already seen some of my abilities. But I don't want to talk about that right now. We have more important issues at hand."

"Was she killed by the same kind of creatures that came after us and Burt Thomas last night? Skinwalkers, are they called?" Diane persisted.

Lee nodded, swallowing to ease the lump in his throat that thinking of Annie always brought. "Their kind have been after me from the very beginning. They can smell vampires as different from other humans—maybe even sense the power, I don't know. Being Navajo makes me especially noticeable to them, I think."

"Suppose I believe you now, or at least go along with this because it fits in with what I've seen. You said skinwalkers are all evil, something to do with what made them shape-shifters. Are vampires like that too, all evil? What about you?" Diane looked him straight in the eye. "You going to attack me next?"

Lee shook his head. "Skinwalkers and vampires aren't the same, though the changes are produced through the work of some kind of similar viruses, or something even more basic than that, passed through something attached to red blood cells, I think. But from what I've learned, which isn't, admittedly, a whole lot, it seems that vampires aren't much different from the people they were before, except for the physical characteristics you've already noticed about me, and the fact that they have to avoid direct sunlight."

"You always wear long sleeves and a cap, and those wraparound sunglasses. Is that enough protection?"

Lee shook his head slowly. "I'm only half vampire, thanks to the Navajo medicine man who was in a position to help me. I use a lot of maximum-strength skinblock, cover up, and work basically at night. But even a full day outside, if I'm careful, won't kill me. A full vampire can be outside for brief periods, maybe a half hour if he or she has on a lot of sunblock and is protected like me."

"You seem to eat like a horse, and don't seem to have an ounce of fat. I thought vampires fed only on blood and weren't really alive. You're alive, aren't you?" Diane reached over slowly and felt his pulse. His skin tingled at the touch, but he didn't flinch.

"I breathe, and my heart is beating, maybe a little faster that usual right now," he said. "I even have a reflection. That blood-sucking, neck-biting, and long-fangs image comes right from Bram Stoker and Hollywood, though blood *is* particularly nutritious for us, like a quick energy food. I get mine from butcher shops, slaughterhouses, and ranchers, a little here, a little there. They think I use it in my garden as fertilizer. I told them it's an old Navajo secret ingredient for growing corn."

"You have a vampire for an enemy. You said you shot Hans Gruber in the head, then later threw him off a cliff. Yet he didn't die. If you'll pardon me asking such a sensitive question, how *do* you kill a vampire? Cut off its head? What are those vital spots you mentioned?"

"Decapitation is one way, and that's the reason I carry the long dagger. You can chop up their bodies in other ways too, or destroy their heart so it can't pump blood anymore and circulate the healing elements. Big wooden stakes actually work if they destroy the heart. Fire works too, *if* it gets hot enough to consume the body. Anything that will stop the heart or shut down the brain completely, like decapitation. We burn up a tremendous amount of energy, so I suppose you could starve a vampire too, a lot faster than with a human. But you'd have to have a strong prison. A vampire has tremendous strength."

"Even more than you? I find that hard to believe."

Lee shrugged. "I've only had to fight two vampires since I took on Hans Gruber. They came after me on separate occasions, and I managed to kill them both. One I shot several times, which rendered him unconscious, then I cut off his head. The second, well, I managed to get him toasted, literally."

"Sounds like a bitch. By comparison, the skinwalkers are almost a walk in the park—with wolves." Diane looked at the .45 rounds in his ammo box, noting they were soft points. "Those bullets have a lot of punch up close."

"Not all skinwalkers use the wolf form. They've also attacked in the form of mountain lions or black cats such as panthers. The one who killed your partner was a jaguar or whatever. Those are the strongest animals for the weight.

They're fast and stealthy too, especially for solo work. When they take wolf form, they usually run in packs."

Diane sat there, thinking for a while, and Lee stared at his coffee cup. He still didn't know how the night would end, now that he'd basically blown a cover he'd had for nearly sixty years. What would Diane do with all this information?

Finally she spoke again. "Which brings us back to the original question, the one that I asked you a while back. The Navajo man you killed on the Reservation, Johnny Tanner. Was he a skinwalker?"

"Yes, and the wolves killed were his missing girlfriend and her sister. They died before they could transform back into humans, so they'll never be found, naturally. Tanner had remained in human form to set up the car accident scenario. Now you know why I had to lie." Lee shrugged. "If I'd have told you the truth without you having seen what you did tonight, you'd have recommended me for the rubber-gun squad.

"But that wasn't the only reason you came to talk to me the other day, was it?" Lee crossed his lean, powerful arms across his chest, never taking his eyes off of hers. She was wavering, finally thinking outside the box.

"No. But if all you've told me tonight is true, I think I know why you wanted to know about the German Air Force pilot. He's really Hans Gruber, isn't he?"

"I think so. And if he is, I need to know why he's returned to New Mexico after fifty-seven years. I have to find out if he somehow knows about me, or if he's here to get the military cargo he tried to hijack so long ago."

## CHAPTER 9

Do you understand what's going on now, Diane? I'm after a superhuman spy who may have killed many Americans, including a young cop with a wife and infant son, and an innocent civilian. I know we've had several wars since then, and the Germans are considered our friends and allies. But I don't think Hans Gruber, if that's who Major Wolfgang Muller really is, has come to New Mexico just to drop practice bombs and work on his tan."

Diane shook her head. "I'm still trying to comprehend the existence of vampires and skinwalkers. Give me a few hours to digest all this, and sort things out in my head, then I'll tell you what I think." Diane looked toward the front door, which was constructed of metal, and had two dead bolts. "Are we really safe here?"

Lee nodded. "We could probably hole up here for days. Unless a den of skinwalkers lives just downwind, we'll be all right."

"How far do skinwalker packs range? You said they normally only bother other Navajos?" she wondered.

"I've never come across any Navajo witches outside of the Four Corners states, and only rarely off the Navajo Nation. Like most of the animals they change into, they're territorial." He stopped, then added with a wry smile, "It's a problem that affects the *Dineh*, and that's why for the past half a century, I kept coming back to Navajo settlements to hunt them down. I owe my people that much for the help the medicine man gave me when I needed him. Skinwalkers have undermined my people for hundreds of years, maybe forever, if you believe the old stories, and I've helped equalize things a bit. They *are* the closest thing I've seen to pure evil since Hitler's time."

"So you've always put yourself in harm's way, like live bait, knowing they can't help but come looking for you. You must have a major death wish. What exactly do they want, besides to kill you? Will your blood make them immortal, healing their injuries and diseases? Would it do the same for me?"

"I don't know for sure, but I doubt it. I'm only half vampire, 'a walker of the night,' as the medicine men say."

"There goes my fountain of youth. Guess I'll still need moisturizers." She smiled wearily, then walked across the room to the hall. He followed.

"We don't need to keep watch, at least not tonight. Take the bedroom at the end of the hall. I'll use the one across from the main bathroom. I leased this place basically furnished, and there are plenty of nonperishable supplies." Lee handed her the flashlight.

"Do you have a laptop? I'd like to do some research?"

He nodded. "You're going to look up vampires and check up on the other stuff I've told you?"

"I'm a federal cop. We do a lot of our legwork from our offices."

He walked back into the living room, unlocked a desk

drawer, and returned with a small laptop and power supply. "Here you go."

"Tomorrow morning we're going to have to discuss what to do about Muller," Diane said, taking the laptop from him.

"I know. Just try to relax in the meantime, and make sure your head is on straight after all you've learned today. Biding your time until the opportunity to strike is right is a good battle strategy. Trust me on that."

"I know. Patience is always a good investigative tool. And I've got lots."

Lee watched Diane go. It felt strange having a woman in the same house as him—one who knew his darkest secrets, even if she probably really didn't believe some of them, not yet. He'd made himself vulnerable by telling her as much as he had, though he'd had little choice after all she'd already encountered. His only hope now was that his instincts about her were on target and she wouldn't betray him.

After living alone for so many years, always in danger from skinwalkers or the discovery of his vampire powers, Lee had become a light sleeper, and with his enhanced hearing, it wasn't a difficult habit to acquire. Sometime before sunrise he heard Diane walk into the living room, and unlock one of the dead bolts on the outside door.

He didn't move, though he knew he could stop her. The choice was really hers, and he couldn't risk having an ally who'd change sides at the worst possible moment. He wasn't so much worried about her telling his story—she'd be laughed out of the Bureau—but she could get in his way.

After about five minutes, she locked it again and went back to her room. Lee rolled over and closed his eyes, knowing he was safe for a while. Whatever crisis she'd had had passed, at least for the moment.

Vampires, even half vampires, didn't need alarm clocks to know it was morning. Lee woke up feeling moody, having dreamed for the first time in years about Annie. He didn't remember much about the dream, only that Annie had been there with him, and they'd been on the road in his old pickup with the camper shell. They'd gone on a lot of trips during their time together, just the two of them. It was those fond memories that had helped block out her loss.

Not one to dwell in his rather substantial past, Lee opened his eyes, saw where he was, and got out of bed. He slipped on a pair of jeans from the closet and walked down the hall past his guest's closed door, and headed into the kitchen. He could hear water running in the shower.

He had a pot of coffee brewing by the time Diane came into the kitchen. She had on a pair of his jeans, which were slightly baggy on her, and an Aggies sweatshirt. It was a common sight in Las Cruces. Diane looked very natural in the casual clothes he'd kept here for emergencies, like the woman of the house on a lazy Saturday morning—except for the nine-millimeter handgun in a pancake holster on her belt, of course.

"Good morning, Lee. Hope you don't mind me tracking down some clothes. Your jeans are a bit large, but I like them clunky."

Diane walked over to the sink and found her cup in the drain rack. "Coffee nice and strong? I can use it this morning." She stared at his chest for a moment, then she must have realized what she was doing and looked away.

"What's mine is yours when it comes to clothes. Sorry about the sizes though, I don't have very many women guests." Lee shrugged, knowing she had to realize that he'd never brought anyone here. "I'm going to grab a shower now. There aren't any towels or soap in the hall bathroom."

"I noticed you have lots of sunblock beside the sink in the bathroom I used. Put that on first thing every day, I bet." Diane sounded almost used to the idea of him being a night walker.

"Be prepared, like the Boy Scouts say." He walked down the hall to the master bedroom and stepped inside, closing the door. The bed was already made, and her clothes were neatly folded on the floor beside the dresser. The room smelled like a woman, and it was a scent he stopped for a moment to enjoy. The trace smell of makeup, a hint of perfume or hand lotion, it all brought back pleasant memories of the one brief time he'd been truly happy with his cursed life.

Realizing that kind of pleasure wasn't something he should start getting used to again, Lee went into the bathroom and stripped off his jeans. A long shower was what he needed, preferably cold.

Later, they worked together to fix breakfast. There weren't any eggs or fresh milk, but they had pancakes from a mix that only needed powdered milk and vegetable oil to prepare, and he paired it with canned ham sliced and warmed in the skillet. He set out a jug of blood from the refrigerator too, and she looked at it curiously for a moment before he explained that no, it wasn't tomato juice, and she didn't have to drink any to be polite.

Diane didn't say much during breakfast, though Lee knew she had a lot on her mind from her thoughtful expressions and lack of attention to his lousy jokes.

Finally, as they were loading the dishwasher—Lee joked he wouldn't have a safe house without one—Diane finally brought up what was on her mind.

"I was raised in Albuquerque's North Valley, the old Alameda neighborhood, and I grew up with all the spooky old children's stories there about La Llorona, the spirit of the mother looking for her drowned child along the ditch banks, and the stories of the Anglo bogeyman as well. The stories all promised that if you were a good kid and listened to your parents, you were safe.

"Then those stories gave way to stories of Frankenstein, the Wolfman, and Dracula—old Hollywood. Good always won out over evil, and the devil's servants went to hell, where they belonged. Even in the films about that guy, Jason, Michael, or whoever it was with the ski mask and butcher knife, good won at the end, though evil would be back in the sequel.

"But no matter what was in vogue, I always knew a real threat from one that was made up. I'd jump and scream at all the right times at the movies, but I was never really afraid. A rational mind protects you to a large extent. I became a cop because the line between right and wrong was clear and everything was predicated on hard facts. Then in the FBI, I learned what a really scary guy is—and what motivates him. Yet even within insanity there was always logic, convoluted as it might be, and it all fit within the laws of nature. But now. . . ."

"Still the skeptic?"

"What did you expect? Even when I was a little kid and we went to amusement parks, I always knew there was a human inside that mouse costume. And the movies; makeup and camera tricks."

"We're real. I'm real, and creatures like me have nothing to do with either magic or special effects. We're a part of nature, just like rabid dogs and serial killers. If you haven't accepted that skinwalkers and vampires really exist, what made you change your mind and stay this morning?"

"You heard that but didn't try to stop me? Why?" Diane was obviously surprised.

"Either I had no real choice after what you've already encountered, or I saw something about you that made me want to take a chance and finally trust someone again. Last night won't be your only test of faith. Things are just going to get tougher now, and stranger than anything you've seen before."

Diane nodded. "I was afraid you'd say that. If it hadn't been for the evidence I'd seen and felt for myself, I'd have been long gone. But now we have to deal with the topic of that German, Major Muller, and the possibility that he's really Hans Gruber. We need to decide what to do next. What if he's not the man—vampire—you're after? And what do we do about the skinwalker or skinwalkers still running around out there looking for you, and possibly me as well? I know you want Muller, and I understand why, but *I* want the creature who killed Burt Thomas." Diana's voice had gone from calm and businesslike to deadly cold by the time she finished speaking.

Lee had no doubt that she'd learned the details of her partner's death last night via the laptop. In spite of having her world turned upside down, this young Hispanic woman had the courage and training to face up to things as they stood now. She might have made a good partner for someone like him in the real world. Hell, she might prove to be an asset in the unreal world as well.

"Conventional justice and the law part company with our investigations now," Lee pointed out. "Are you ready for that? You've seen that skinwalkers are vicious predators. They will kill even if placed in prison, until they are themselves killed. There's no way we can ever take them to court, for obvious reasons. And Muller? He could never be brought in for the crimes he committed in 1945, and even if jailed, he could probably get out quite easily."

"And kill a handful of those trying to stop him, if he's even stronger and faster than you."

She obviously was following his logic, so he continued. "We both know where we stand, but before we decide who to go after first, the skinwalker pack or the vampire, we need to pool what information we have."

He brought out a map of the Alamogordo area. "I know where Muller lives, some of his routine off base, and the names of his associates—mainly his crewman and that crewman's wife. He's easily our most dangerous prey, and will be very hard to kill. For all I know, he's been around for hundreds of years, and a vampire with that kind of experience can have many skills. If he even suspects we're on his trail . . ."

"He'll come looking for us, or slip away again. So what you need to know from me is what contact, if any, the Bureau or any local authorities have had with him that might have tipped him off." Diane reached into her purse and pulled out a small notebook, flipping through it to find her working notes on that aspect of his case.

"Basically, my boss, Raymond Lewis, the Special Agent in Charge in Albuquerque, told me to interview you and find out why you were using FBI sources to check out a German Air Force pilot training in New Mexico. If there was something the Bureau needed to know or act upon, I was to follow up on it. If it turned out you were the problem, I was to keep an eye on you in order to keep you from embarrassing the country. He said it could be a real career maker for me." She paused, then added, "That's what I get for being ambitious."

Lee nodded, having pretty much guessed as much. "So following up on the shooting of Johnny Tanner was just an excuse to interview me without tipping your hand right away."

"Exactly. But now I know that particular incident hasn't been settled either. Agent Thomas had a wife and three children." Her eyes narrowed. "Whatever we do about Muller, I'm still going to get the bastard who mutilated my partner."

"You'll have my help on that. But getting back to the first matter; what, if anything, do the Germans or any other personnel, including the U.S. military at Holloman, know about the Bureau's activities and my inquiries concerning Muller? More importantly, what has Muller been told?"

Lee walked over to the window, and looked outside without disturbing the fall of the curtain. If he was paranoid, at least he had plenty of good reasons for it.

"The Bureau, to my knowledge, hasn't communicated any of this to base officials or the German government, and especially not to Muller, his crewman, or his commanding officer. You gave the excuse of not revealing your suspicions on drug dealing or espionage because you had no real evidence, just odd circumstances. The Bureau is even more paranoid when it comes to giving out information, especially when it could all blow up in our faces politically. I could destroy my career just by telling you this, you know." Diane looked through the rest of her notes before looking up again. "Trust works both ways now."

"Well, if we both make it through this alive, and stop Muller, I'll find the nuclear material for you, and you can present it to the authorities," he said. He was looking forward to the day when he could finally turn that responsibility over to others. "Hopefully, you can come out of this smelling like a rose. I don't want to draw any more attention to myself than I already have. Just keeping my job is going to be tricky now."

He stopped and remembered something Diane had said just before the skinwalker-wolves had attacked.

"Wait a moment. You mentioned yesterday that you had done a background check on me. That's when you found the connection between my past and present. Who else knows about that? If that info is available to other Bureau agents, and they go to interview Muller, he'd know what was going on for sure, even though they'll still think it's just an odd coincidence or similarities between generations of families."

Diane thought about it a moment. "I have notes on the information, and there's a log in the system that would indicate what searches I'd done, but the information itself has never been printed out. Unless another agent decides to run it again, that information is still safe, and certainly not in any report of mine. If I can stay in contact with my supervisor, I think I can get him to focus away from Muller. Then you—we'll be a lot safer."

"You think you're going to have to meet with him face-to-face?" Lee knew that this would be the ultimate test of her loyalty.

She nodded. "An agent has been killed, and the shit's already hit the fan in the Albuquerque office, count on it. SAC Lewis has got a chip on his shoulder about me already. I don't think he likes Hispanics, and I know he'd like me to look like an idiot so he can get rid of me. He'll be willing to give me just enough rope to hang myself as long as he doesn't think I'll bring him along with me. I'm going to have to call him. You suppose he'll trace the call and try to locate me?"

"I'd count on him trying. He's going to want to know your location, particularly since you'll want to hold it back from him. He's already lost one agent."

"You're reading Lewis correctly. The last thing he wants to do is lose control of me—his only link to what happened yesterday." Diane looked around. "You don't have a phone here, apparently. And I wouldn't want to use it anyway. My cell phone, or maybe a pay phone somewhere?"

Lee walked over to the kitchen drawer, removed the contents, then turned over the drawer and removed a cell phone attached to the back with duct tape.

"There's a charged battery plugged into the outlet in the hall bathroom. Use it and this to call him. It's a cloned phone, and he'll have problems tracing it. Just keep your call short, under a minute. Let him know where to meet you, maybe in front of the main library on the State campus, then hang up."

"You think of everything?"

"Not yet. Eventually I will." He smiled, and she smiled back.

## CHAPTER 10

Two hours later, Lee drove down the alley behind a college area apartment complex. Halfway down the block he stopped, and Diane, who'd come back from her meeting, stepped up to the passenger door of the pickup and jumped in. He drove down the alley, pulled out into the street, then drove slowly around the neighborhood for several minutes to check for a tail. Diane crouched down, so it would appear that he was alone in the vehicle.

"Think he followed you?" Lee asked, keeping his eyes on traffic. "I thought we had a tail for a moment, but the car turned away a block back."

She peeked out from under the coat, still slouched low in the seat, and gave him a wicked grin. "Ray couldn't find his butt with a global-positioning system. And I doubt he'd risk devoting manpower to tail me when he'd trying to find the wild animal that killed an FBI agent."

"Put on the hat and jacket I brought, then you can sit up."

Diane put on the western-style, red-satin windbreaker, tucked her shoulder-length hair into the hat, then shifted to sit normally. "Starting to get an achy-breaky back, sitting like that."

"What did you find out?" Lee asked, scratching the fake beard he'd attached before leaving the safe house. The sunglasses were a different brand than he usually wore, but dark lenses were a necessity outside, where he'd eventually be unless he remained inside the vehicle until nightfall.

"The body is already at Albuquerque in the Office of Medical Investigators' morgue at University Hospital. The pathologist says that the wounds on Agent Thomas's body were probably inflicted by a large carnivore, and the animal hair found at the scene, and enormous paw prints found outside the window, support that theory. Couple that with the dead wolf and the bodies of two naked humans found in your apartment, and there is a real mystery going on. SAC Lewis is anxious to keep the details out of the press, and he kept insisting on getting more information from me."

Lee nodded, looking in the rearview mirror to check for anyone who looked like he might be tracking his pickup. "You stick to the truth as much as you could?"

"I made it consistent with the evidence. I repeated the story about the big cat, informed him that you and I defended ourselves in your apartment by killing the wolf and those fanatics, and that you had driven off after the cat. I told him that I hoped to find you, then team up to track down the animal. I mentioned that you spoke Navajo and understood the culture, and that you had reported seeing a Navajo near the cat, who was probably its trainer."

"Kind of true. How much of it did he buy?"

"I think he believes I've gone around the bend after being attacked by an enormous wolf and two naked fanatics, but Lewis is willing to let me make the trip as long as it's clear he's not with me on it. I'm to report in every four hours unless something critical prevents me from doing so. He also wants a written report. I promised him one tomorrow at the latest."

"Do you trust him?"

"He suspects I'd like his job, and I would. I've made it clear that I have a career with the Bureau in mind, and expect to climb the ladder quickly. That makes any trust conditional at best. He'd sell me up the river in a second, though I doubt he'd deliberately put me in danger or risk getting caught in a lie. Loyalty to a fellow officer out in the field comes before politics for him, but just barely. At least that's my estimation."

He looked around the neighborhood they were passing through heading north again, skirting most of the city to the east by following roads beside the Rio Grande, on their left. "Now you see why I like working alone."

Diane looked disappointed, but didn't speak.

"I hate dealing with paperwork . . . or assholes." He grinned and went on. "Glad you were with me yesterday, though," he said in a more serious tone. "I've never taken on three wolves in my living room before. It was a bit close for comfort."

"Way too close. I have the scratches and bruises to prove it." She looked down at the scrapes on her hands that she'd gotten when she'd held the wolf's throat just inches from her own. Apparently trying to shake the memory from her mind, she looked up into the pale blue sky, where the sun, this being New Mexico, was perpetually shining. "How much sunlight *can* you stand? Do you tan, or does your skin start smoking, like in the movies?"

"May I never find out. I think my naturally dark coloring helps protect me a little, and the fact I'm not a full vampire helps too. But I do tan quickly. When I notice a color change beginning I know it's time to cover up and get more sunblock."

"So you and vampires are essentially the same, except by degree. They are faster and stronger, and barely age at all?"

He nodded. "But full vampires are much more vulnerable to the sun."

"How do you know?"

"I went to Germany back in 1990, right after the re-unification of East and West, searching for Hans Gruber. I was posing as a tourist looking for German soldiers that may have encountered my father during WW II. I stumbled across an unemployed, ex-East German soldier, who was also a vampire."

"Doubly dangerous and now unemployed?"

Lee nodded. "The ex-soldier had heard me asking around and knew I was an American. He stalked me in the dark, thinking I had money and would be easy prey. But I could hear and see him, which was a real shock. Not only was I aware of his presence, I was much stronger than he expected."

"He still had the advantage, didn't he?"

"But I had superior training from self-defense instructors, including a Japanese martial-arts master. I was able to break free from his grasp, and put some distance between us. Then, for about an hour, we stalked each other in a large, urban apartment building."

"Why didn't you just take off when you had the chance?"

"He was a vampire, and I knew he hadn't been born in that condition. I thought he might know Gruber, or know of him. I had to take that chance."

"So what happened?"

"I managed to ambush him on a balcony, and in the

struggle, we both fell two stories onto the parking lot. I landed on top, and kept him pinned until the sun came up. I was hoping to make him squirm until he told me all he knew. I'd learned to speak some of the German language years earlier."

"But he didn't talk, or didn't know anything?"

"He never got the chance. The East German didn't have any sunblock, and had become totally dependent on daytime shelter from the sun. The guy died within a few minutes from terrible burns, and all I got was a bit of a tan on my exposed skin."

"You feel guilty about it?"

"I have my own baggage, but not from that guy. I found out he made his living robbing and killing people in that apartment complex—a simple enough trade for someone with a vampire's abilities."

"Care to talk about your baggage? Besides your fellow state policemen, and those soldiers?" Diane said.

"Not really. It's better now to stay focused." Lee thought about Benny Mondragon, the young lieutenant, and all the rest of the dead soldiers. The memories were still there, but compared to Annie's memory, they *were* history. Annie represented something much more lasting, and as eternal as his own life could be. That baggage would always be a part of him.

"Like now?" Diane teased.

"Sorry. You're right, we need a plan. Any suggestions?"

"If Muller is Gruber, he knows about sunblock and wears it religiously. If you want to confirm that Major Muller is Hans Gruber, the vampire you're after, why don't you use an old FBI trick? Search his trash and look for empty sunblock bottles. Messy work, sometimes, but relatively low risk," Diane offered.

"Nobody outside weapons labs guards his trash." She paused, then added, "But there's a fundamental flaw in your theory about Muller being Gruber. The German Air Force wouldn't have allowed a guy who can't be outside in the sun to enlist."

"Unless Gruber has assumed someone else's identity relatively recently, I really don't know the answer to that. There's record of him having reported a skin condition that makes him sensitive to light—but maybe he reported that after he was in. That still doesn't explain it, mind you. He would have been discharged for something like that—it would interfere with the part of his job spent *outside* an aircraft cockpit." He looked at her and shrugged. "I just don't know." He paused, then continued. "But first we have to decide—do we go after Muller or the skinwalkers first."

"I've already told you I'm not going to stop looking for those skinwalkers, but we already know where Muller is. We don't even know what the skinwalker who became that panther looks like in human form, much less where to find him. It just makes sense to begin with Muller while local authorities and the rest of the local Bureau look for Tanner's relative and whoever was the panther. Besides, I think the German Air Force rotates their units when they complete their training missions here in New Mexico, so we don't have forever."

"Agreed, partner."

She looked at him strangely for a second, then nodded. "I guess we are partners—for now. I suppose that makes me Scully to your Mulder. Only you're an X-File all by yourself, Lee."

"Ain't that the truth? Let's return to the safe house, do what we can over the Internet, then call and see if we can learn what day is trash day in Muller's neighborhood. After that, we can plan a garbage harvest."

"All right with me. But while we're on the way, would you remind me again about the best way to kill a vampire?"

"Sure," he said, nodding. Diane had good survival instincts. As long as they worked together, they'd need to protect each other. Her best resources would be knowledge and courage.

"Hang on, I think we may have a tail. That van has been following us for several blocks." Lee looked in the side mirror.

Diane leaned back in the seat, watching out her side mirror. "That's a Mudde Pie delivery van. You're just hungry," Diane moaned, but she checked her seat belt, then brought out her pistol and held it on her lap.

"They're closing in, hang on!" Lee looked ahead, swerving to the right onto a narrow side street. To the left was the high concrete wall of a mobile home park, and to the right a fenced-in industrial park. The van followed at high speed.

Suddenly a sedan appeared at the next block, cutting across the road, blocking their way. They were boxed in!

"Fake left, go right!" Diane shouted.

Lee accelerated, heading for the narrow gap in front of the sedan. The sedan moved forward to cut them off. At the last minute, Lee swerved to the right.

The tailgate of the pickup slapped the rear end of the sedan as the truck lost some traction, but Lee managed to squeeze through.

"We're not running!" he shouted, cutting to the left and sliding to a stop fifty feet from the sedan and parallel to it. Tires screeched from somewhere on the other side of the car as the pursuing van was forced to stop.

Lee leaped out of the pickup, and sprinted to the sedan before the startled occupant, Devon Blackhorse, could exit on the driver's side. Lee had his Beretta out already, and fired on the run just as Blackhorse, startled by Lee's quickness, desperately swung his weapon around.

Blackhorse's head trembled slightly as Lee's nine-millimeter pistol round struck him in the throat, and he fell sideways out onto the pavement. Lee ducked his shoulder as he bounced off the side of the sedan, unable to stop in time.

"Stay down!" Diane yelled from behind, and a burst of automatic weapon erupted from the van, tearing into the sedan, riddling the interior and shattering the windows.

Lee, ducking the flying glass, took a grazing bullet strike across his shoulder blades, and felt the sting. He turned to look behind him, and Diane, using the pickup's engine for cover, returned fire over his head toward the van.

There was another three-second burst of automatic gunfire, mostly too high, but the windshield of his pickup was chipped away, the rounds ricocheting into the air. Diane had already ducked down again.

Lee moved at a crouch toward the front end of the sedan, and peeked out just as the van raced off. He started to stand and return fire, then thought better and stayed down, not wanting to be hit by Diane, who was still behind him. He turned to look at her and noticed she'd avoided shooting as well.

"Shit!" Diane yelled. "They're getting away!"

Lee stood, raised his pistol, then realized it would take a lucky shot to put the fleeing vehicle out of action. The van swung out into the boulevard, then turned south and disappeared from sight.

He ran around the front end of the sedan, and confirmed

that Darvon Blackhorse wouldn't be moving anytime soon—
except in a body bag.

Diane ran up. "You want to go after the van?"

"Probably too late for that. Make the call!"

Diane dialed the police on her cell phone, and Lee took
a quick look around the car without touching anything. It
was apparently stolen, because it had a Las Cruces parking-
lot sticker on the fender, along with a decal of a local gun
club. That explained the firepower, probably stolen along
with the car.

Lee realized how bright it was and looked down at his
slacks, which had a tear in them and a bloody scrape. It was
already healing, but there was a danger of sunburn now,
even more so from his back wound.

"You need to get out of the light, and away from anyone
who'll see you healing up so fast. Take the pickup and try
to find the van. I'll handle the cops," Diane said, discon-
necting the call. "I'll cover for you, then call and arrange for
you to pick me up somewhere."

"Good idea." Lee hurried back to the pickup, and was
already a block away in the direction the van had fled when
he heard the sound of approaching sirens.

Three hours later, Lee picked up Diane at a shopping center, having stopped at an auto-glass shop after failing to locate the missing van. The windshield had been replaced
while he waited.

"How did it go at the scene?" Lee asked as soon as they
were moving again.

"The Las Cruces PD was happy to have one suspect out
of action, and so was SAC Lewis until I told him that he'd
probably been followed by the shooters and used to locate

me and you. He said he'll be more careful from now on. But nobody liked not being able to speak with you. I got your Lieutenant Richmond on the line, and he wanted a full report, in writing, ASAP.

"The delivery van was found within the hour, abandoned in a minimall parking lot near a residential area. Crime scene people are still going over the vehicle. Nine-millimeter shells are everywhere inside it, apparently. Officers are questioning local residents, but I doubt they'll get anything."

"And the sedan? Stolen from the same person missing a handgun and assault rifle, right. What was that weapon, did you find out?"

"The man who lost his car and weapons is a registered gun collector, and owns several firearms, including an AK-47. That and a Walther P-38 were missing, along with several boxes of ammunition. The guy came by to see his car, and was really pissed when he found blood all over the driver's side. The bullet holes and broken glass didn't seem to bother him as much as the blood, oddly enough."

"We still have another skinwalker out there, from the van," Lee reminded. "Did you notice anything about the driver?"

"Just a person with an assault rifle. With all the bullets flying by, I didn't stop to take a good look for facial features."

"Is that what you told the Cruces PD?"

"I said the person had darker skin, like an Indian. Think I should have?" Diane looked over at Lee, then checked in the rearview mirror for the tenth time.

Lee nodded. "Bound to be a Navajo. We'll have to keep checking on Blackhorse and Tanner acquaintances and relatives for a likely suspect."

"I advised that to the detectives I spoke with, and to

SAC Lewis. Do you think Darvon Blackhorse was the panther who killed my partner?" Diane asked.

"Who knows? Maybe we'll find out when we finally track down the other skinwalker. If we see them in animal form, that should tell us for sure."

"Right. Well, if you have no other firefights planned for today, I'm ready to take a break. How about we head back to the safe house?" Diane said. "And on the way, refresh my memory again on how to kill a vampire—if we live long enough to try."

Lee continued the lesson he'd begun hours ago, but waited until he'd had a chance to clean up and change clothes. When he was ready, he opened a vent in the master bedroom, held in place via magnets on the inside but with phony screw heads to mislead anyone searching. He brought out a hand towel, and unwrapped it. Inside was a sturdy lockback knife with a simple but deadly looking four-inch blade.

"Sears Craftsman. Lifetime guarantee, no doubt." Diane examined the sturdy brass-and-polished-oak handle of the knife, curved slightly to accommodate the hand.

Lee watched her pull out the blade and heard it snap into place. "It's not just for fishing or around the construction site anymore. Find a way to carry it so you can bring it out quickly in total darkness, if necessary, but never resort to it unless you're without your pistol, or have already disabled the vampire so he can't resist. This is just for removing his head, which *will* kill him. You could also stab him in the heart with it, but if you do, make sure you hit the heart several times so it'll quit functioning completely. Of course there's always fire, but a flamethrower is harder to conceal in your boot."

"Maybe I'll pick up some hair spray and a lighter." She shrugged. "Come to think of it, that might not be a bad idea." Diane worked the blade open and closed several times without looking down, getting a feel for it. Finally she gave it one more look, then placed it in her jeans pocket. It bulged out suspiciously, and she reached inside, shifting it around.

He smiled. "That's why I carry my knife in my boot. Gets a *lot* less attention than a front pocket. If I'm using an identity where carrying a firearm arouses suspicion, and have to go through metal detectors, I carry a tough plastic or nylon blade. But I try to avoid these situations. I don't trust knives like that as much as a firearm or steel."

"Anything to incapacitate the vampire long enough to be able to finish him off. Or her?" Diane said, raising the gender question.

"I've met only one vampire woman, in France, and she didn't have an ounce of evil in her. Sounds kind of strange saying that. But, to her, I was the curiosity." Lee raised an eyebrow.

"She must have never met a Navajo half vampire, poor sheltered girl," Diane said.

"Never met a Navajo, actually." He laughed, then walked to the closet of the master bedroom. She watched as he opened a shoe box and took out several maps. One was a detailed chart of a housing area northeast of Holloman AFB in the city of Alamogordo. He unfolded it upon the bed.

"What do you know about Major Muller's daily routine?" Diana walked over and sat down on the bed beside the map, looking at the details Lee had added lightly in pencil. He sat down on the opposite side of the bed and pointed out the location of Major Muller's house, the route he generally took out of the neighborhood when he drove to the base, which was southeast. Then he gave her a general description of the neighborhood.

Looking up to judge her reaction, he noticed that they were seated less than two feet apart. He stood up, and awkwardly reached for the map. "Maybe we should look at this at the kitchen table. I feel a cup of coffee calling me." His hormones were scrambling his thinking. He needed to put space between them.

"Right. And one of us still needs to call to find out about the day the trash is picked up in that neighborhood."

Lee walked out of the bedroom, and she followed.

After a look at the Alamogordo phone book, one of the many things he'd acquired in preparation for this hunt, Diane made the call. It didn't take her long, posing as a new resident in the same area, to learn the days of refuse pickup.

"The last pickup day was Tuesday, and this is Saturday. How much skinblock do you think he uses? How much do you use?"

"You can't buy the stuff by the gallon, and between the needs of his occupation and being a full vampire, I'd say he uses a bottle every other day, depending on how often he's forced to be outside during daytime. I use two containers a week and work a night shift as a state cop."

"So, assuming he bathes and sweats regularly, we should be able to find two or more bottles of sunblock in his garbage. Sound right?" Diane had noticed the scent of the lotion on Lee and wondered how Muller covered his intense use of the products.

"You know, more than one vampire out there may be using the excuse that he's got a skin disorder that makes him extremely sensitive to sunlight. Could you check through the Bureau and see if any other Germans in Muller's unit have a similar condition?"

"Think he might have turned some of the people he worked with? Is 'turned' the correct term?"

Lee shrugged. "Works for Hollywood, works for me. Vampires and skinwalkers are very secretive, for obvious reasons. Skinwalkers, because of their animal instincts, seem more inclined than vampires to form packs, so it's unlikely that he's taken the risk of involving several other people to that degree. I doubt there's a vampire club with a secret handshake. But there's no way for me to be sure, and family groups seem likely. I think it merits checking."

"I'll have to figure out a way to do that without tipping our hand," Diane said, "or creating problems with my supervisor. I don't want SAC Lewis involved at all in this."

"Just remember that we don't know if we're running out of time. I checked the area where the box is buried just recently, and as far as I could tell, it hasn't been disturbed. At least there's been no signs of digging beyond the usual animal dens."

"And Muller doesn't know exactly where you hid it either. If that's what he's here for, he'll have to search blindly, probably with some kind of radiation detector," Diane pointed out.

"Are you sure it's still buried, and wasn't discovered and removed decades ago by the military or civilian authorities?" she added. "The whole state has been explored for uranium, basically, especially in the Grants area," Diane pointed out.

"I've been checking regularly over the years, not just the past few weeks. I think I'd have noticed if the area had been disturbed. Let's just target Muller for now. If he goes out searching, we'll know what he's planning. If he doesn't head out that way, he's after something else. Whatever it is, I'm sure he's up to no good. Either way, following him may give me a chance to deal with him alone, away from witnesses and potential victims."

"All right. It's a plan."

Lee reached over and touched Diane's arm, hoping to make his point very clear. "I don't want either of us meeting up with him, except on our terms. He's quite possibly the most dangerous man on the planet right now, especially if he's after the makings of his own A-bomb."

## CHAPTER 11

Lee had traveled through Alamogordo many times while on patrol as a state police officer, and knew that there were long stretches of highway empty of adjacent man-made structures.

Nearly the entire route northeast from St. Augustine Pass was on White Sands Missile Range land, composed of an extremely dry, high-desert basin bordered on one side by the barren Andres Mountains.

The vast White Sands National Monument eventually appeared to their left, off to the northwest. Glistening in the moonlight, the vast dune fields made a perfect postcard of this section of New Mexico. With his sharp, clear vision, the rolling, drifting hills were easy on his eyes this time of night. But during the daytime, even with his windows up and his dark sunglasses, the glare off the sand hurt his eyes like a snowfield did in winter.

"I'm a native New Mexican, and I've never been to White Sands. You believe that?" Diane said.

"Yes. Neither have I. I've been hoping that some special ceremony won't come up and I have to help provide state police security for the governor or other dignitaries. Way too much brightness for me."

"I see your problem. When I was growing up in Albuquerque, we preferred going into the mountains on vacation rather than even drier places. Have you been to Carlsbad Caverns?" Diane asked.

"Yes. Definitely my kind of place. During the part of the tour when they turn off the lights and everything is totally dark, it's interesting to watch people's expressions. I remember seeing couples sneaking kisses."

"You don't miss much, do you, Lee?"

He shook his head. Just real companionship, he thought but couldn't say. Diane was the first person since Annie that he didn't have to hold back on what he said, though his thoughts still had to remain censored. But their association couldn't last long either, and he wondered, if they both got out of this alive, what would she do with the secrets he'd shared.

After passing the main Holloman Air Force Base facilities, also to their west, they finally arrived at the town of Alamogordo, a name that means fat cottonwood in Spanish. Most of the road was lined with old, huge trees that required careful attention during the spring winds. Cottonwoods were "self-pruning," as many natives joked, and branches often littered the streets following storms.

When they arrived at the crosstown housing compound where Major Wolfgang Muller and some of the other German officers were living, they were disappointed to see that instead of individual trash containers and curb pickup service that Lee had seen before, the complex had recently converted to large, centrally located bins.

"It's not really practical to search through these bins filled with garbage bags looking for empty sunscreen containers," Lee said, looking over at Diane. Today, she was wearing a seedy-looking auburn wig, phony glasses, and a shapeless dress two sizes too large for her.

"You mean I put on the bag-lady look for nothing?" Diane joked.

"Seriously, I think we'd be wasting our time since we don't know which of the bins Muller uses or how many other people use the same one. We'd also look really suspicious filling the back of this pickup with putrid-smelling plastic bags. I have a better idea, as long as we're here."

"I hope it doesn't include breaking and entering." She shook her head slowly. "That's a real career-breaker for a woman agent hoping to shatter the glass ceiling in the Bureau. Tell me you're thinking of something else, Lee."

"We try to avoid actual breaking, of course, which would definitely arouse suspicion. But I'm sure we can put our heads together and get into his apartment for a little reconnoiter. If he's a vampire, we should find several bottles of sunscreen there. Nobody else stores it up, do they? And there might be a stash of blood in the fridge too."

Lee looked around the parking lot as they passed Muller's apartment for the second time. "The coast looks clear. Let's go find out if Muller is Gruber."

"This is going to be messy . . . particularly if we get caught."

"I can't see any other way of verifying his identity. You don't really think we're going to catch him sucking blood from someone's neck, do you?" Seeing Diane's wary expression, he shook his head. "Just not done. It's impractical and messy and no self-respecting vampire would feed that way. You've seen what I eat. It's the same for them."

"If it is Gruber, once he'd dead I want you to find that plutonium, if that's what it is, and turn it over to the authorities. Agreed?"

"Of course. I don't want the responsibility of knowing it's out there, unrecovered, one second longer than it's absolutely necessary." Lee pulled into the parking slot farthest from a lamppost. "Let's shed the street-person look now. We'll have better luck passing as a young couple coming back from a movie." He gestured to the old, oversized flannel shirt and coveralls he had over his ordinary clothes. She nodded and started pulling her baggy dress over her head.

He couldn't help but watch, at least out of the corner of his eye. Underneath, she had on form-fitting leggings and a dark blue sweater.

"Do you change clothes much in a pickup?" she asked, ducking as he tossed his shirt behind the seat, nearly knocking off her wig.

"When I was a teenager, we had to sneak everything. I couldn't date a girl unless I took a woman family member along, usually the girl's aunt. And we went almost everywhere on foot or horseback, or caught a bus. Boy, have things changed."

He slipped the overall off by sitting sideways, turned away from the steering wheel, trying not to kick Diane as he untangled his legs from the large garment.

"My father didn't let me go anywhere in a car alone with a guy until I was seventeen. Even then, he preferred me double dating," she said.

"Smart father. Didn't discourage the boys though, did it?"

"Not completely. But I appreciate his intentions now. Not that I did at the time. We argued a lot."

"Some things never change, but I think tough parents are the best. Ready?"

"No. But I'll go anyway."

"Come on," he cajoled. "Haven't you ever wondered if vampires wear boxers or briefs?"

She smiled, but her gaze was already taking in the area, and her mind was on the job. "There aren't any security cameras, at least, unless Muller bought his own. Shall we make small talk in case someone sees us?"

He climbed out of the truck and walked around, helping her out like on a real date—at least like a date in his generation. "Only if we know we're being seen. Let's act like we're a dating couple, but keep it quiet. No sense in attracting attention. When we get to his door, keep a sharp eye out for anything he may have left as a trap, or to indicate that the place was entered in his absence. I do that."

"I noticed."

They walked up to the sidewalk that ran alongside the parking area, then strolled casually toward the closest building, which contained eight apartments, four of them on a second story. Muller's, according to Lee's information and observations, was downstairs and on the side closest to the parking lot.

The buildings were typical of local construction, unremarkable wood frame and beige-tinted stucco, with a tile roof of composite material made to resemble red clay. The doors were recessed four feet under an overhang, creating a rudimentary porch in combination with a concrete pad.

The porch light was off, as were the lights inside the apartment. At least they appeared to be with the drapes drawn. Lee stopped in front of the door, pretending to be fumbling for his keys while checking around the door opening. If someone was inside, he'd pretend to be drunk, thinking this apartment was his.

"There." He pointed to a small paper match stuck into the doorjamb about six inches down from the top, on the doorknob side.

"How did you see that?" Diana whispered, then swore softly and added, "Never mind."

Lee checked around, and found a small stick that looked like a straw from a broomstick on the hinge side. "Thought there would be two. Try and remember exactly where they are. We'll have to put them back when we leave."

"I don't see any signs of an alarm system but if he has an interior zone alarm, we're screwed," Diane whispered. "Just don't leave any fingerprints behind." She handed him a pair of latex gloves, then put some on herself. They were both accustomed to wearing them during crime scene investigations.

Taking a small set of lock-picking tools, she went to work on the door lock. He positioned himself so nobody from the street could see what she was doing, and worked on the dead bolt. It was relatively easy for him, having acquired lock-picking skills many years ago from an expert.

The dead bolt clicked open after twenty seconds. Diane lacked his experience, and she kept working.

"You're fast," she whispered.

"I've had fifty years to practice," he answered.

A second later, the door lock clicked. "Okay," she whispered, relieved.

He grasped the match and straw from their locations as she opened the door. They entered quickly, closing the door behind them, and waited, listening.

Lee gave the room, which bordered on total darkness, the once-over. "Don't see any alarms. You can use your flashlight if you have one. I don't need mine." He set the straw and match down carefully upon a magazine stand by the door.

She took out a small penlight, and stepped across the carpet to check a stereo system on a metal rack. "Make sure there's no sound-activated recorder here," she murmured after a moment.

Lee closed the door but left it unlocked. If Muller returned, he'd probably try to unlock it, not realizing it was already open, and lock it instead. That extra click would give them a few seconds more warning that he was there.

"I'll check the bathroom, you take the bedroom," Diane suggested quietly, and went down the short hall, checking inside the doorways until she found the bathroom. Lee followed her down the hall, and went into the bedroom.

On the nightstand was a half-empty sixteen-ounce bottle of a SPF forty-five rated sunblock brand Lee used frequently. It was very effective and lightly scented. It was a kid's product, and since there was no sign of children here, that made it even more suspicious.

In the nightstand itself was another unopened bottle of the same brand, and it had the price sticker of a local discount superstore. He checked the closet and dresser drawers, but didn't find anything unexpected. Going back to the bed, he lifted the mattress, and between it and the inner spring was a military-style combat knife in a nylon sheath, and a large softcover book full of maps of New Mexico. He located the pages for the Fort Wingate area, but there were no marks or notes written there, which was disappointing.

Lee replaced the mattress, making sure the bed appeared undisturbed before he moved away. There was probably a pistol or other firearm within reach, but he didn't really have the time or a reason to look for it. There were no family photos anywhere, which to Lee seemed perfectly natural for a vampire, where family ties were few and risky. He searched for more detailed maps of the area around where the convoy had been ambushed, trying to figure out if the vampire's mission was really to find the missing plutonium, but he found nothing of that sort either.

He went into the kitchen and found Diane looking through the refrigerator, using its interior light to guide her search.

"What is it with you people? A large jar of 'tomato juice' that's really blood, I understand. But other than that, there's nothing but high-calorie food in here. Not even margarine—like you, he uses butter."

"So, does that imply that those supermodels are all really vampires?" Lee whispered back, lifting up a pasta TV dinner and pointing out a pistol and clip of ammunition in a plastic freezer bag behind it.

"It would explain a lot," she muttered. "Damned skinny women. I should stake them all."

Diane closed the refrigerator door, and waited a few seconds in the dark beside him. "I lost my night vision, but really thought the refrigerator was a logical hiding place. By the way, there were at least five bottles of different brands of sunblock in the bathroom. All were rated at least forty-five on that scale they use. I think he buys only one bottle at a time to avoid gathering attention."

"I found two bottles in the bedroom. All that sunblock, plus the blood in the fridge, confirms he's a vampire, all right. And it looks like he lives alone. There's also a combat knife under his mattress that would serve as a good emergency decapitation tool," Lee pointed out, "and a book filled with New Mexico maps. But nothing in the right area was marked."

Diane moved out of the kitchen area and bumped into a chair. She took her flashlight back out of her pocket, but he reached for her hand. "Don't worry about the flashlight, it's time we left anyway." He led Diane by the hand back across the living room toward the door, then let go long enough to crouch down low to the floor.

"Did you drop something?"

"No. Just verifying that we didn't leave any footprints in the carpet. It's worn enough to prevent that. Can you get the door?"

She opened the door while he retrieved the match and straw, then helped him replace both in the doorjamb as they closed it carefully.

Lee was relocking the dead bolt when he noticed a light beam on the wall beside them, and realized somebody had noticed their presence. "Stay cool," he whispered. "We're going out for a late-night snack."

Lee put his arm around Diane and together they walked down the sidewalk toward the parking lot. The beam of light continued to illuminate them. He could see the man approaching, a private security guard in his early twenties in a blue uniform. The man carried a portable radio on his belt, but no weapon was visible.

"Good evening," Lee said good-naturedly. "I haven't seen you around here before. I usually work evenings."

Diane smiled at the man, who'd stopped and was watching them approach. "That light's so bright, I can't see. Could you aim it at the ground, Officer?"

"I'm with Guardian Security," the young man replied. "Do you live in that apartment? I thought it belonged to a German Air Force pilot. A tall, blond guy."

"It does. His name is Wolfgang Muller. I'm a friend of his. My name is Orlando. He gave me his key so I could come and bring in his mail when he was away on a training exercise."

"That's all right then," he said, glancing over to make sure the door hadn't been forced.

"Good night," Diane said as they walked away.

They walked to Lee's pickup, and were soon heading southwest again toward Las Cruces. Neither spoke for a while, then finally Diane broke the silence. "Do you think the security guard will tell Muller about us? He's likely to suspect it was you if the guard says you were Navajo."

"Some people get Native Americans and Hispanics confused, and I used a name he'd associate with Hispanics, so that probably will stay in his mind. I think he'll keep quiet, at least to Muller. Though he may mention you to some of the other guards, especially in that hot-looking outfit and fiery wig. You look like someone who might be available," Lee replied.

"You mean cheap and easy. Well, that was the desired effect, I suppose. Maybe he'll hope to meet up with me again without you around." Diane laughed.

"Hey, the boy can dream, can't he?" Lee was grateful for the lightness of their interaction. He'd been on edge as soon as they'd entered Muller's apartment, remembering what the vampire had done to Benny Mondragon, and to him as well. Finally, knowing that he'd located the man/creature he'd been after for nearly a lifetime, the pressure was off just a little, at least for the moment.

"I thought about bringing out my FBI ID and doing some heavy b.s. about an official investigation, foreign spies, or drug dealers, but decided that would make it even harder for him to keep quiet. He'd want to brag about it. This way it's more mundane. I thought it was the right decision." Diane looked over at Lee, who seemed intent on the road right now.

"I think so too."

"What worries me now is that I'm supposed to keep supplying progress reports to SAC Lewis, and I don't have a clue what I'm going to be saying next. I certainly can't mention entering a suspect's apartment without a warrant." Diane took off her wig, shook out her hair, then began to straighten out the tangles with her fingers.

"I have the same problem, though technically I'm not working at all right now. The news people still don't have the details on what happened at my old complex, at least the truth, anyway, and I don't know how much pressure your people are putting on the state police or the governor. But when my commanding officers get pushed, the push will quickly come down on me. I'd hate to have to go underground again. I've enjoyed being a cop again."

He thought about the death of Annie, and the newspapers, and the police coming around. It had been a terrible time for him, and despite having come so close to having his secrets revealed, time had passed and people had eventually forgotten.

These days, with technology so far advanced, he was having a harder time keeping his night-walker secrets. Backgrounds and IDs were getting harder to fake with current terrorist threats making everyone justifiably paranoid. He didn't want entanglements in his life anymore, but the more he was around Diane Lopez, the harder that became. Even though he knew she would never replace Annie in his heart, Diane was rapidly becoming his companion. And, unlike anyone else since his wife had died, this woman knew most of his secrets.

Diane looked over at him, her face light-skinned compared to his even in the dark. "What is it really like for you, Lee? Never able to remain who you are or who you've become for very long. You're so easy to be around, pleasant and intelligent. People must want to be with you. Do you turn away from them eventually, or do you remain distant and aloof around other people from the very beginning? How can you ever have a relationship with such a big secret?"

He thought about it for a while before answering. To Diane's credit, she waited. Navajos usually didn't expect other Navajos to respond immediately when spoken to—like good teachers, they gave people a chance to think before voicing an opinion. But most of the non-Navajos he met were less patient.

"You're the first person since . . . well, almost forever, that I've been able to talk to honestly and completely about my life. I usually can't afford that. It gets obvious pretty quickly that I have a secret, then people start trying to figure it out. The better someone gets to know me, really know me and be around me, the harder it gets to keep that secret. If the wrong person discovers who and what I am, it could end my chance for any kind of life.

"I gave up on normal a long time ago. I only broke my rule of silence once when I fell in love. I knew she loved me so I took the biggest chance of my life. I told her exactly who and what I was. It took more courage to do that than to face a dozen vampires."

"Your wife, Annie?" Diane's voice was soft, understanding.

He nodded, but was unable to speak further for a while. The center dashes in the road passed by for several minutes in the silence, the only sound coming from the pickup engine and the whine of the tires on the asphalt.

"I didn't know whether she'd run away, or treat me like some kind of monster. But I got lucky. She loved me enough to stay. We got married, and she kept my secret for eight years. Then she was killed . . . because of my secret." Lee barely managed to get the last few words out, like the last few breaths of a dying man.

"Can you tell me what happened? How she died?"

He shook his head. "Maybe, someday. But not now. You know that you hold my life in your hands, don't you, Diane? And if you get caught in a lie, your career could be shot to hell over this. I know we haven't known each other long enough for you to do it because we're friends. Why are you sticking with me?"

Diane thought about it for a moment. "Right now, Lee, trust is what we need most from each other. I just hope that when the time comes, I'll be able to make the right choices. This whole experience—vampires, skinwalkers, a hidden cache of plutonium, potential German terrorists—it scares the living hell out of me. But it's also my job to deal with it when the security of our country is at stake. I believe we have a common goal here, no matter how strange the circumstances or how brief the acquaintance. That's a pretty good basis for trust." She reached over to the steering wheel and placed her hand upon his for a moment.

When she finally took her hand away, he didn't look directly at her. It had been so long since he'd trusted anyone, he'd forgotten what it was like.

## CHAPTER 12

Lee used a pay phone at a convenience store outside Las Cruces to call Lieutenant Richmond, his immediate supervisor. When he got back into the pickup, Lee was still shaking his head.

"Let me guess, your lieutenant is pulling you off leave and wants to see you first thing in the morning." Diane tried to interpret his expressions.

"Close. He wants to see me right now. He's getting a hell of a lot of pressure from your SAC Lewis to bring me in for an interview with him and Captain Huckabee, Richmond's boss. Your SAC wants to hear all the details of what happened at my apartment, what went on when we met, where you and I have been and what we've been doing, what happened when Blackhorse and the person in the van ambushed us, everything we've learned so far, and what we plan to do next." Lee shook his head.

"You left out the meaning of life and the next winning lottery number. That sounds like something Ray Lewis would do. He's looking for more answers to all the deaths, especially because the Bureau lost an agent, and it was an agent from his office." Diane cursed under her breath. "He's also pissed that Blackhorse obviously used him to track us down and attempt a hit. He sure doesn't want that showing up in any report I file.

"Lewis is just afraid it'll look like he's losing control of the situation. As if he ever had control," she added.

Lee waited to allow an eighteen-wheeler to pass, then pulled back out onto the highway. "Lieutenant Richmond is really a decent guy, and usually backs up his officers. But I was afraid this was going to happen sooner or later. The people behind the desks always get nervous when those of us out on the street take the initiative."

"So, when are you going to meet with your lieutenant? At least he sounds more reasonable than SAC Lewis."

"Tonight." Lee looked down at his watch. "Or make that this morning, now. He wants to make sure nobody in the Bureau tags along."

"At his home, or some neutral location? Maybe an all-night coffee shop?" Diane suggested.

"Unfortunately, no. I would have picked one of the truck stops, myself, but he wants to meet at the district office. There is a dispatcher there, of course, but otherwise, it'll be just him and me."

Lee turned to her. "I can take you back to the safe house but I'd rather keep you close in case there's trouble. Do you mind driving around the area while I talk to the lieutenant? I don't recommend you park and make yourself a stationary target right now."

"Agreed. We need to watch each other's backs. I'll drop you off close to the office, then meet with you at another spot, or the same spot, later on. Do you have a preference?"

Lee nodded. "There's a little park, not much more than a grassy lot with several trees, two blocks north of the state police district office. I'll head for the north end of that park when I'm through. If the lieutenant gives me a hard time, it may be a while."

"I'll drop you off a block or so south of the office, if that's possible, just in case the place is under surveillance. SAC Lewis is not to be trusted and I know you don't want your truck spotted," Diane pointed out.

"Sounds like a plan. Be careful about being seen passing through the area too many times. Maybe one pass every five to ten minutes, randomly timed. If you see any feebies, just leave the area and head for the safe house. I showed you where the key is. I'll get in contact with you later to arrange for pickup. I'll call on the cell phone hidden under the sink in the master bathroom," Lee said.

"How many different phones do you have hidden around that house?"

"One in the garage, and another in a plastic box buried beneath the trash barrel. You can use one of the batteries I have charging in the garage for that one." Lee smiled. "See, I do think of nearly everything."

"Do we have time to stop for something to eat? If you're getting set up here by my cohorts, you'll want to be at full strength. Besides, I'm feeling hungry."

"Are you sure you don't have a little vampire in your family?" Lee teased.

"Are you kidding? We just like to eat. No skinny super-models in my family at all. Everyone is well rounded," Diane responded with a smile.

"How do I respond to that without getting myself into trouble? Just let me say that you are pleasing to the eye, and leave it at that." Lee smiled.

"Thank you for your excellent taste. Now, where can I find a good burrito?"

When Lee arrived at the entrance of the Las Cruces district office—the state police headquarters building was far north in Santa Fe—he could see Lieutenant Richmond through the glass panel, in street clothes, talking to the dispatcher, a buxom, attractive black woman in her thirties named Iris Worth that Lee knew, but not well. The entrance was locked, and Lee pressed the buzzer.

Iris looked up, saw who it was, then pressed the buzzer. Lee entered. "Thanks, Mrs. Worth." He nodded to the woman, who smiled back. "Officer Hawk, based on the body count, it looks like your vacation has turned into a small war."

Richmond looked up with a scowl, but didn't say anything.

Lee gave her a sheepish grin. "Sure has." He then looked directly at his lieutenant. "Good morning, sir. I suppose you want to talk in your office?"

"Let's go back there now, Lee. Thanks for the coffee, Iris." Richmond smiled at the dispatcher, then motioned Lee ahead of him down the narrow hall. There were only two rooms in that direction, one a cramped storeroom with an outside door, and the other a small office with two desks, several filing cabinets, and a large map of New Mexico that covered one end wall. The state police emblem and the yellow flag of New Mexico with its red zia sun symbol were against the back wall, one above each desk.

Richmond started to take a seat behind the desk with his nameplate on it, then decided to stand, which made his great height seem even more imposing. "I need to get an update, for the record, on anything that might even remotely be connected to what transpired on and since the day you met Special Agent Lopez. I want the details of that shootout included. When you mention my visit with you, leave out everything except the papers I brought for you to sign, okay, Lee? The Bureau is breathing down everyone's neck since they lost that agent, and we're not too happy about it either, especially with one of our own involved. I'm going to record this and make a text copy available to SAC Lewis, so keep that in mind when you're speaking."

"Thanks for your support, Lieutenant. There are some aspects of this case that are obviously out of the ordinary, but I'll keep to the facts and resist any speculation."

"Good idea. Much as I'm eager to hear it, save your speculation until after the formal part here is done and I turn off the recorder." Richmond reached into a desk drawer, pulled out a small tape recorder, and checked the cassette. Then he turned it on, nodded, and sat down. Lee remained standing, though the lieutenant gestured toward the other desk.

Lee described his meetings with Special Agent Lopez, stating that she had since indicated that she'd been using the previous incident on the Rez as an excuse to find out why he'd done a background check on a German pilot temporarily stationed at Holloman. While he'd been busy explaining why he'd been curious about the major, the attack on his apartment had occurred. A wolf had come crashing through his window followed by two crazed Navajos behaving as if they'd been high on PCP.

Lee measured his words carefully, telling the lieutenant that the man and the young woman had been unarmed, but had attacked them with hands and teeth. It wasn't a lie— of course he wasn't about to explain that they'd been wolves at the time.

Lee continued, telling him how they'd received a call for

help from Agent Thomas at the other apartment. Agent Lopez had taken a blow and was still in the process of recovering, so he went to check out Agent Thomas's situation. At the apartment, he encountered a large panther and another Navajo. After realizing that Agent Thomas was dead, he'd asked a neighbor to call the authorities, and hearing more gunfire coming from his apartment, he'd returned as quickly as possible. That's when he'd learned that Agent Lopez had been forced to fire when the male Navajo, though already wounded, had attacked her with a piece of plate glass.

"And that's when you decided to leave the scene and go after the black panther and the Navajo working with the animal?" Richmond asked.

"Yes. Agent Lopez wanted to go to her partner, but when she learned he was already dead, she agreed to help me try to catch the attackers before they left the area completely."

Lee could see that his story sounded strange at best, and knew it left a lot of questions unanswered. For now, he wouldn't give Richmond any more details about what had happened since the attack, or about Muller. The lieutenant had enough to think about.

Lee knew his supervisor would have a hard enough time swallowing the story he'd been given about wild animals that had been trained and used in an attempted murder. On the other hand, the lieutenant would have had even more trouble with the truth. So this was the way it had to be.

Forensic evidence would show Lee's blood on the nails of the dead Navajo man, but on the face of it, without knowing the humans had attacked in wolf form, it looked like Agent Lopez and he had killed two naked, unarmed people who'd become insanely violent and had behaved like animals.

The shootout with Blackhorse and the person in the van, though extremely serious, was almost an anticlimax. Of course Lee didn't mention the fact that he was wounded and had subsequently healed, or couldn't stay around because of danger from sunlight.

Finally Lee finished what he had to say, answered a few more questions, then the lieutenant reached over, announced the time and date, then switched off the recorder. He labeled the cassette, and stuck it into his shirt pocket.

"Damned incredible story, Lee. I'd like you to know that the Office of the Medical Investigator has put a rush on this, working with the FBI crime lab facilities in Albuquerque, and so far, your story is backed up by the evidence, unlikely as it seems. The FBI apparently has some snapshots Agent Thomas took of the surveillance of your apartment—which I gather don't show the attack itself, though they won't confirm or deny it. They are looking for a wolflike animal, though, and a black panther as well. They've even brought in an animal expert and a professional hunter as consultants. They don't like it, and are apparently really pissed off about you and Agent Lopez working together undercover, but so far, your and her stories seem to be consistent with the known evidence."

"I haven't heard the news or read the papers lately, but how much of this is going out to the public?" Lee wanted to know how much Muller would hear. A vampire was more likely to spot events of a supernatural nature, even when they were carefully couched in rhetoric. Lee knew his one advantage was that Muller probably had never come across skinwalkers and had little knowledge of them.

"Not much, except that wild animals, possibly a wolf cross and a black mountain lion or jaguar that had come out of the mountains attacked two men and a woman at a local apartment building. At least one woman saw the black cat." Richmond shrugged.

"You think you have a lead on who trained the animals that did this?" Richmond added. "Maybe that Blackhorse character, who'd gone for you the night before? And what about those naked fanatics? Do you suppose they were on some kind of drug trip? The drug tests still aren't back yet from the lab."

"Once somebody gets a confirmation on the identities of either or both of the dead perps, we'll have a better idea where that trail leads. Please don't let this out of the room, but you know how secretive some of the tribal groups are, especially with outsiders. I believe, and Agent Lopez agrees, that a secret Navajo sect is behind all this, and it goes back somehow to that attack on me that happened over near Shiprock a few months ago. That ties in with Darvon Blackhorse, we're certain of that."

Lee continued. "If anyone else gets involved, and the Navajo group knows they're in danger of being uncovered, they could go underground for years or strike out violently on a large scale. People up in the Four Corners, and anywhere there is Indian land, can be very tight-lipped with outsiders. I plan to see what I can find out unofficially. Please do what you can to give us a chance to nail these guys and their animals, will you, Lieutenant?" Lee tried to sound as credible as possible.

"Is this in any way connected with that German pilot?" Richmond asked. "That possibility is what got the feebies interested in you in the first place."

"I don't see how. But if there is a connection, we'll find it. I just hope the FBI doesn't go to the man and stir up things prematurely. They could tip him off if he is involved.

Try to find a way to discourage that, if you can. I understand SAC Lewis is ambitious, and prone to running over anything that gets in his way."

Lee hoped to leave this angle open without getting anyone else watching Muller, at least for the moment. If Muller became suspicious, however, plans might change.

"I won't bring it up and I'll downplay the possibility of a connection if they ask. But be aware that you and Agent Lopez aren't going to have more than a few more days before the feds push the issue. What kind of officer is Agent Lopez, by the way? Are you sure you can trust her?"

"My instincts say yes. But she does have higher aspirations in the Bureau, so I'm keeping both eyes open in case she's a user. I think in the long run, she'll do what's right." Lee actually trusted Diane a lot more than that, she'd proved her courage in dangerous situations already, but he figured if he sounded too positive, it would make Richmond suspicious.

"Anything you need, Lee?"

"Let me know if the LCPD lab people find out anything new regarding Blackhorse and the driver of the van. But try and discourage any officers—especially the feebies, from trying to track me down. They should continue searching for the driver of the van, who could also be the Navajo who brought the panther—or not. Whoever killed Agent Thomas was really after me, I believe, and I need to maintain low visibility. I'm being hunted, but so are they. And I plan on getting to them first."

"You have the physical and mental skills to do the job, Lee. If you need backup, call in and I'll make sure you have it." Richmond shook Lee's hand, then lowered his voice. "I'm going out front and stand around for a while before I leave to attract attention. I'll have Iris unlock the back door for you. If anyone is watching the front, you might be able to get a few steps ahead of them."

"Good idea. Thanks."

Three minutes later, Lee stood outside in the alley, waiting in the shadows, watching and listening. Patience was a quality a hunter needed, but even more important, it was a survival trait for someone or something being hunted. Usually, in the wild, the animal that moved first was spotted and became the prey, or went hungry.

He doubted that the FBI actually had someone in or around the alley. They'd simply be watching the block for movement, probably through night-vision devices. It was even more unlikely that they'd actually have been tailing Richmond or watching the local state police office in the hope that Lee would show up. If they'd wanted him, they could have just insisted Diane bring him in one way or the other, assuming she could pull it off.

But the streets were empty, except for an occasional late-night patron going home after the bars had closed, or because he'd run out of money or energy. Lee walked in the opposite direction from the park that was his goal, keeping an eye on the rooftops as well. No one could hide from his vampire eyes, even in total darkness, and his hearing was exceptional.

At the end of the alley, he waited before stepping out onto the sidewalk. No cars passed by, and nothing at all could be seen moving around the area.

As he started across the street, intending to keep in the darker zones below the awnings of storefronts there as he circled east, then north again, Lee saw a shadow moving to his right, behind a low hedge.

A big cat was following him, not a tabby or an alley cat, but a huge black panther. The animal froze as he made a casual sweep of the neighborhood with his gaze, and it was difficult for Lee not to stop and stare, giving himself away.

There couldn't be two cats like that loose in the same area, so this had to be the skinwalker that had mauled Agent Thomas, and maybe the van driver as well. Now the shapeshifter was tracking him with the intelligence of a human hunter and the quickness and strength of an agile animal predator.

Fortunately for Lee, the human intelligence behind the actions of the cat could be used against it. A wildcat had natural instincts that made it wary and skittish, while humans, especially those feeling powerful and cocky, made mistakes that were all too human. On the negative side, the skinwalker knew he was armed, recognized the threat that presented, and would be watching for any sign that Lee was reaching for his weapon.

Careful to continue to give the impression that he was cautious, but not give away the fact that he'd discovered he was being hunted, Lee continued across the street at the same pace he'd been setting for himself. He then stepped into a doorway that was completely in shadow far from the streetlight at the end of the block. He scanned the area again, his eyes moving past the cat without acknowledgment, while noting it had slipped farther down the street on the opposite side and was poised behind a newspaper stand, watching him.

The skinwalker/creature was trying to guess which way he'd be going, and was waiting for Lee to move laterally east or west before committing itself. Lee looked in both directions, and saw that there was a narrow gap between two buildings just down the sidewalk to his left, which was west.

He stepped out onto the sidewalk, and headed casually west. When he reached the gap, he turned around as if to make sure nobody was around, then stepped into the gap, completely out of sight from the road.

At the end of the narrow passageway between the buildings was an eight-foot-high chain-link fence, a barrier he could easily scale. But that wasn't his intent. Couching low about ten feet back from the sidewalk, Lee took out his nine-millimeter Beretta and waited, the barrel pointed toward the sidewalk and narrow gap.

If the skinwalker was going to follow him, he'd have to move quickly or Lee could be out of sight within seconds. If the skinwalker was going to play it smart, he'd run around the block, hoping to catch Lee coming out, or at least get him back within sight.

Lee waited, making sure he was downwind, and giving the cat plenty of time to cross the street and enter the narrow passage. If the cat took a look around the corner, the darkness wouldn't shelter it. Lee would be able to get off a lethal shot to the head.

Once he was certain that the cat wasn't coming, Lee stood and moved the ten feet back to the street in less than two seconds, standing tall as he peeked around the corner. The street looked clear in both directions. Just as he moved out, the lights from an off-duty taxicab appeared at the end of the block, crossing the intersection perpendicular to him. Lee was forced to slow to a human-scale jog, and wait for the vehicle to pass before crossing the street to head back east.

Suddenly he heard a light thump somewhere behind him, and saw that the big cat had leaped down from a rooftop onto a metal awning. The structure groaned, but the cat quickly leaped onto the sidewalk. The skinwalker now knew that Lee was on to him.

Turning, Lee brought out his pistol, but the cat was

watching, and cut to the right, out of sight around the corner. Lee took advantage of the big animal's evasive tactics to run directly across the street. He could hear a vehicle coming in their direction, and the sound of the engine was familiar.

Diane pulled up next to the curb, nearly hitting him before she realized Lee was coming up so fast. He jumped onto the running board, holding on to the side mirror.

"Was that . . . ?" Diane shouted.

"Yes!" Lee answered, stepping in through the passenger-side door and rolling down the window so he could look and aim outside. "The skinwalker must have staked out the local HQ, or followed Richmond to his office, just like with your SAC, Lewis. Circle the neighborhood. Maybe we can catch sight of the cat again. I'd like a clear shot."

"What do we do if he comes at us from my side?"

"Keep the window up. That'll slow him down if he hits the glass." Lee searched each yard they passed. They'd entered an area where old houses had been converted to offices or shops, and most had front and back yards, though one or the other had usually been converted to a small parking lot.

He didn't know the name for this style, but the mostly converted houses had probably been twenty years old in the forties, and were wood-framed with steep roofs and large, covered porches extending the width of the front. Trees ranged from saplings to giant cottonwoods big enough to hold the cat they were hunting. "Slow down whenever we pass a big tree. I want to take a careful look at the lower branches when we pass."

They circled the first block, then stopped at the alley after failing to see anything on any of the four sides. "He went down this way, I saw the cat before he went around the corner and out of sight," Diane reported. "Should we try the alley?"

"It's too narrow, and too good a place for a skinwalker ambush. That beast could be through the window before we could react," Lee advised. "It's time to call the cavalry."

They'd circled the neighborhood for less than five minutes before local police cars began to arrive. As Lee had advised in his call on the cell phone, the responding officers used a silent approach, with emergency lights and sirens off.

Using their spotlights, the officers began to search trees, shrubs, hedges, and every dark corner, porch, and alley for the big cat. Lee had advised bringing in a helicopter, and soon one appeared overhead, checking rooftops.

Trying to remain as inconspicuous as possible, Diane held her badge up to one of the city officers asking her to clear the area, then she drove another block away from the neighborhood where the intensive search was taking place.

"What if he or she has changed into human form again?" Diane asked, turning to Lee. "Has there been time?"

"I don't know. It varies. But the officers would be quick to spot a naked man or woman," Lee said. "Particularly a woman, I'd think."

"Unless the skinwalker hid clothes nearby. The cat probably didn't travel too far in that form, I'd guess," she pointed out.

"Maybe the skinwalker has an ally close by, driving around in some vehicle so the cat can hop right in, then shape-shift back into human form while out of view. All they'd need then is a blanket."

He punched out a number on his cell phone, contacting Iris at Dispatch directly, asking her to pass on a request for the searching officers to stop *any* vehicles in the search area, and detain anyone believed to fit the suspect's description, a male or female Native American.

They drove a widening search pattern around the neighborhood, looking for places where a big cat could hide, or where someone in a parked vehicle could change clothes.

After ten minutes, they were about to decide on another plan when they saw the flashing light on the dashboard of an unmarked vehicle parked by the curb. The driver was talking to the passenger of another vehicle, a station wagon, that had apparently been pulled over.

"That's SAC Lewis!" Diane said, turning the corner quickly before the man noticed her.

"Pull over and switch places with me, then keep down low so he can't see you. I'm going to circle around and see what he's found," Lee said.

"He probably heard a report about the cat on his radio and came directly here. Don't hang around for long. If he sees I'm in the car, he's going to wonder what we've been up to, and I don't want to have to answer any more questions yet."

"Okay, just keep low." He took off his jacket, and placed it over her after she scrunched down low under the dashboard.

"Don't take too long. This is damned uncomfortable."

"Be grateful that you're not my size."

Lee turned the vehicle around, then approached the FBI SAC's vehicle from the opposite direction. The station wagon was gone now, and Lewis was back in his vehicle, involved in paperwork or something.

Lee pulled up beside Lewis, stopped, and stuck his head out the window. "FBI, right?"

Lewis, a short, stocky, red-haired man with the eyes of

a weasel and a conservative dark suit, glanced over, a disinterested expression on his face. Seeing a Navajo, he jumped and reached for his handgun.

"Easy, Special Agent. "I'm State Patrolman Leo Hawk. You recognize me, don't you?" Lee held out his badge, the gold shield glittering in the streetlight. "I was the one who called in the report about the cat. I spotted it stalking me after I left a meeting with my lieutenant at his office, not far from here. He has my latest report to share with the Bureau. Any luck so far in tracking down the cat or a suspect?"

Lewis glared at Lee angrily. "Hell no. Couldn't you get a shot at the beast before it got away?"

"Unfortunately, no. Have you seen any civilians in the area walking or driving around within the past few minutes? Somebody who might have let the animal out, or picked it up?"

"Hell no. Just some sturdy-looking hooker half in and half out of her dress. She was afraid I was going to arrest her, so she offered to get in the backseat with me. I told her to leave the area, and go home where it's safe." The SAC rolled his eyes. "She's lucky she didn't run into that animal. Probably kinda wild herself, though."

"Let me guess. Was she Indian?"

"Yeah, don't know what tribe. Attractive woman, I suppose, but she looked mean as hell. Probably specializes in bondage and discipline." The SAC almost smiled, then decided against it.

"Well, then we have to keep looking. Maybe we'll get lucky tonight in a way that counts." Lee nodded, then drove off just as the man said something in reply.

"Damn, damn, damn, damn, damn," Lee cursed as he drove down the street, heading north again. He lifted the jacket off of Diane, who looked up at him in the half-light.

"That woman was the black panther, wasn't she?"

"I'd bet a month's pay on it, Diane. Your SAC is lucky he didn't meet that wildcat about ten minutes earlier. He seems kind of slow on the draw. I should have figured that out when it was obvious the skinwalkers used him to track down you and me earlier for their little ambush."

"I think he's a bit slow at everything, except when it comes to taking advantage of opportunities for self-promotion. Probably was hoping to bag the cat himself and make the national news. Still, I'd hate to lose another officer, even him, and he'd never believe the woman he met could be the perp we're after." Diane rubbed her shoulder.

"Next time, you get to be the one who hits the deck," she groaned.

"I guess it depends on who we're ducking, doesn't it?" He laughed. "Now let's head back to the safe house. I'm hungry, and it's been a hell of a long day."

## CHAPTER 13

It was early morning when Lee went on-line with his computer, Diane looking over his shoulder. He could feel the warmth of her breath as they both read the electronic version of a local newspaper, and he remembered how Annie liked to come up behind him and put her arms around his chest.

It was a moment before he could speak, the memory had come on so strong. "Muller's unit has had their temporary duty here shortened. They're only going to be here another two weeks."

"So, if he came here to retrieve the plutonium, he's suddenly running out of time," Diane said.

Lee nodded. "We'll know real soon if that was the reason he returned. If we can get details of his training schedule, we'll know what hours he has free to roam. If he's going to search the area with Geiger counters or other radiation detectors, he'll have to spend every free moment looking between now and when he leaves. And it's going to have to be at night."

"Are there any agents you can persuade to help you get that information from the military?" he added. "SAC Lewis is out, you don't want to get him started checking into Muller."

She thought about it for a moment. "There's a woman agent stationed in Phoenix I can ask. She was my supervisor when I first went into the field, and now she's the SAC in that city. By now every FBI agent in the country knows about Burt Thomas's murder, and she'll even know he was my partner. If I tell her this is part of the investigation into Burt's death, I'll get the information." Diane gestured toward one of the cell phones they had charging at an electrical outlet, clearly asking if she should use one.

"Let's go for a drive instead. You can make the call while we're away from here, just in case the Phoenix office traces all their incoming calls." He checked his Beretta, put on his sunglasses and cap, then grabbed a second phone. "Ready?"

She took the big lockback folding knife Lee had given her, and placed it in her jacket pocket. Her pistol was already at her waist. Looking around for her wig, she took that too. "Okay."

They timed their entrance onto the main road outside the driveway of the safe house so that no cars would note where they'd come from. Lee headed south toward the city, and Diane looked for a convenience store with an outside pay phone. Ten miles away from the safe house, they stopped at a gas station minimart and she made the contact. Lee waited in the pickup.

Diane was on the phone for less than five minutes before she returned, her eyes lit up with a smile. "It's all set. She'll send me the information and I'll pick it up on my handheld organizer. I have a wireless modem."

"Sounds great. Before we do anything else, though, I want to ditch this pickup. Your SAC saw it last night, and probably took down the license number." Lee eased the pickup back into early morning traffic, headed across town west, toward the river valley.

"Another emergency backup?" Diane sounded impressed.

"Hey, I've had over fifty years to try out different ways of protecting myself. I've had to change identities a dozen times. After a while I learned to set up places like the safe house, and keep a backup vehicle or two handy. I also keep money in several bank accounts under different names, which makes it a lot easier if I suddenly have to go on the run from skinwalkers, like I've had to do three times already."

After a fifteen-minute drive, Lee turned down a narrow road into a poor neighborhood where the crumbling adobe houses looked ancient, and pulled up beside a boarded-up gas station that was right out of the sixties.

"This reminds me of when I was a child," Diane said.

"Right. Gas was cheap then, and a uniformed attendant actually pumped your gas, checked your oil, and washed your windshields. Instead of beer and bread, you bought tires and could get an oil change. The good ole days." Lee shrugged.

"You should know."

"Sounds like faint praise."

He parked on the concrete pad where pumps had once been installed, but left the engine running. "When I pull out, park this pickup in its place." He climbed out of the truck, glanced around and adjusted his sunglasses, then pulled a key from his wallet. He walked over to the structure, which was painted in different-colored, varying-sized blocks along the bottom six feet or so to cover up gang tagging, and unlocked a big padlock on one of the bay doors.

Stepping inside, he walked over to a rusting water pipe,

reached around behind it, and unwound a key from a wrapping of duct tape arranged to resemble a hasty repair.

It took a little while to start the older-model sedan, but he managed, driving it out so Diane could pull the truck inside, out of sight. They moved their gear into the sedan, locked up the bay, and were gone in less than five minutes.

"Dusty but comfortable," she said, settling into the faded bucket seat and looking around the four-door sedan, an inexpensive Honda Civic in a faded chocolate brown.

"Doesn't gather a lot of attention, and it's economical. If I needed to travel several hundred miles, I'd prefer this to the pickup anyway," Lee mentioned. "The vehicle legally belongs to another identity of mine, and won't send any flags up with the tag numbers. I even have the minimum required insurance."

"You're doing better than a lot of New Mexicans, just having insurance." Diane nodded. "All this is planned to reduce calling any attention to yourself, I suppose."

"Exactly. And I try never to return to a community where I might be recognized by old neighbors or coworkers. Well, I've done it a few times before, but I waited twenty years or more first. Then I can say I'm a younger relative of whoever might be remembered there, if anybody thinks they knew me."

"Do you think you'll ever be able to live a normal life?" Diane spoke softly. "Spending time with friends, dating, family outings, that kind of thing?"

He waited a long time before answering, not really knowing what to say. "This is the closest I've come to a normal life in decades. It's great just having someone to talk to who knows my secrets and can accept me for who I am."

Diane looked at him curiously, but didn't say anything all the way back to the safe house. There were moving vehicles within view of the turnoff when they approached, and Lee decided not to risk being seen going down that road. If he was being followed, whoever was doing it was beyond damned good.

He circled the neighborhood, passed by again, noting there weren't any cars within sight this time, and quickly turned around to pull up the drive.

That afternoon, they got ready to stake out Muller's apartment and, if necessary, follow him if he left. Hours went by, and they took turns catnapping while the other kept checking Diane's handheld assistant for the E-mail from her FBI mentor.

Lee found himself unable to sleep. Having Diane around had reawakened memories of living with a woman, and Annie had been his wife and companion for several years. He kept trying to visualize Annie in his mind, and realizing he'd forgotten exactly what she looked like, having idealized her memory for so long. There were two things he remembered vividly, however. One was how happy he'd been when they were together, and the second was discovering her body after she'd been killed. That image would never go away, even if he lived to two hundred.

Finally, he got up off the sofa where he'd been lying down and went to sit at the table, sipping coffee and focusing on his plans.

Lee kept going over and over again what he knew about the neighborhood where Muller lived, and the layout of Alamogordo and the route to Fort Wingate. He'd been over that stretch of highway road that passed near where the box was buried hundreds of times, and knew it with his eyes closed. Too bad his memory about where the box was, exactly, was so dim. He might have a hell of a time finding it.

"Can't sleep?" Diane walked into the living room rubbing

her eyes, wearing one of his long shirts and a pair of jeans that had been cut off as shorts. She was barefooted.

For some reason, his heart started beating faster, and he looked away, reaching for his coffee. "Too much caffeine, I guess."

Together they discussed their general strategy, and finally the message they'd been waiting for came in from her FBI contact. "Too bad we can't print this out, but let me read the training schedule off to you and you can write it down." She started giving the dates and hours on- and off-duty, also relating what times the German flight crews were in class, briefings, and on practice missions.

Ten minutes later, they knew what Muller officially had to be doing the remainder of his tour in New Mexico.

"He's only got three more night exercises, and the rest of his duty time will be spent in debriefings and short day flights," Diane pointed out. "And he has tonight off. He's not due back for duty until six P.M. tomorrow."

"So, if he leaves town and heads toward Fort Wingate, we'll have a good idea what he's planning on doing with his time." Lee nodded. "We need to follow him from the base and see where he goes. Then . . ."

"If the opportunity presents itself, you plan on making your move, with me backing you up? You know . . . killing him?" Her voice trailed off as if she had a bad taste in her mouth.

She probably did. After all, they were planning cold-blooded murder. He thought about it for a moment. "Are you okay with this? I don't see that trying to take him alive is a viable option. It would be impossible to link him with the crime he actually committed back in 1945, unless we catch him digging up that box. Even then, he'd probably go free or be deported unless he turns out to be an actual terrorist or drug dealer. Anything short of his death would have no long-term effect. He'd break out of lockup, go into hiding, and I'd have a hell of a time finding him again. A lot of other people could get hurt along the way if we don't act now."

"I don't look forward to killing a man, even a vampire, in cold blood," Diane admitted. "It's just not in my nature, no matter how valid your argument is. And I do accept your argument, you know, or I wouldn't be here now." Diane looked away, checking her extra pistol magazines.

"It doesn't come easily for me either, but I've learned to accept the necessity, like a soldier does during wartime. But if he sees us coming, or guesses what is going down before I strike, it may be the last thing we do. He's stronger than me and quicker than a gazelle. He's also smart, and he's had decades of experience hunting and being hunted. If you manage to disable him, don't hesitate. Finish him off completely before he can recover. He'd kill you without a thought if he thinks you're any danger at all. If you can, stay well clear of him and let me do the . . . work."

"I've seen you in action, and you are very quick and capable. It's hard to imagine anyone faster or stronger. You ran from the pickup to Blackhorse so quickly it was absolutely amazing. But do you have it in your heart to do this in cold blood to another man? He's not an animal, like those skinwalkers have become." Diane looked up, reading his face.

"I was around Muller just long enough to see him for what he really is. Muller is evil. He's a pathological killer who enjoys his work. He developed those traits differently than the forced madness a skinwalker is subjected to. They can't help themselves, but he can. Killing a skinwalker is putting a violently disturbed creature out of its misery. Killing Muller would be a service to mankind. He was that way long before he became a vampire."

Diane looked a little paler, but nodded her acceptance. They were ready to leave within a half hour. From another hiding place in the garage, Lee brought out a .30-06 hunting rifle with iron sights. He hid it underneath the backseat along with a box of 180-grain solid-point ammunition.

Lee touched up his sunblock, made sure he had an extra bottle stashed in the car in case he was unable to return to his supply at the safe house, and Diane helped stow extra food and water in a small backpack to bring along. The last thing Lee did was take out his medicine pouch and sing a brief blessing. Diane watched politely, saying nothing.

The trip to Alamogordo was comfortable in the Honda Civic this time of year, before it got hot, and Diane drove. She wasn't wearing the wig anymore, that image belonged to the woman in the pickup. Like Lee, she was wearing a baseball cap. Hers was a maroon NM Aggies cap, and he had a black one with no image or logo at all, a rare find in the age of perpetual promotion.

They passed White Sands National Monument, and pulled off to the side of the road within sight of the turnoff to Holloman Air Force base, which was ahead on their left. Lee kept watch through a telephoto lens on a camera, pretending to take photos of Diane, who was posing as if they were tourists.

Fifteen minutes later, while pretending to change the film in the camera, Lee spotted Muller's small sports car pulling up to the highway from the turnoff. It was a hardtop, and the windows were darkly tinted, though Lee knew glass alone was enough to filter the damaging radiation. It was the ultraviolet rays that actually did the damage. He'd learned through experimentation, grateful that such activities hadn't cost him the finger he'd used for the tests.

"Time to go, dear," Lee shouted to be heard over the sound of young men passing by in a pickup. They were whistling loudly at Diane.

"Okay, dumpling," she shouted back, hurrying toward the car. Lee was ahead of her, already opening the door.

Lee checked to make sure no cars were approaching, then pulled out quickly, gaining speed in order to keep Muller's sports car in sight, while maintaining a paranoia-safe distance. Diane took the camera, and used the magnified lens to check out the car. "GXX-184. That's the right tag, all right."

"Hopefully, Muller will remain true to form, stop by a convenience store for a six-pack of beer, then go straight to his apartment. At least that's been the routine he's followed the five times I've tracked him from the base. On two of those occasions, I waited for hours before I saw him coming out again, and was afraid someone would think I was a terrorist staking out the base. Glad you were able to get his schedule. Every time I thought I knew his routine, it would change. I'd figure it out again, then it would change again."

"How long have you been monitoring him?"

"I've been watching him off and on, depending on my patrol schedule, for about three weeks now."

"Why didn't you make your move before?"

"I was looking for a way of verifying he was really *the* vampire who killed the rookie state policeman assigned to me, and that civilian that he carjacked. I'm like you. I can't kill an innocent man."

"How could he have gotten into the military—a vampire? Basic training out in the sun should have killed him." Diane shook her head. "I know we talked about it before . . ."

"I've given that some thought. The only thing that I can figure is that he must have killed the real Major Muller, or paid him off and took his place right before a transfer to another unit where he wasn't known by sight. The lure of immortality and immunity to disease and illness could be a powerful incentive, and the switch could have been a willing one. And he's in a branch of the military that doesn't require him to be outside for long stretches of time, at least at the rank of major, I suspect. A cockpit would insulate him well from sunlight, especially the ultraviolet wavelength that burns vampires. He could have paid for private flight training. With enough money, he might have traveled to Russia and flown high-performance military aircraft," Lee suggested.

"You said Muller is intelligent and resourceful. I wonder why he chose to come to the U.S. now. He could have come long ago as a German tourist and searched off and on for years, rather than maneuvering and manipulating to come as a military pilot."

"I have no idea. At this point, we don't know if his return has anything to do with me or the cargo I took from him. Unless the spy that tipped him off about the plutonium back in 1945 was able to let him know I never turned it in, Muller doesn't know for certain it's still hidden. We'll find out this morning. If he is after the plutonium, believing it's out there, it's possible his politics have changed and he hopes to conduct some terrorist act, or sell the radioactive material to a Middle Eastern client. Maybe that's where he got his high-performance aircraft training. Or maybe he already knows pretty closely where the container is, and plans to use his military status to get it out of the country conveniently—

like in his aircraft. Whatever the reason, this is the end of the road for him."

They remained silent for a while after that, following just within visual range, which wasn't hard, even with the undulating but relatively low-profile terrain between the base and Alamogordo. To the north and west were ancient lake basins, with mountains farther west, northeast, and east beyond the city.

The trip to Alamogordo was only around ten miles from the base, so it wasn't long before they entered the community from the south end on highway seventy. Muller's apartment was near the New Mexico State University branch so they followed his car from a distance as he skirted the downtown area, circling east, then headed north on Scenic Drive.

"Okay, we're getting close, let's not get spotted now," Diane advised, watching Muller pull up into a numbered parking slot less than fifty feet from his apartment.

Lee followed a road that led deeper into the complex, knowing he'd be able to keep Muller in sight until he entered the apartment. The man hadn't made his customary stop for beer tonight, another indication that he'd be on the road again soon.

They drove around to a visitor's space nearly opposite Muller's apartment, and waited, watching. Many cars were arriving and departing now, with day workers coming home from work or going out for dinner. No one gave them more than a quick glance.

They almost missed seeing Muller leaving ten minutes later.

A van had pulled up behind his vehicle, and he'd rushed out to it in a wide-brimmed boonie hat and dark green hiking clothes and boots, carrying a large duffel-type bag. The sliding side door of the van had opened, and he'd placed the bag gently inside, then jumped into the passenger seat.

"With that tinted glass, I can't make out any details of the driver, can you?" Lee asked.

Diane, who had the camera out again, shook her head. "No, I was hoping the polarizing lens would help out by cutting the glare, but all I can see is another shape. Any idea who the van belongs to?"

"From the check I did initially, I think that belongs to his crewman—Kurt Plummer, the guy in the backseat of his airplane. Who better for him to team up with than the man he depends on during flight operations?" Lee said.

"Could he be a vampire too?"

"Sure. But the man doesn't have to know what Muller is to work with him to recover the missing cargo."

"Well, according to our basic scenario, if Muller is heading toward Fort Wingate, they'll take the fastest route— north on fifty-four to Carrizozo, then west to I-25, and north again to Los Lunas. Once they hit I-40 west again, they'll make good time on the Interstate all the way to Wingate." Diane looked up from a highway map she'd brought along.

"Looks like we may be in for a long ride. Think you can sleep for a while?" Lee asked, glancing over at Diane, who looked tired. She must have had as much trouble sleeping earlier as he had.

She nodded, then reached over and moved the lever adjusting the seat back so it reclined to about forty-five degrees. "I've been in the Bureau long enough to learn to catch some Z's whenever I can. If I don't wake up on my own by seven, wake me up and I'll drive for a while."

"Good enough."

. . .

Lee let her sleep until eight. His strong constitution, a by-product of his half-vampire blood, could keep him going at full strength for days at a time, if necessary, as long as he had food, and a quart or two of calves' blood. He'd munched silently on high-calorie granola bars, washing them down with blood from a thermos, knowing that in tonight's encounter with Muller, he'd need any advantage he had.

He'd had to stop once, outside Las Lunas, when the van had pulled into a station for gas, and Diane had instantly awakened. Once she'd seen what was going on, however, she'd gone to sleep again within minutes.

Lee changed places with her, and slept while she drove. By the time he woke up, they were passing through Grants and were less than a half hour from the area he believed Muller would start his search.

"The walker of the night lives," Diane joked, hearing him yawn. "They seem to have slowed down a bit, do you recognize the area?"

Lee smiled, yawned again, then sat up and adjusted his seat, glancing out at the railroad line and the surrounding mesas, most topped with mixed stands of piñons and junipers. "It looks like home, at least to an Navajo boy like me. We're less than ten miles away from the old turnoff leading to where I hid the box. Do you suppose they've narrowed down the location somehow?"

"Maybe they've gotten hold of some geological surveys that have target sites with higher radioactive activity. I understand that much of New Mexico has some radioactivity in the rocks, with so much uranium around. But maybe they're simply checking out the hotter spots, hoping one will be the jackpot."

"They might also have some good equipment in that bag Muller loaded into the van," Lee said.

"You don't think that was just their dinner?" she joked. "Raw liver and coolers full of iced blood?"

"Trust me, it's really quite good, and nutritious. There's a tribe in Africa, I think, where the male warriors feed on blood almost exclusively."

"I think that is the Masai tribe. But I personally don't even like my steaks rare. Where did you put those granola bars? I ate two, but couldn't find the rest without waking you up." Diane looked over at him.

"I'll hand you one. They're on the floorboard behind your seat." Lee reached between the two seats and brought back a peanut-flavored bar. "Want me to unwrap it for you?"

"Never mind. It'll have to wait. They're really slowing down. There's a freeway exit ahead. Want me to go on past them?" Diane slowed down, hesitating.

"No. Pull over quickly, then turn off the lights."

Diane took her foot off the gas immediately, checked in the rearview mirror, saw it was clear behind her for the moment, and worked the brakes, slowing quickly but keeping control. The Honda responded well, and they were soon on the shoulder of the Interstate, sitting there with the lights out.

"They took the ramp off, and are driving down to the intersection of the exits. Let's wait until we see if they go north or south, or just parallel the freeway on the frontage road." Lee squinted, then remembered and picked up the camera with the telephoto lens.

"I can't see a thing," Diane mumbled.

"They're at the intersection, now they're heading north . . . no, they're going down the frontage road, continuing west. There are several small roads there, leading to a trading post, hogans, and wells. The turnoff to the Church Rock Uranium

Mine is farther down." Lee watched for another minute.

"Should I follow now?" Diane checked the mirror, let an eighteen-wheeler roar past, the wind from the big trailer tugging at the Honda, then she accelerated onto the Interstate again, headlights on once more.

"Right, but once we take the exit and reach the intersection, stop and we'll switch places. I can drive with the lights off, remember?"

"Old owl eyes, right?"

"Owls are considered bad omens for Navajos."

"Okay. *Hawk* eyes." She chuckled.

A minute later, they played red-light green-light, running around the front of the car, switching places with the headlight and dome lights off. The moon was behind a cloud, so Diane couldn't see very well and collided with the door as she was getting in. "Ow! I bumped my elbow."

Lee was already inside and at the wheel. "Sorry. Ready to roll?"

"Yeah, dammit."

He put the Honda into gear and accelerated, trying to make sure they didn't lose track of Muller, their quarry. Somewhere ahead, in the distance, was the van, also running with the lights out. "Muller must be driving."

"Unless his crewman is also a vampire," Diane reminded Lee softly.

Within a minute they saw the vehicle again, stationary on the shoulder of the road about a quarter of a mile ahead. Lee pulled over to the side of the two-lane asphalt road beside a drainage ditch and stopped, turning off the engine. After hours of engine noise, the silence was deafening except for the soft *tick-tick* of cooling metal.

Diane rolled down her window, and listened. A truck roared by on the Interstate two hundred yards to their left. Then, as it rolled on into the distance, the night grew quiet again. The van was just sitting there, but she could hear the faint rumble of its powerful engine.

"Do you think they spotted us following them?" Diane whispered.

"I doubt it. They're probably just looking for the right road, or using some equipment in the van to try to track the cargo. This is very close to where I hid it, less than two miles, I estimate. I wonder how they could have narrowed down the search so quickly?" Lee whispered, not taking his eye off the van. If anyone got out, he'd see them, but they'd also see the Honda too.

"They might have gotten lucky on an earlier search, before you found out Muller was back in New Mexico. Or maybe they had a way to do an aerial survey to narrow it down. Aren't there aircraft geologists use to map the surface minerals with special instruments? There are probably instruments that can search for radioactive spots too," Diane suggested. "I saw this film about minerals on public TV. They use the same technology NASA uses to analyze the surface of planets when doing flybys with space probes."

"I should have thought of that," Lee mumbled. "They may have the spot narrowed down to the size of a football field or less. At least it'll take some time digging out the box, even if they do find it. And, while they're preoccupied ..."

"It's around midnight already. Do you think they'll try to work past dawn?" she whispered.

"Not a chance, unless the man with Muller isn't a vampire. But Muller is going to have to stay in the van once the sun comes up, except for a few minutes at a time. Unless they brought a portable shelter or tent of some kind."

The van started forward again, and the vehicle turned off onto a narrow rutted road leading up into the woods to the north.

"Is the hogan where the medicine man lived still there?" Diane reached down and checked her pistol while she spoke.

"Yes, but that's farther down the road. Bowlegs, that was his nickname, abandoned the old one when a patient died in there, and constructed a new one close to where I buried the box. Later on, he died, and that hogan was abandoned as well. Remember, I've been checking up on the location from time to time."

"Do you think the medicine man built his second hogan near where you hid the box by accident?" Diane asked.

"He could well have seen signs of where I'd been, or the truck tracks, and wondered. But he never messed with it. I would have noticed signs of digging, I think."

Diane nodded. "Maybe he was protecting it too, in his own way. Did someone else move in after the medicine man died?"

"No. His relatives punched a hole in the north side to remove his body. Then the hogan was abandoned." Lee thought about it a moment. "I just realized something from last time I was here. There were tracks around the hogan, and signs that somebody had been patching holes in it with mud. So a vampire . . ."

"Could hide inside the hogan during the daytime," Diane finished. "That might be their base camp, a place no Navajos would go, if I'm right about the aversion to death. It's a good place for them to take shelter from the sun, and still be in a great position to continue their search for the cargo. Are they heading in the right direction?"

Lee checked and nodded, starting the engine. "We'll go

down past where they turned off, then continue on a short distance until we find a place to hide the vehicle. I don't want to get too far uphill. We could get stuck. There are still some shady, damp, low spots ahead where leftover moistness from late winter snows collects. The sandy ground in those areas makes it impossible for the tires to get any traction."

Lee waited until he could no longer see the van, then drove slowly past where Muller and his companion had turned off, until they were out of sight of that position. Then he drove off the track and inched slowly uphill until they were hidden among some tall junipers.

Within a few minutes, they were standing beside their car. Lee had the rifle out now, loaded, and Diane was checking her pistol again. "The abandoned hogan is about a quarter mile upslope, roughly parallel to us if we were to head directly uphill. There is a small meadow around the hogan, and a few old fruit trees—dead, I think." He was whispering, knowing how good Muller's hearing must be.

"Other than some sagebrush," Lee continued, "there is little cover within fifty feet of the hogan entrance, which is on the east side, according to custom. The hole punched in the side where the body was removed is on the north. If they plan on staying the whole day in that hogan, then they must have brought something to cover both that hole and the entrance to keep out direct sunlight."

"Even if they already know where the box is, unless they plan on digging it out tonight, they'll probably get the hogan ready first," Diane speculated.

"You may be right. They're not due back until Monday, so they might plan on getting set up tonight and doing a little work, hiding out in the hogan tomorrow, then working tomorrow night, and maybe Sunday night as well. It would be too dangerous for us to make a move on them while they're in the hogan itself since there's only one way in. So let's get close enough to see exactly what their strategy is for tonight."

"Okay." Diane nodded.

"Remember that Muller can see as well at night as you can in daylight, and we don't know if his crewman is a vampire too. So stay hidden, and move around as if it was the brightest time of day. And their hearing is super-sensitive."

She nodded. "You want me to watch your back while you get close enough to take them both down with the rifle. Then we can move in and . . . cut off their heads?" She shivered at the thought.

"Something like that. If we can pull that off, I'll still want to stay around to watch for a while, just to make sure Muller doesn't somehow find a way to reattach his head." Lee shrugged. "If that happens, I'll burn the bodies, or put them out where the sun can do it for me."

He wondered, now that he had said it out loud, if he could actually go through with it. He'd never considered himself an assassin, and despite the loss of all those soldiers, there had been a war going on at the time of the ambush, and the other Germans with Muller had all died that night too, some of them at Lee's hands.

Then Lee remembered Benny Mondragon and his wife and young son, and he knew he had to go through with this. Muller had to be killed. Who knew how many people Muller had murdered since then, and why he wanted the plutonium now?

Muller may have gone back to what later became East Germany, and functioned as a spy or soldier for the communist government, gathering information from his original

American contact. He might now be on his own, hoping to sell the plutonium to a government hostile to the United States. Or maybe Muller was simply a terrorist. He'd have had to do something underhanded to even get into the German Air Force with his little problem with sunlight.

"Let's go. Just be careful, watch my back, and stay extremely quiet. Remember to move as if it were daylight. Watch my hand signals," Lee said. "Ready?"

Diane took out her pistol and nodded. Despite her experience as a field agent, she looked positively grim at the moment. But he remembered her quick reactions and combat skills when the skinwalkers came in through the windows a few days ago, and knew she had the right instincts around danger.

He turned, looked around one more time, then moved silently uphill across the rocky ground and thin grass, his rifle loaded and the safety off. He had extra ammunition in his right jacket pocket, in a cartridge box so the shells wouldn't rattle against each other. In his pants pocket was his medicine pouch, with the hunting bear and other sacred items Bowlegs had given him around the middle of the last century. And, just in case he got pinned down somewhere for a long time, there was that small plastic bottle of sunblock.

## CHAPTER 14

As they climbed slowly up the slope, moving among the piñon and juniper pines, pungent sagebrush, and lean, pale green and yellow grasses, Lee kept a constant watch for the van and its occupants. He had to make sure they wouldn't be walking into an ambush.

Lee's instincts told him otherwise. Diane's belief that Muller had narrowed down the search area using sophisticated technology, and perhaps an aerial survey, made sense.

Although he was used to moving quickly when no one was around to see, he'd slowed down so Diane could keep up. Exhaustion could impair her shooting accuracy and that was one problem neither of them needed.

He paused, standing still to listen. There were no vehicles operating nearby, but a mile or so downhill, the hum of a distant truck passing on the freeway was clear.

He turned, and saw Diane searching the area behind them and to their flanks. She caught his eye, and pointed toward a house or hogan about a half mile farther east and a little closer to the road. There was a light on there. It was the home of a Navajo family, probably someone related to old Bowlegs.

If Lee did any shooting tonight, whoever was in that house would certainly hear. But he doubted anyone would come to investigate unless they had cattle or horses running loose. It was possible they'd call the cops, but even then, it would take them a long time to respond.

He heard a vehicle door slam somewhere ahead, and Diane heard it too, judging on her reaction. He started toward the sound, and she followed, silently, remaining behind and enough to his right so that he could see her position by checking to his side.

Crouching low now, Lee inched forward, looking through breaks between the trees for the van or any figures on the move. Stepping beneath the branches of an ancient piñon, he glanced up and saw a barn owl staring down at him, its big eyes following his every step. He automatically touched the leather drawstring pouch in his pocket that contained his fetishes. A blessing from the Navajo gods would be welcome now.

Diane passed on the other side of the tree, and the owl flew off, its wings flapping in a quiet rush that couldn't be heard ten feet away. She startled, and swung her pistol around toward the tree, but had the good sense not to fire without checking the target first.

She looked to see if he'd seen, and shrugged her shoulders when she saw him watching her. Diane was as nervous as a cat, for obvious reasons. He held up his hand, signaling that she should stay in that position.

He moved ten feet farther, and heard the distinctive sound of a zipper. Kneeling on the ground beside the van, about fifty feet away was a man removing a small electronic device, probably a radiation detector of some kind, from an athletic bag. It wasn't Muller, Lee knew that right away. Where was the vampire?

Shifting slightly on his knees, Lee took a step to his left and looked again, sweeping the forested area ahead. Beyond the van was the old log hogan, an eight-sided structure larger than Bowleg's first structure and suitable for ceremonies and the work of a medicine man. On top of the mud-sealed roof a man was spreading some kind of tarp over the smoke hole. It was Muller.

Lee turned to check on Diane's position, and noted she was watching him. He pointed toward the men, and held up two fingers. She nodded so he'd know that she understood.

He checked back, and saw that Muller was inching down from the roof of the hogan. Raising his rifle, Lee got ready to take a shot as soon as the angle was right. He figured on taking Muller down with a head shot, switching to the crewman, then going in to finish Muller off before he could heal himself. If the other man was a vampire, he'd have to be decapitated as well, but Muller was the main threat.

Muller walked around to the far side of the hogan before Lee could get him in his sights, and he had to wait. Checking the crewman again, he saw the man was taking a second radiation detector from the bag.

As silently as he could move, Lee slipped past the trunk of a juniper and brought his rifle back to bear on the hogan. The next time Muller was visible, he'd take the head shot. A quick glance back at the crewman almost stopped his heart. The man was gone. He couldn't have moved that fast unless he was a vampire too!

Turning, he looked for Diana, who had whirled around to her right, her pistol up. The muzzle blast of a gunshot flashed somewhere to her left, striking the tree beside her in line with her shoulders. She fired two quick shots in return, and Lee heard the sound of movement from the location of the muzzle blast.

Expecting a quick reaction from Muller, Lee whirled to his right, anticipating his opponent. But Muller went forward, moving so quickly, he almost ran right past Lee.

Lee fired instinctively, grazing Muller, who dove to the ground and rolled.

Knowing he had little chance of getting a second shot, Lee crouched low and ran quickly to Diane, who was looking around wildly, her pistol extended in a combat stance.

"It's me," Lee said, warding off her pistol as she spun around at his approach, too late to hit him but sending another two rounds in the direction of Muller.

"I got one," she yelled. "The crewman."

Lee raised his rifle and sent another round toward Muller, who'd crawled to their right in the direction of the van. Muller snapped off two shots in response, and they whined overhead.

"Break off. I'll follow." He knew they'd lost the initiative and a night fight wasn't a good idea. He pushed her in the right direction, then whirled, looking for Muller. The vampire was nowhere to be seen, so Lee decided to shoot both the front tires of the van. He got one shot off, then had to change positions when another shot whined by dangerously close.

He racked another round into the rifle, as he ran downhill. Suddenly, another gunshot rang out from up the hill. He felt a tug at his right shoulder and searing pain. His arm jerked in a spasm, and he dropped his rifle. Lee jumped down a small embankment and ran parallel to the drop-off for twenty feet, then continued downhill, catching up with Diane.

"Damn, you can run," she gasped, aware of who it was before she could bring her pistol around.

A bullet whined past them just to their left, and Lee grabbed her hand, pulling Diane to the right just as another bullet struck the ground beside her and ricocheted off downhill.

"Forget going back to the car. We need to hide and set up an ambush," Lee said as they ran around a low outcropping of rock, effectively hiding them for the moment.

He reached over with his left hand and pulled out his Beretta, then slumped down behind a waist-high rock resting between two sturdy pines.

She dropped down prone behind a nearby boulder, glanced back in the direction they'd come from, then looked over at him.

"My God, you've been hit. There's blood all over your arm and shoulder," Diane rasped, struggling to catch her breath.

He groaned. "No big deal, if we can keep them at a distance long enough, it'll heal. I only wish I hadn't dropped the rifle."

"Forget about the rifle. We need to get you a little farther away. I hit the crewman squarely, and he went down. Is he a vampire? Will he get right back up?" Diane sat up and moved behind Lee, trying to see how badly he was hit.

"The way he moved, he's a vampire. He must have heard me moving to get a sight line on Muller, and ran down to outflank me. That's when he came across you unexpectedly."

She nodded. "I saw him before he saw me, but he still managed to get off the first shot. Fortunately he missed, and I didn't."

They waited a few minutes, then she whispered, "Will Muller come looking for us now?"

"Maybe. His crewman may be out of commission for an hour or more, *if* he was critically hit. Muller may choose to watch over him instead. With them both being vampires, they'll have the advantage, especially now that they know what they're facing. Muller will know he hit me when he spots the blood."

"In the dark? Oh, right. Then maybe we should try to put more distance between us, if you can move."

"Good idea. I shot out a tire in their van so if they plan on getting out of here before morning, they have to fix the flat before it gets light. That means they only have about an hour to look for us. If we can avoid Muller until then, he and his partner will have to hole up somewhere, either in the hogan or in the van."

"Why don't we go after them now? The odds will be better, with the vampire I shot having to heal himself before he can make a move. Muller will be watching for us, but at least there's just one of them operational now." Diane stood up and looked at Lee.

"No, I'm not fully functional now and his vision is much better than yours. With the rifle, he'll have a tremendous advantage. We need to get far enough away so they'll run out of time looking for us. Let's get moving." Lee didn't look at Diane, afraid he'd give himself away. He'd lost Annie because he'd gotten complacent. It wasn't going to happen to Diane. He didn't want anything to happen to her, and if they went after Muller now, the German would be in a good defensive position and could pick them both off.

His shattered upper arm was starting to heal now, from the inside out, and it hurt like hell. Lee was a pretty good pistol shot even with his left hand, but the odds were too close to make an attack. They'd have to be careful if they wanted to live through the night.

Lee and Diane walked quickly downhill, picking a route diagonal to the hillside and away from where the car was parked. Lee was no longer leaving a blood trail, but they didn't want to ruin their chances of getting away later by vehicle, and the best way of keeping Muller and the other vampire from finding the car was by leading them away from it.

"How long do you think it'll take before the one I shot is conscious and able to defend himself?" Diane whispered as they hiked quickly across a sandstone outcropping, hoping to conceal their tracks for a while.

"Do you think his wounds would have been fatal if he'd been human?"

"Without immediate medical care, probably. That's just a guess. I hit him solidly twice in the upper torso."

"Muller could probably leave him within a half hour then. I'm healing up now, I can feel it, but it sounds like he was hurt a lot more than me. But if Muller decided to just hide the man somewhere, he could be coming now."

"Then let's go straight downhill. The closer we get to the highway, the less likely Muller is to take action where he could be seen. And we can make better time." Diane grabbed his left forearm, and pulled him in the direction she was headed.

"Let's pick up the pace." She broke from a quick walk into a jog, and he did the same. "I could run downhill forever."

For another ten minutes they jogged along, not looking back, and eventually came upon a shallow stream less than six feet wide, running across the hillside, winding downhill. Diane stopped, and Lee came up beside her.

"The bottom is pretty rocky, we can hide our tracks by

wading awhile," Lee suggested, looking back uphill, but not seeing any movement among the trees.

"Upstream or down?"

Lee thought about it a second. "We can make the quickest time running downstream, so that would be the most logical choice. Muller is smart, so he might think we'd go the opposite to throw him off."

"Upstream? So we really go downstream anyway, at least there's the advantage of making better time." Diane thought about it for a second. "And Muller would do the same. So we go upstream after all."

"Okay. Trying to outthink an outthinker always has me flipping a coin. Let's go upstream. Move slowly at first, then we can pick up speed later." He stepped into the water, and it was ice-cold. Diane had done the same, and she'd gasped.

"Like playing in iced tea," she muttered, and began to pick her way carefully upstream. She slipped and nearly fell in, but he caught and hung on to her until she was steady again.

"Let me lead. I can see the bottom, and you can't." Lee let go of her and stepped ahead, making sure to push his feet forward rather than picking them up, avoiding noisy splashing.

The stream curved gently uphill, and he got the idea that the local Navajos had adjusted its bed over the years to slow down the flow, which would make it less vulnerable to erosional effects. The route took them in a direction that put them closer to the car, and that might be an advantage when sunrise approached. He looked over at the eastern horizon, hoping he was wrong and it would look brighter. But a vampire knew sunrise and sunsets almost by instinct, and Lee knew even before checking his watch that daybreak was still some time away.

"Put your pistol away," he whispered.

"Why? I won't drop it even it I fall," she whispered back.

"Someone is ahead, and he doesn't look like an enemy. Just trust me," Lee whispered. He remembered that a *hataalii* lived in the area. Though he'd never met the man, he'd heard that he was well respected.

They continued up the stream, barely stirring the frigid melt waters that originated in snowpack way up in the Cibola National Forest. Lee's feet were numb, and he admired Diane for sticking with his chosen route without complaint.

"*Yáat'ééh, hataalii,*" Lee said softly as they both got close enough to see the middle-aged Navajo man standing beside a pine tree less than ten feet from the stream. Lee had seen him clearly a minute ago, and recognized the Navajo man's long hair and sweatband as signs that usually identified the traditional *Dineh*. The leather pouch at his belt, the handmade knife in his belt, and the blue color of his sweatband suggested he was also a *hataalii*, or medicine man. There was a familiar look to the man's face as well as he scrutinized Lee carefully.

"I don't know you, stranger," the Navajo man said softly, "and there is something not right happening out here in the darkness. Are you here to harm me?"

"No, sir. The Anglo world knows me as Leo Hawk—Patrolman Hawk of the New Mexico state police. May I show you my badge?" Lee waited for a response, accepting the lapse into Indian time despite the need for fast action. Showing patience was a necessary sign of respect, especially to a medicine man. If they wanted this man's help, they'd need to play by his rules.

Lee reached into his jacket pocket, and brought out his gold shield, now clipped to a leather holder.

"Can't see it that well in the dark, Officer, but I've heard your name, and that you have patrolled the highways here and on the Navajo Nation up by Shiprock," the man said. "Why don't you come out of that water now? You must be freezing."

Lee grabbed Diane's hand and helped her climb up onto dry ground. She was shivering from the cold. "Thank you, sir," she said to the medicine man. "We're sorry to disturb you." Diane could see a hogan not far away.

"Let's get inside. From your expression, it looks like you're being hunted, especially when you're walking in such a cold stream to hide your tracks." The medicine man shrugged, then reached around the tree and retrieved a lever-action .30-30 rifle he'd propped there, out of sight.

None of them spoke as they walked quickly down to the hogan. Another hundred feet beyond the eight-sided structure was a small wood-frame house with a light on in one of the rooms. Lee knew that this was the source of the light they'd seen not long after leaving the car.

The medicine man stood beside the entrance a moment, took something out of his medicine pouch that Lee suspected was corn pollen, and softly said a blessing over his medicine hogan. Then he turned and blessed both of them, surprising Diane, who said nothing. After that, he held back the blanket, and motioned the two of them inside. A small piñon fire crackled in the fire pit of the medicine hogan, and in the glow, the notched and carefully positioned logs that comprised the eight-sided traditional structure were prominent.

Lee waited to be asked to sit, and Diane just stood there, looking around. It was obviously her first look inside any form of hogan, much less one of a medicine man. From what Lee knew, this was an uncharacteristic privilege for the *hataalii* to offer a woman stranger, particularly a *bila-gánna*—white woman.

"Sit here by the fire and warm your feet," he said to Diane, gesturing to a spot on the south side, traditionally "belonging" to the women. She took the opportunity to sit down on a sheepskin and direct her feet toward the coals. Lee noticed that she kept looking to her right, toward the entrance, which was covered only by the heavy blanket, and she kept her hand close to her pistol, now under her jacket in its holster.

"You are protecting this Anglo woman, I suspect," the *hataalii* said, this time in Navajo, motioning for Lee to sit at the north side of the fire. "Someone is after you, and you've been wounded. I heard many shots about an hour ago, not long after two vehicles went up toward the killed hogan where my old uncle once lived."

The medicine man glanced at Diane, then back at Lee. His attention seemed to center on the large amount of blood that had caked on Lee's upper arm.

Lee's eyes must have given away his reaction to the mention of the old hogan, the one Bowlegs had constructed late in the forties after a patient had died in his original structure. He nodded, and answered back in Navajo. "The two men from the van are dangerous killers out to do harm. If they find us here, they won't spare any of our lives. If you wish, we'll leave."

The man was listening to Lee, but his eyes were fixed on his wound. His words were in English now. "If that's your blood, you shouldn't even be able to walk. Yet you hold your arm as if healed already." The *hataalii* looked at Lee, up and down, then thought about it for a moment before speaking.

"The one who once lived at the hogan up the hill. My uncle. Do you know what he was called?"

Lee nodded, suddenly suspecting old Bowlegs had taught his nephew the ways of the medicine man, and even shared his knowledge about night walkers. The man was still studying Lee's shoulder, which was nearly healed, and he'd taken a step back, reaching for his medicine pouch. He took out a small fetish, perhaps his ward against evil.

Lee responded in English. "I'm a friend, and I think your uncle may have told you about me, and that time many years ago, when the Germans were our enemies. Your relative was called Bowlegs, and he did much to help me that night." Lee smiled at Diane, who was looking back and forth between the two men curiously, but obviously relieved that she was able to understand what was being said.

"I was told about a state policeman who'd come to him after being contaminated by the blood of those called walkers of the night. My uncle had done all he could, and protected that man from the curse of the sun, though not completely. Are you that man? Tell me what he was named." The medicine man was agitated now, practically shaking with excitement.

"Your uncle was very kind, though he shook like you do now at first. But walkers of the night, like most men, are good or evil from their hearts, not from this affliction. As I said before, you have nothing to fear from me, or from my companion. I was called Lee Nez at that time, but I've had many names since that night in 1945. Did your uncle find the rations I left for him?" Lee recalled the case of C rations he'd set off the truck for the man.

"He did. Bowlegs shared it with my mother and my brothers and sisters. We lived closer to Fort Wingate, just north of the railroad tracks. My uncle only spoke of you one time, and that was years later when he was telling how to counter the affliction, and how to fight night walkers who were bad men." He smiled for the first time.

"I'm called John Buck by the state of New Mexico, though many of the *Dineh* around here follow the Way and don't use names that much." He nodded to Diane. "You have been blessed with the protection of a powerful man/creature. Are you a policewoman, miss?"

Diane nodded. "Diane Lopez." She brought out her shield.

John Buck's eyebrows rose. "I didn't know the FBI believed in night walkers."

"I didn't at first. Sometimes you have to see something to believe it. Like you did tonight." She smiled weakly, then turned to Lee. "Are you ready to travel now? I've warmed up and we shouldn't hang around here much longer, or we'll put our host in danger." She looked at the medicine man. "Sir, I would recommend that you leave the area as soon as possible. If anyone else lives here with you, we should try to warn them too."

"I live alone, but it'll be daylight soon. None of us will be in danger then."

Lee nodded, and had just turned to thank John Buck when a dog started barking outside.

John Buck reached over and grabbed his rifle, motioning for Diane and Lee to move to either side of the entrance. As they did, they drew their pistols and crouched down low to the hardened earthen floor.

Buck walked around to the opposite side of the smoke hole, the west side, putting himself in the shadows and aiming his rifle toward the blanket covering the entrance. He whistled sharply once.

The blanket moved at the bottom, and a brown mutt

rushed into the hogan and ran around the fire pit, sitting beside the medicine man and growling toward the covered entrance.

Lee flinched when the dog ran in, and noted out of the corner of his eye that Diane had reacted the same way, but kept her pistol still.

It became very quiet, and the only sound was the soft crackle of burning pine and the nearly imperceptible, deep growl of the dog. The mutt's ears were lowered so far they almost disappeared into his head.

The sound of a footstep just on the other side of the blanket was only slightly louder than Lee's beating heart. At least it sounded that way to him.

The medicine man pulled back the lever on his Winchester, cocking the weapon loudly as it sent a cartridge into the chamber.

They waited a minute, then three minutes. Even the dog never took his eyes off the wool blanket hanging from the top of the doorway. It occurred to Lee that if a piece of wood in the fire popped, that blanket would be full of holes in two seconds.

The thought made Lee remember the smoke hole above. He looked up toward the center of the wood-lined ceiling, caught John Buck's eye, then looked up again.

The medicine man nodded and, holding his rifle as steady as he could with one hand, reached over with the other and grabbed a piñon log heavy with yellow chunks of pitch. He set it in the middle of the fire, and scooted back slightly. The dog looked at his owner, then scooted back too. The mutt had finally noticed Diane and Lee, but his focus soon shifted back toward the entrance. He crouched down low to the ground. His mouth was halfway open, showing sharp, healthy fangs.

The pitch in the wood caught fire quickly, flaring up and putting out a spitting flame that reached three feet off the ground toward the smoke hole. Anyone peeking inside would either be temporarily blinded or scorched, perhaps both.

Nobody moved for another five minutes, but finally everyone relaxed a bit. Diane lowered herself to the ground, going from a painful crouch to a sitting position, relief evident from the expression on her face when she finally sat.

Still no one shifted their weapons' aim away from the entrance, and John Buck kept the fire going a bit longer. Eventually the fire died down and Lee noticed light starting to appear in the sky outside the smoke hole.

Not long after that, the dog inched up to the blanket, sniffed, then went outside.

Diane sighed, and lowered her weapon. "My arm is tired," she whispered. Lee nodded, and motioned with his head toward the medicine man.

"It's over for now," Buck said.

## CHAPTER 15

Diane went to the blanket serving as the door to the medicine hogan and peeked out. The sun was just coming up, and Lee stood back to avoid the direct rays.

"Sorry, Lee. I forgot." Diane looked contrite.

John Buck gently lowered the hammer of his Winchester, setting the weapon down on a sheepskin. "The one at the entrance. He was one of the night walkers?"

"Probably the same one who made me one of them so long ago," Lee answered. "He's after us because we know about him. He's a German who came to this state during World War II and killed several soldiers, my partner, and a shop owner in Albuquerque. At the time, the vampire was with other German spies. He and I were the only survivors of the ambush he arranged back in March of 1945."

"I heard about that from my uncle after I'd grown old enough to learn the ways of the *hataalii*. The government said it was a terrible accident, and that you had drowned later in a ditch, but he knew they were lying about it. Has this German night walker come back to hunt you down after all these years?" Buck stood slowly, stretching to ease his cramped muscles.

"I don't think he's after me, unless I get in his way. He wants something the soldiers were protecting back during the war, something very much a secret, even today." Lee looked at Diane, who shrugged.

"But he didn't get it then, apparently. Was it something you hid, and is that why you've been coming back here as long as I can remember?"

"So you'd seen me, and already knew who I was last night."

"My uncle found a small hole that had been covered over with dirt, and never looked inside, but he built the hogan near there so he could be close. He kept watch too, thinking you must have had a good reason to hide whatever it was inside there. Do I want to know what it is?" Buck looked at Lee, then Diane.

"It would only put you in much greater danger." Diane shook her head. "We hope to remove it as soon as we can, and finally return it to the government." She came up beside Lee. "Don't you think that's the best way to handle things?"

Lee nodded. "Your uncle was quite a man. It's good to see his nephew has followed in his footsteps. You saved our lives last night. Now we can go. Just be very careful around strangers," he said, giving him a description of the vampires, "and stay close at home at night. Your dog serves you well, give him plenty of food and water."

"I'm always careful at night. My uncle also told me about the evil ones, those who hunt their own kind while in the skins of wolves and wildcats. He said they would hunt you, in particular, now that you've become a walker of the night. Has that come true as well?"

Both Diane and Lee nodded at once, and Buck was surprised. "You've seen these Navajo shape-shifters, and they've attacked you, a non-Navajo?" He shook his head slowly as Diane nodded again.

"They've attacked more than once, and one woman, in the form of a black panther, killed my Anglo partner in Las Cruces." Diane's voice grew cold and calm. "I'm going to hunt down that bitch."

"There have been many stories, but they are never mentioned outside a hogan. These creatures are said to be strong and smart, but they lack the cunning of the animals they become. They still think like humans. That is their one weakness, I have heard." John turned around, and began to put kindling on the dying embers of the fire.

"Yes. I've been hunting these creatures for many years, and have always prevailed. But their packs keep coming, and I've never been able to have a moment's peace near the *Dinetah*, Navajo country. These Navajo witches can smell the part of me that is a night walker, and they crave my blood to make them immortal." Lee finally put his pistol away, and wiped the perspiration off his brow with the back of his sleeve.

"Is there any way for Lee to cover his tracks and avoid their detection? Perhaps you've learned something as a medicine man than can help him?" Diane watched John as he placed a sturdy wire grill upon four strategically placed rocks, then began to search along a small wooden shelf attached to the bottom of a log. She wondered if he was going to prepare some sort of herbal remedy and smiled when she saw him reach for a jar of instant coffee.

John placed a speckled blue coffeepot onto the grill above a hot spot. "Human scent is powerful, well known to all animals, and a good predator like a wolf or mountain lion can smell humans far away. The unique smell of a night walker must be even stronger to the skinwalkers when they inhabit the bodies of animals. Maybe if you had a dog, your animal could smell them coming as well. But you have your own qualities to defend yourself, don't you, enemy-slayer?"

"My abilities have served me well against the Navajo witches. They pose a threat to me, but it's one I've been able to handle. The ones who are more than a match for me are the walkers of the night. They're more powerful than I am. The ones after us now are killers, and we need to find them again so we can settle this once and for all." Lee brought out the bottle of sunblock from his pocket, took off his baseball cap, and began to rub lotion onto his face, neck, and hands.

"Don't forget the spots where your jacket is torn, you'll have exposed skin there," Diane reminded.

"You are welcome to stay here until night again," John Buck suggested.

"Thanks, but no. We have to leave soon. They can't face the sun for as long as I can, so they must be holed up somewhere, perhaps the old hogan, or their van," Lee pointed out.

"More likely they've left. They didn't have time to hunt for us, find the hidden container, and fix the tire all before sunrise," Diane said.

She continued. "I doubt they'd remain in the hogan where we could find them. We wouldn't need to assault the place, just burn it down or crack it open to let the sunlight in. That would be enough to fry them, wouldn't it?" Diane checked Lee's expression for an answer.

"I'm glad you're on my side. Those methods would have worked against them, I'm sure." Lee smiled. "You're right, they've left in the van. I would have done the same thing.

And I wouldn't have gone back to my apartment either."

"They might decide to remain on base, at least until tomorrow night. They know it wouldn't be easy for us to follow them there. Then they can risk coming back later for the you-know-what." Diane smiled at John, who understood why she wasn't being specific.

"Being on base would protect them from me, that's for sure. They're protected from civil authorities there unless we go through channels, and neither one of us has any evidence to go in and arrest them," Lee said. "We'll have to wait them out, but they'll be ready for us next time."

"I have a plan, and I'll tell you about it on the way back," Diane said. "But first I need to get our car back. How about if I bring it over here so you won't have to expose yourself to sunlight for more than a few minutes?"

"Check to see if they found and booby-trapped it first. Assume nothing."

John Buck cleared his throat, and they both looked over. He held out two glass mugs. They were a shiny carnival glass like gold, looked brand-new, and were brimming with steaming coffee. "You can't leave before you have your morning coffee. I got these mugs inside boxes of oatmeal years ago, and now have a special occasion to use them. I've always doubted the stories my uncle told me about the deepest secrets of the *Dineh*, but last night I found them all to be true."

"Is that good news, or bad?" Diane asked, accepting the first of the offered mugs.

"Like everything else in nature, I can't judge its value. To me, it's just a fact of life." John handed Lee a mug, then picked up a third, an old coffee-stained cup with the faded logo of the Washington Redskins.

"Thank you for your friendship, and the friendship of your ancestor," Lee offered, raising the cup to his lips gratefully.

Lee drove skillfully down the Interstate, eyeing each van he saw closely, not expecting to spot the one he'd seen last night, but knowing from Murphy's Law that a vehicle with no spare tire was more likely to have a flat than one equipped for an emergency.

Diane had postponed telling him her plan. She wanted to make sure it felt right to her first. Now, exhausted, she was asleep on the backseat, her head resting upon her jacket, and he saw no need to awaken her, though they'd agreed to take shifts on the driving, two hours on, two off, so they'd both get a chance to rest.

Diane had found the car, which had not been disturbed or tampered with, apparently, and when they left John Buck's home, they went by his uncle's last hogan just to verify that the vampires had cleared out. The van was gone and the hogan open to sunlight as Diane had predicted.

Wearing his cap and sunglasses, Lee backtracked quickly to check for his rifle, but it was gone. That was not unexpected. Muller or his crewman had taken it with them.

Diane checked the spot where she'd hit Muller's partner, and his blood had oxidized, leaving only a brown, rusty spot on the ground. Deeply indented footprints showed that Muller had found the injured vampire and carried him inside the hogan. There they found another spot of blood, not affected by sunlight, where the vampire had lain until he healed.

Diane had used a cell phone to contact her Bureau SAC, Ray Lewis, asking him to contact law-enforcement agencies statewide and have them keep an eye out for the vehicle. If they spotted the van, they were to avoid contact, but inform Diane and Lee. Diane promised to give her SAC more information later that day, and gave him her cell number. Though he pressured her unsuccessfully for details on the two men in the van, she refused to identify them, though she gave descriptions.

Lee munched a granola bar, the last one of his share of the remaining snacks, while downing the rest of the calves' blood from the thermos. He still had plenty of strength and mental awareness remaining. The animal blood and high-calorie intake helped compensate for all the energy he had used to heal himself last night.

He'd had an extra change of clothes in the trunk, and wore them now instead of his bloodstained attire. Those clothes had been placed in a plastic trash bag and thrown into a restaurant Dumpster in Grants.

There was the sound of movement behind him, then Lee saw Diane in the rearview mirror, sitting up and yawning. She checked her watch.

"Hey, you let me sleep an extra hour."

"How do you feel?"

"Less sleepy. But you need to get some rest too, if we're going to be watching for Muller and his crewman tonight." Diane reached for a granola bar from the pack on the rear floorboard.

"You mentioned earlier that you had a plan. Ready to talk about it now?" Lee glanced back at Diane again. "Remember there are two canteens, no blood in either one. Just water. Drink up, you don't want to dehydrate."

"I'm going to contact SAC Lewis again. This time I'll name names, and tell him that we suspect it was Major Muller and his crewman on Navajo land last night, in that van, and that they fired some shots at a tribal elder, according to our contact. We were alerted because we had obtained a Navajo informant who said Muller was connected to the training of the animals that attacked us and killed Agent Thomas. I'll remind him that *Schutzhund* training is a German tradition. We just want to keep Muller and his crewman under surveillance because we have reason to believe either he'll be contacting those Navajo animal handlers, or they'll try to contact him. It's too sensitive an issue, especially because the Germans are guests at a military base, to act without more information."

She sat forward, her head next to his. "How's that?"

He thought about it for a moment, enjoying her proximity.

"Well?"

"Usually Navajos give other Navajos time to think about things. We don't rush."

"I'm not Navajo, I'm Hispanic. We all like to talk at the same time, and never wait for answers. Where's your cultural awareness, Indian?"

Lee laughed. "Okay. The idea is a good one and your speech sounds plausible. There is even a lot of truth mixed in there. It'll give the authorities a reason to watch Muller, and maybe restrict his movements, especially with the present threat of terrorism. That will make it hard for him to leave the base without us finding out about it."

"Exactly. He'll have a hard time looking for that plutonium with people watching him." Diane sat back and began eating her granola bar. "Whenever you want me to drive, just pull over."

Hours later, just outside Las Cruces, Diane received a call on her cell phone. After a few minutes, she ended the conversation, and spoke to Lee, who was driving. "Muller and the van arrived at an Alamogordo car-rental place, then he and the crewman, whose name is Kurt Plummer, were picked up by a woman who turns out to be the crewman's wife, Ingrid. The rental van was rented under a phony driver's license."

"Both men are at the Plummer apartment now, under surveillance," Diane continued. "And my guess came through on that aerial survey. Major Muller rented an aircraft used by a mining company to conduct aerial surveys. He needed his pilot credentials to get the aircraft, so he used his real ID for it. The flight plan said he flew in the area of Mount Taylor."

"We know he didn't go there, Mount Taylor is too far east of Fort Wingate, but it explains how he got his information on the location, or possible locations. Depending on how many hot spots he found, if that's the way it works, he may not know for sure he was so close. Either way, he hasn't dug up the plutonium," Lee answered.

"What did your SAC say about the survey? He's probably curious about what Muller is looking for, isn't he?" Lee added.

"That was the part where I answered 'I have no idea.' You know what kind of reaction we'd have gotten if Lewis thought there was buried nuclear-weapons material sitting out there someplace."

"The place would be crawling with feds, Muller would probably go deep undercover or leave the country, and I'd be back at square one."

"Why don't we just get the plutonium ourselves, if that's what it really is, or in case it's too dangerous to handle now, tell the Department of Energy or whoever? They could have a busload of experts from Las Alamos and Sandia Corporation out there in a few hours," Diane suggested.

"I've thought of that many times, but always go back to the same selfish answer. I'd been putting it off for years, but now I think I know why I never dug it up."

"I have an idea. It's the one thing you hold over Muller's head. Something you have that he wanted badly enough to risk his own life, and take the lives of many others. Is that it?"

"I'm afraid so. Worrying about who to trust in the military stopped being a concern years ago. But for a long time, keeping the box from him was the single victory I had over the man—the vampire. I'd hunted him, of course, but never gotten close, not until now, but that was the only possible bait I had to lure him back. When I realized he was probably after it now, for whatever reason, I knew where he'd have to go. I only wish things would have gone differently last night. Another few seconds one way or the other, a direction he might have turned, and I could have taken him down."

Lee was angry at himself, wondering if he'd held back for some deep-seated reason. He'd blown his best chance, after waiting over half a century for it. Revenge, best served cold, was now going to heat up considerably.

"But you didn't know Kurt Plummer was a vampire too, not for sure. He moved so fast, I barely heard him in time. If . . ." Diane shook her head. "I guess I still had my doubts, in spite of all I've already seen."

"That might have been my problem as well. If I could have taken out Muller at the same time you were handling his partner, we wouldn't be having this conversation now."

"No, we'd have dismembered their bodies, then waited for the sun to burn them up. And we'd have had to live with killing two more people, humans despite what they'd become." Diane sighed softly. "Now we'll have to try something else."

"With the Bureau and local officers keeping an eye on Muller and Plummer, I think we should remain on standby in case they make a move on Bowlegs's hogan again. We should be able to get there before them, even," Lee proposed. "At least we'll get advance warning."

"Then let's get to the safe house, shower and have a quick meal, restock our supplies and get back onto the road. It could be a busy night. You vampires never seem to get tired." Diane yawned, then laughed. "I never thought the word 'vampire' would ever become so large a part of my vocabulary, much less my thoughts."

"Just never forget that there are skinwalkers out there too, literally gunning for us," Lee added. "Any large animal you see after sunset could be one of their kind, and unlike vampires, they are *all* predators. And, as we know now, they'll attack non-Navajos too."


It was sunset, and Lee and Diane were on I-25 heading north toward the town of Truth or Consequences. They planned to reach the Fort Wingate area first, and have a trap waiting for Muller and Plummer if they made another move to locate and recover the box.

Diane's cell phone buzzed. She picked up the small unit and looked at the number of the caller. "It's my SAC," she said to Lee, who was driving. "Hello?"

"Lopez, this is SAC Lewis. Wolfgang Muller and Kurt Plummer just left Plummer's apartment in a dark green Ford Expedition with tinted glass and a rental tag. I'm with Agent Harris and we're following at a safe distance. They're headed north. Any ideas about their destination? Northwest again?"

Diane nodded automatically, despite being on the phone. "Northwest, toward the Thoreau area, would be my guess at the moment. We're going to attempt to place ourselves in a position to intercept them. I'd advise you not to tip them off by getting too close. These are military men, and are probably armed, especially if they're consorting with cop killers. And they're going to be watching for trouble."

"I know how to tail a suspect, Agent López. Just keep me informed of your position."

Diane rolled her eyes. "Yes, sir. Let me know the route they take once they reach Carrizozo."

Ray Lewis disconnected the call.

"This SAC of yours, Ray Lewis. When I met him, he seemed a little overconfident, maybe too complacent. Will he be able to maintain the tail without letting Muller spot him?" Lee asked. "Lewis doesn't know how well the vampires can see at night, and he missed the tail the skinwalkers put on him in broad daylight."

"He and I have always been at odds, and there might be a tendency for him to be a little overeager, I suppose," Diane admitted. "Whatever his skills as an administrator, he's just not a good field agent."

"That could get him killed. He'd have to be very lucky to take down Muller and Plummer, and even if he managed it, that would only be temporary unless he got them both in the heart or blew their heads off."

"Unfortunately, I can't be honest with him, Lee. He'd yank me off the case and confine me to a desk, answering the phone. Ray wouldn't believe a word I'd said. You know that."

"Then we have to make sure we do the job. Still have your knife?" Lee asked.

Diane nodded. "But I still don't know if I can cut off anyone's head. That's so . . . calculated."

"He'd do the same to you, or me. Muller may even think

I've turned you, or am thinking about it. Until he knows for sure, he's going to treat you like a vampire too."

Diane looked at Lee for a long time. "*Are* you thinking about it?"

"No! I don't even know if I *could* turn anyone into a vampire. What the *hataalii* did for me changed what I am." Lee kept his eyes on the road.

"But if it's in your blood, isn't it in all your body fluids too? You said you thought that whatever did this to your body was like a virus. And you were married. Didn't you and your wife . . . ?"

Lee didn't say anything.

"I'm sorry. I shouldn't be prying like this. Forget the question."

He looked over at Diane, who was obviously embarrassed. "I've told you more than I've ever told anyone in my life except for Annie. If I ever decide to talk about Annie, it'll probably be to you. But not now, okay?"

Diane nodded.

As they rode down the highway, Lee thought about something that had bothered him for so many years, always in the back of his mind. *If* he had turned Annie, she'd probably be alive today. They'd discussed the possibility, of course, but Annie loved her teaching, and didn't want to do anything that would force her away from that, so she'd said no. He had wished a thousand times since then that he'd tried to convince her otherwise.

After getting a call from SAC Lewis reporting that Muller's vehicle was, indeed, headed west across Socorro County, which was a repeat of the vampire's earlier route to Fort Wingate, they increased their speed, and Lee's thoughts returned to their mission.

"Muller is going to be expecting a trap. We don't know

for certain that he recognized you as Lee Nez, but he does know we're after him. Even if he doesn't know you're a night walker, we got away, and he has to assume the hunt will continue. Do you suppose he realizes that we know what he's after?" Diane asked.

"We have to assume so. Even if he doesn't fear us, there is John Buck to consider. Muller may believe that the medicine man told everyone, including local deputies, about someone roaming the forest near his place at night, taking pot shots at something. Let's just hope Muller doesn't go after Buck." Lee liked the *hataalii*, and trusted him immediately, just as he had the man's uncle, Bowlegs.

"So when and where do we make our move?" Diane asked. "We discussed a lot of possibilities earlier, but now we know what he's trying to do, at least initially."

"I figure we'll have to nail Muller right by the freeway, just off the exit when he's still out in the open. I'll use the backup rifle I brought, and shoot from the underpass as they're coming down the ramp. It'll be less than a hundred yards. Inside the vehicle, they won't be able to take advantage of their mobility."

"You want me to disable the vehicle, then? Shoot out the tires?"

"Exactly. Once they're disabled, we'll move in and I'll set fire to the SUV with the cook-stove fuel I put in the trunk. We'll just have to hope a passerby doesn't get caught in the middle or try to interfere."

Lee knew it was risky, but he didn't want Muller to get loose in the forest. It would be nearly impossible to track him down, and Muller's ability to run would make him a hard prey to catch even if Plummer wasn't with him.

"You should contact SAC Lewis and try to send him on

a wild-goose chase at the last second to avoid his interference. He and whoever is with him won't understand the need for overkill when it comes to eliminating a vampire," Lee said.

"Neither did I, until Kurt Plummer walked away after what I did to him. I'll take a position in the drainage ditch beside the intersection," Diane suggested. "They'll be in a crossfire."

"Okay. Just don't miss, and don't stop shooting until I do. Go for the head shots unless you're so close you can't possibly miss the heart. These guys are tough, and they'll be ready. Hopefully, they'll be expecting us to hit them when they reach the forest or are around the hogan."

"Well, if we pull this off, at least no one will ever find the bodies. We can simply maintain that we found the van empty."

Lee looked down the road, spotting an exit ahead, but kept his mind on working out the details for tonight's operation. Now that the FBI was watching Muller, Lee had to strike when the opportunity came.

Diane had contacted the SAC again, and Lewis had agreed to continue down the Interstate once Muller exited, then stop at Wingate Village and set up a roadblock where the frontage roads merged. They would catch Muller's vehicle between them that way. It was a diversion, of course, to keep the rest of the FBI away from the scene, because Muller would turn off before he'd gone that far.

Now Diane, who'd had little sleep for two days, was trying to rest, but her eyes were open. Lee was wide awake, driving an extra shift, eager to bring Muller to face ultimate justice. Most of his life, Lee had been a walker of the night, and he couldn't remember anymore what it was like to experience the darkness of night. Only by closing his eyes could he block out the light. He wondered if this was the reason he was seldom sleepy anymore.

"We're getting close. The next exit is the one we want to take," Diane spoke, her voice taking on the matter-of-fact tone of an experienced cop. She was obviously resigned to the plan, and apparently had no more doubts about doing what had to be done. Last night's experience had taught her a lot, Lee thought, looking at her out of the corners of his eyes.

Lee checked his watch. "We'll be there in three minutes, give or take. According to your SAC, they are about fifteen minutes behind us. We should have plenty of time to get set up." He looked ahead for the exit sign on the right side of the Interstate.

When they reached the exit, it only took five minutes for Lee to get into position, parking the car inside the wide, shallow tunnel on the northbound lane of the access road that passed beneath the freeway. He had a heavy-barreled Winchester varmint rifle in .30-06 caliber, again with iron sights. No scope was necessary with eyes like his.

He'd fire across the hood of the Honda, using the engine block for protection. Diane was farther out, lying in the drainage ditch beside the culvert where the exit lane intersected with the road passing under the Interstate. If things got too hot, she could duck inside the culvert.

He waited ten more minutes, then realized something was wrong. His cell phone rang, and he grabbed it instantly, looking up the freeway ramp, keeping watch.

"Yes?" he answered.

Diane spoke excitedly. "I just got a call from Lewis. Muller took a freeway exit farther back this time, and my SAC changed the plan. He's decided to follow them off the Interstate and down the frontage road. I couldn't change his mind."

"We need to saddle up. Hurry," Lee answered, then put the phone back in his pocket and set the safety on the Winchester before setting it on the backseat. Jumping inside, he started the car. Diane was running in his direction, and he pulled over and stopped long enough for her to jump in.

"Now what?"

Lee started to speak, but his words were lost in the concussion of an explosion somewhere close by that shook the light sedan. A fireball lit up the night sky, and he turned to see an inferno just off the freeway.

"That's at the other exit!" Diane shouted. "Muller!"

"Hang on!" Lee spun the Honda around, and accelerated down the frontage road east, back toward Muller's SUV and his FBI tail.

Diane grabbed her cell phone and started pushing buttons. She listened, and tried again. "I can't get a response from Lewis. I keep getting an out-of-service message."

As they raced down the frontage road east, flames and black smoke continued to pour from a single object directly in front of them.

"Lewis and his partner should have stuck to the plan. Do you think Muller spotted them?" Diane kept trying, but couldn't get a response on the cell phone.

"What kind of car were they driving?" Lee said, his voice sounding distant and detached. Below the billowing black smoke and the flames reaching twenty feet into the sky was the wreckage of a sedan. The doors had been blown off, and the interior was a wall of fire. Puncture holes were everywhere on the shell of the vehicle, but the vehicle tag was still readable.

Diane set down the cell phone and started shaking her

head. Lee could see she was biting her lip, trying to control her emotions. Looking down, he saw his own hands were gripping the steering wheel so tightly nobody could have pried them loose.

"Call for backup, Diane. Muller and Plummer did this, and we have to find them before they get away." Lee pulled up to within a hundred feet of the inferno. The body of the front passenger was ten feet away from the fire, his clothes still smoking. At least one arm appeared to be missing, and his pockets had been turned out, showing the body had been searched. The driver, still mostly inside, had been blown apart. Both men had probably died within a second or two.

He looked around, but no other vehicles were in sight. There were skid marks, however, that indicated a vehicle had accelerated away quickly, headed south beneath the freeway toward the east-bound on-ramp.

Diane had tears in her eyes, but she was speaking calmly and coldly on the cell phone as she put in an All-Points for Muller's SUV.

"Diane." She didn't seem to hear him. "Diane!"

This time she turned in his direction.

"They're headed back east. Let everyone know that they're using explosives, probably a grenade or a big pipe bomb. Something that throws a lot of shrapnel."

Diane relayed the information, never taking her eyes off the smoking body of the passenger, Ray Lewis. She turned to Lee. "We can't afford to wait for the fire department. If Muller is heading east, that's where we're going. I want those bloodsucking bastards."

## CHAPTER 16

Shit! I wish we had a radio." Diane was on the edge of her seat, her cell phone in her hand as she looked out the window to her right for signs of Muller's SUV.

Every few minutes she'd get a call routed through the Albuquerque FBI office. Roadblocks had been set up at Grants and farther west as well, and local deputies and the Navajo police were alerted to check secondary roads throughout a hundred-mile radius.

"They'll be getting rid of the SUV. They obviously knew the people they saw tailing them were cops who'd reported the vehicle description. Keep an eye out for the thing," Lee advised. "If they're thinking clearly, they'll probably steal another vehicle, so maybe we'll get an auto-theft report that we can follow up on."

Diane nodded. She had been agitated for a while, suggesting possible moves made by Muller and his crewman to avoid detection. Now she was calming down, obviously trying to get inside the heads of the German vampires.

"What about the wife of the crewman? Ingrid Plummer." She punched out another number on the cell phone. "This is Agent Diane Lopez again. I'd like a report from the team assigned to watch Kurt Plummer's apartment. What is the wife doing?"

Diane listened for a minute. "What? When? Why didn't somebody notify SAC Lewis and me? Put out a bulletin on that woman. She might lead us to her husband and Wolfgang Muller. Also notify Base Security. They are to consider Muller and Plummer extremely dangerous, and be ready to use deadly force. Let me know immediately if any of these people or their vehicles are located."

She disconnected the call, and released a long stream of obscenities.

"Let me guess. The wife has disappeared." Lee sighed.

"The team that was supposed to take over the apartment surveillance for Lewis and his partner when they followed Muller arrived a few minutes late. The dumb asses assumed the wife was still in the apartment, but didn't get around to checking on her vehicle until an hour ago. It was missing. They checked with the neighbors, who heard her drive off a few minutes after her husband left."

"Are they looking for her vehicle?"

"Yes. And her as well."

"It's my fault. I didn't include her in the picture at all. She's probably in on everything. There's no way she wouldn't know her husband is a vampire. She could even be one herself." Lee used some of the curses Diane had employed earlier.

"She may have followed her husband in a loose tail, spotted Ray Lewis, then contacted her husband. They knew we were looking for them. They just outsmarted us. We can't afford to let that happen again." Diane kept her eyes open, looking at every side road that might have been used by Muller.

"Check and see if they have a cell phone listed. Maybe

we can track down their calls if they try to get in contact with each other," Lee suggested.

Diane nodded, and within five minutes had the answer. "A call was made from the cell phone in the same general area where Ray Lewis and Agent Harris were killed. Who do you suppose got close enough to throw the explosive device, the woman?"

"She may have pulled up behind Lewis's car at the intersection where he was attacked, flagged them down, and then just walked up to the window and tossed in a bomb or grenade. They probably didn't even recognize Ingrid until it was too late," Lee said. "Like us, they probably only have a description of her."

The cell phone rang again, and Diane listened briefly, then disconnected after only a moment.

"They found Ingrid Plummer's car. It was in a supermarket parking lot in Alamogordo. Local officers are checking the area, trying to find her, or anyone who may have seen where she went," Diane reported.

"She just switched vehicles. You might ask the officers to check and see if any car-rental places are within walking distance of that parking lot, and if she could have rented a vehicle during the right time frame."

"Good idea."

They continued on for another ten minutes, then Lee pulled over at a gas station west of Grants. Parked back in the darkest spot of the lot was a Ford Expedition of the right color. "I just happened to notice. Good eyes, remember?"

They approached the vehicle cautiously, but it was empty and unlocked. The rental paperwork inside revealed it was the one they were looking for.

"Diane?" Lee caught her eye and indicated a man approaching. She kept her hand near her pistol, but quickly realized it was only an employee of the gas station.

"You cops or something?" the young man asked. He was Hispanic, wearing oily olive-green coveralls, and had dusty grease on his hands.

"Right." Lee had his ID out before Diane could reach into her pocket. "We're from the state police. A car was firebombed tonight near Thoreau, and we believe the occupants of this vehicle were involved. What do you remember about the driver, and was anyone else with him?"

"I remember hearing them drive up in a hurry, but I was working on a muffler at the time. There was a brief argument, somebody got slapped, and doors slammed. When I came out, the Ford was here, and a red Chevy Suburban was laying rubber east."

"You see the tags?" Diane asked.

"No, ma'am. Too dark. But it looked new."

"Did you examine the SUV, or look inside?" Lee asked.

"Sure did. It was unlocked, and I wanted to see if there was registration or some kind of address inside. These suckers are expensive." The mechanic smiled, eyeing Diane.

"When the officers show up, make sure they get a sample of your fingerprints so they can match them against those found inside. It might save you some trouble later on," Diane said, reaching for her cell phone again.

While she contacted local officers, Lee questioned the young mechanic about any details he remembered about the argument and anything he might have seen. After a few minutes, the man admitted hearing a man call someone an idiot. A woman had said something, then yelped. She was the one slapped, probably.

Lee and Diane were on the road again soon. While a local crime-scene team searched, then impounded the vehicle, other officers would scour Grants and surrounding areas for the red Suburban.

"Do you think they will be going back to Alamogordo?" Diane asked after they'd been on the road several minutes.

"Not really. There are too many people there who might recognize them, and now they're on the run for something we can actually arrest them for," Lee pointed out.

"Which means they're going to go into hiding. I don't think the heat will die down very soon, do you?" She thought about it for a moment. "They're going to be going back for that box, if they really want it that bad. If they wait much longer, they have to assume you'll finally turn it over to the authorities or hide it somewhere else. By now they realize you've been hoping Muller would come back for it, which is why you never turned it in. They know it's your bait."

"These are very smart people, at least Muller is," Lee said. "I doubt killing Agents Lewis and Harris was his idea. The woman probably did it to protect her husband. That would explain the slap and the argument. I bet they're going to hide out until night, or try to travel by daylight in a covered vehicle."

She nodded. "They've become federal fugitives."

"Where would you go if you wanted to hide out a few days, Diane?"

"Me? If I hadn't lived in Albuquerque half my life, that's where I'd go. Lots of housing, plenty of strangers to hide among, and thousands of choices if you're looking to steal some transportation. It's also the biggest city anywhere close to Fort Wingate," Diane replied. "Gallup is quite a bit smaller, and they would have to pass by us."

"I agree. Then that's where we go tonight," Lee said. "Maybe, in the meantime, we'll get lucky and somebody will spot that Suburban."

• •

There are more than a dozen tiny communities between Grants and Albuquerque, and though the trip normally took less than an hour, they had to pass through roadblocks manned by heavily armed officers at McCartys on the Acoma Indian Reservation and again at Laguna for that tribe's officers. Both villages featured several side roads that the German Air Force fugitives could have taken.

Once in Albuquerque, though it was not yet sunrise, Lee and Diane were ordered to meet with a combined task force of federal, state, and local officers concerning the bombing of SAC Lewis's automobile and the dragnet out for Muller and the Plummers.

The multistory FBI building was a few blocks from what was considered downtown, with easy access to I-25, which was only a short distance east. Lee had never been in the building, but Diane had her cubbyhole office on the second floor, he learned as they drove into the basement parking garage of the modern structure.

"The meeting is in the big conference room on the first floor," Diane explained as they jogged up the single flight of stairs. She stopped at the stairwell door and adjusted her clothes.

"You look fine. Is my tie straight?" Lee said, and she turned to look automatically. He hadn't worn a suit in years.

"Go to hell."

"I think I'm about to," he replied, pulling the door open for her.

They emerged in the lobby, and discovered reporters and cameramen from at least two television stations hanging around, apparently waiting for a press conference or the opportunity to interview anyone who'd speak to them. "Who are they?" one of the civilians said to her companion, and camera lights came on.

Lee kept his face away from the cameras as much as possible without appearing too obvious, following Diane across the room to a door where a tall, grim-looking man in a brown suit was standing.

"Gabriel," Diane said as the man opened the door for them, blocking the press at the same time.

"Agent Lopez, Officer Hawk." The agent spoke softly, nodding to both of them as they passed through the doorway onto the gray-carpeted hall beyond. Lee moved quickly, glad to be out of the sight of the press. He didn't like the idea of so many people, especially FBI agents, having a good look at his file photo either, as the agent named Gabriel had obviously done.

The conference room was surrounded on four sides by hallways, and that section of the building was overflowing with uniformed officers and men in suits despite the hour. The low tones of conversation reflected the grim atmosphere, which was further enhanced by the darkened lighting in the halls.

Diane entered the room first, with Lee right behind her, and the room grew silent within a few seconds as every face turned toward them.

"You're finally here, Agent Lopez. And, Officer Hawk, I presume . . ." A wide-shouldered, towhaired agent probably ten years older than Diane broke the silence. "I'm Acting SAC Vernon Logan. Would you two please have a seat? I'll handle the introductions, then you two can give everyone here the background needed to get us up to speed on the current status of these cop-killing bastards."

Lee noticed one empty chair beside Lieutenant Richmond, although several officers from outlying agencies were standing. Another seat was empty beside Logan. Diane was motioned toward that chair, and Richmond nodded to Lee. The Lopez and Hawk team was already being split up, apparently. He'd have to do something about that. Hopefully, Diane would recognize the strategy and make the same move.

Someone placed a cup of hot coffee in front of Lee as soon as he was seated, and he nodded without turning around, instead watching the faces of the officers and officials as Logan quickly gave their names, ranks, and agencies. Most were executive officers—their captains or superiors were out on duty, coordinating the intensive search for the Germans and the skinwalkers.

Logan nodded to Lieutenant Richmond, who turned to Lee. "Officer Hawk will now give us a brief synopsis of the situation, which seems to connect two cases, each of which has resulted in homicides where the victim or victims were law-enforcement personnel."

Lee took a sip of his coffee to help clear his throat before speaking. He kept his narrative as brief as possible, first of all relating the events leading up to the death of Agent Thomas, Diane's partner. The bodies of the nude Navajo couple, the wolf, and the presence of a black panther raised a lot of eyebrows immediately. The shooting involving the van and Darvon Blackhorse was much more straightforward, fortunately, and there was a round of nods and murmurs at the mention of Blackhorse's death.

Then Diane joined in, at Lee's request, and she spoke with emotion about the activities concerning Muller that first got Lee's attention and led to the FBI involvement, then the German response, including the murder of SAC Lewis and Agent Harris and their arrival on the scene just after the bombing.

Many of the officers were skeptical of their stories and the unusual nature of the crimes, and had questions and doubts, yet nobody could deny the violence and the deaths themselves. Officers began to argue back and forth about the events and possible strategies, and Acting SAC Logan looked back and forth between Lee and Diane, not certain how to respond to their stories, or the group. An agent in white shirt and tie came into the room and handed Logan a piece of paper. He read it quickly, then stood to get everyone's attention.

"People." He held up the paper. "I've just received some confirmation regarding officer Hawk's theory that these German airmen are here with a terrorist agenda. Bureau contacts with Interpol have obtained descriptions and sketches that identify Muller and Plummer as members of a freelance terrorist gang operating in Europe and the Middle East. They are believed to be highly trained operatives specializing in the assassination of government officials. Muller and Plummer—nobody knows their real names—managed to penetrate the German Air Force and assume the identities of airmen, who are now listed as missing. Ingrid Plummer is also believed to be part of that group."

"SAC Logan?" Lieutenant Richmond spoke. He had that little Texas accent so common from a native of southeastern New Mexico, and it came out in conversation occasionally. "Any idea what is motivating these terrorists? Anything else known about them? What does the CIA have to say about all this?"

Logan replied, "The CIA is in the dark about Muller's gang, apparently. But European and Middle Eastern law-enforcement agencies believe the group made an unsuccessful attempt to take out an Iraqi general intensely loyal to Saddam Hussein. One of their people was taken alive, apparently, by Hussein's guards."

"And this terrorist is *still* alive?" Diane said.

"Apparently, though the assassination attempt took place several months ago. Israeli intelligence sources linked with Interpol hint that the Iraqis are trying to cut a deal to bring these terrorists into their own service. Muller has a sister somewhere, and the captive is supposed to be her husband," Logan replied.

"Exactly what is Muller's gang doing here in New Mexico?" Logan continued. "That's what we need to uncover. Although they have conducted aerial surveys of certain areas, we don't know what they were looking for. Agents are in contact with the survey company now, seeking more information. The CIA and other federal agencies have been contacted, but have yet to provide anything we can use."

Lee looked at Diane, and she was obviously thinking the same thing. Plutonium could be used to coerce Iraq or, alternately, buy a hostage back. It would explain the presence of Muller and some of his group, certainly.

Diane stood, and Logan scowled, but gave her the floor. "This information is consistent with Officer Hawk's original assessment. I recommend at this point that we continue with our current strategy, which is to use all available law-enforcement resources in a coordinated effort to locate and neutralize these three individuals before any more lives are lost. I will continue working with Officer Hawk, who seems to have the most success in predicting their next move. SAC Logan, I know you will want to continue to coordinate state and local law-enforcement personnel in our statewide manhunt through our mobile command centers."

Lee realized that Diane was making her move to shape operations so they could work together before Logan could do otherwise. She knew the real score, and that the two of them were the only ones capable of dealing with Muller's group.

It was his turn now to motivate the gathering into action before he and Diane were put behind desks or in tactical headquarters, but he also had to make sure that any other officers actually confronting the vampires weren't going to be slaughtered by underestimating the threat. He'd have to come across as ruthless and emotional, which went against his nature—at least the emotional part.

He stood before anyone else could speak. "We've lost enough of our fellow law-enforcement officers to these terrorists already. I'd like to remind everyone here that we are dealing with violent, merciless individuals who are totally without conscience. I suspect that Muller's people are wearing body armor, and are so hyped up emotionally, perhaps through mental discipline and/or drug enhancement, that they literally feel no pain. They will be hard to bring down. Warn every one of your officers in the field. If anyone is forced into an armed confrontation with these perps, I strongly advise an overwhelming lethal response. Multiple shots to their heads and hearts are not inappropriate. I honestly feel it will take that kind of firepower to bring them down. Do I need to remind anyone of a street battle several years ago in Miami, when amped-up perps already suffering from lethal wounds continued to resist, killing several FBI agents? This is the motivation of the terrorists we're after, people. They don't want to be taken alive. I suggest they get their wish."

Heads were already nodding, and by the time he finished, nearly all the officers in the room were voicing their agreement. In the flurry of excitement, with nearly everyone speaking at once, Lieutenant Richmond turned to Lee. "Hell of a pep talk, Officer Hawk. I think everyone's ready to kick ass."

Lee looked across the table at Diane, who nodded imperceptibly.

A half hour later, after settling on tactical arrangements and sharing specific details with their fellow officers, Lee and Diane were transferring the gear they had with them into her old Bureau unit, which had been brought to the Bureau's underground garage from the parking lot of Lee's apartment.

"I had to preempt Logan before he assigned me to direct a task force," Diane said, "regardless of how it might help my career. I'd be tied to a desk or some mobile van while everyone coming into contact with them goes down in a firefight they have very little hope to win."

"You timed it right. At least we've warned everyone the best we could about the danger facing anyone who encounters Muller's little gang. We know they won't be taken alive, that's for sure," Lee commented, placing his rifle and ammunition on the backseat under a blanket.

"I was impressed with the reaction you got when you suggested the best way to end this investigation," Diane said, climbing into the driver's side. "Scary."

"Idiots. They bought into it because they thought I was speaking from emotion after losing comrades to these killers. Too bad I couldn't tell them that's the only chance they have of actually killing these vampires."

"I just hope we don't lose any more officers." Diane shook her head as they drove out of the underground garage of the Albuquerque Bureau office just east of downtown. She was exhausted, obviously, and Lee had noticed her yawns several times the past hour, even during the tense moments in the conference room. It had been stressful having to stick to their cover story to avoid being locked away in padded rooms.

"Well, we need some rest, if we're going to be able to track Muller down. It may be our last opportunity before they give up and try to leave the country. I'm glad that we now know Muller's motivation for getting at the plutonium."

"I'm too tired to even think about it now, as you can tell. Come and stay at my place. We have to keep working together if we expect to defeat these killers. If we go anywhere near a law-enforcement agency now, we're going to run into more reporters. I sure wish they hadn't been in the Bureau lobby. If they run your photo, it'll make things even more difficult for you next time you need to establish a new identity."

"At least we were able to go back out via the elevator and they didn't get a second look. The problem with today's technology is that secrets are becoming harder and harder to keep all the time. As a Navajo, I've always been noticed in any small, off-the-Reservation community, but in a large city, I'm just another foreigner to most people. Except in the Southwest, of course." Lee had to remain philosophical, though the repercussions of what had happened worried him. It could have been worse. At least their names and addresses hadn't been given to the reporters.

Diane headed west, passing under some freeway construction, then five minutes later, turned north down Rio Grande Boulevard past Old Town, which was filled with early morning traffic, most heading the opposite direction into the downtown area.

"There's something we need to keep in mind here in Albuquerque," Lee decided to mention.

"What's that?"

"There are a lot of Navajos living between here and To'hajiilee—toward Grants—and some of them might be skinwalkers. Remember, they can sense my presence from quite a distance, like bloodhounds. And my picture might be on the news tonight. If any of Tanner's pack or that shooter in the van sees me . . ."

"You'll be inside during the day anyway, and we'll be out of here again before dark. We'll just have to keep our eyes open. In the meantime, there's no way you can tell them in human form?" Diane asked.

"Well, the only ones I've ever known were Navajo, for some genetic reason, I suppose. Other than that, unless you happen to see them shape-shifting . . ."

"But they can only do that at night?"

"That's what Bowlegs told me, and I've never seen any evidence contrary to that."

"Okay. If I see any Indians or any big dogs or cats, I'll be ready." She started to smile, then apparently changed her mind.

"You live on the west side?" Lee changed the subject as he scrunched down in the seat, adjusting the visor to block out as much as possible of the rising sun. It had been hours since his last application of sunblock, and he was wary, despite the window glass that filtered out the harmful radiation.

"How you doing on sunblock?" She noted his reaction to sunrise.

"I could use a new bottle. Once we cross the river, maybe you could stop at one of those twenty-four-hour groceries."

"Glad to. I'll get us some heat-and-serve breakfast too. It's been a while since I've been home, and I don't remember what's in the fridge . . . but whatever it is probably won't be edible now." Diane slowed the unit to thirty, entering Los Ranchos de Albuquerque, a village that included many fancy homes in the North Valley, and had only recently come into the clutches of the big developers. The speed limit was twenty-five to discourage commuters. All it had accomplished, she suspected, was to give drivers the chance to play cat-and-mouse games with the local police.

"You grew up not far from here?" Lee offered. He loved the bosque, the local name for the wooded areas running alongside the river valleys in New Mexico. The old, gnarly, self-pruning cottonwoods reminded him of San Juan County, where he'd spent his own childhood.

"Just north and east of here, between Second Street and the river. When my father died, my mother moved to Los Lunas, but the old family home is just off Fourth Street. It's now an antiques shop, of all things."

"Hell, I'm almost an antique. Don't knock it." Lee chuckled.

Diane turned to catch his eye. "You look just like new to me."

"Ah, but I'm old inside." Lee thought about Annie for a moment, remembering how they'd joked about him never looking old, and the time when she'd catch up and pass him.

They rode in silence, the only noise coming from the thump thump of oversized stereo speakers in slow-moving cars, or the swoosh of vehicles as they passed. Soon they were crossing the new Corrales bridge, a broad expanse of concrete alongside the old metal-truss structure, now a footbridge for people, horses, dogs, and an occasional llama.

"You're usually pretty upbeat, despite what we've been going through the past few days. Something on your mind?" she commented.

"Just browsing through my memory. Nothing to talk about." He sat up straight now that the sun was behind them. "Remember, we want to stop on the way."

"I didn't forget. I'm starving." Her stomach growled.

"I heard that."

"Won't be the last time. Remind me to eat whenever possible while we're hunting these cop killers. If I'm going to die, there's no sense in dying hungry."

"If I have anything to say about it, you're going to die in your sleep long after you retire, Diane."

"Thanks for the sentiment." Diane smiled. "Partner."

It was nearly five-thirty in the afternoon. Plans made, they were making preparations to leave her apartment when her cell phone rang. Diane listened for a moment, then protested. "No, tell SAC Logan I can't come down there now, I have to be somewhere else. Sure, I'm thinking about my career, but right now I'd rather stop the people behind these killings than worry about my next promotion. I'm working with Patrolman Hawk. He knows his way around the area, and he has the trust of the locals."

Diane looked over at him in desperation. It was obvious someone in the Bureau was making a second attempt to place her in a command position. If that happened, he'd be working alone again. He'd done it before, but not against two, maybe three vampires, each one stronger than he was.

He appreciated her attempt to stick with him, despite the damage it might have to her career possibilities. Diane no longer seemed to be so eager to break that glass ceiling.

"Okay, tell Logan I'm coming down there. I can give the SAC a half hour, no more." She hung up. "Damn secretary.

Screw my chances for promotion. If I can't lead from the front, I don't want the job."

"The pressure is increasing, Diane. Must have been the news coverage." Lee turned and waved toward the TV screen. The set was on, though the sound had been muted. The lead story on the early local news was the deaths of Agents Lewis and Harris, and the station had already twice shown segments from film shot in the FBI lobby, though most of the video was from a brief statement made by Acting SAC Logan. His face and Diane's had only flashed for a few seconds, and though he wasn't mentioned, she was identified by name.

"I've got to go back down there to FBI headquarters for a while. SAC Logan is having second thoughts, according to his secretary. I won't be long, even if I have to resign before they let me leave. We have some unfinished work to do, and I'm not going to trust it to anyone else." Diane looked around for her wallet and badge, sticking them into her jacket pocket.

"Drop me by the state police motor pool first. I can borrow a unit there, and maybe even a spare uniform, which might come in handy later. Call me when you're done. We can meet in Grants and go from there together, or make some other arrangement. I don't see any other way. We pretty much know what they intend on doing tonight, as soon as it's dark." Lee put on his cap and dark glasses, then checked in his pockets. He had a spare cell phone, as usual, in case a battery went bad.

"Let's go now, then. We're on a time crunch." Diane looked around the room quickly.

"You'll be back." Lee smiled, opening the apartment door.

A few hours later, Lee was lying on the roof of Bowlegs's old hogan, his rifle by his side as he watched and listened. It was dark, and he was waiting for Muller and the couple with him to arrive. They'd be watching for him, but he was invisible to anyone approaching unless they came by helicopter.

Diane hadn't called, but Logan's secretary from the Bureau had contacted him on the cell phone, reporting that Agent Lopez was still in a meeting, and would meet up with him later at his destination.

Lee had expected Diane to call him once she was on her way, but she hadn't done that. Maybe she was in a blackout area, but a half hour had gone by already. It was too soon to worry, she was a trained agent and could take care of herself. Still, he couldn't quite get her out of his mind.

Finally he reached for his cell phone, and punched out the numbers of the FBI office in Albuquerque. "This is State Police Officer Leo Hawk. I need to know what time Agent Diane Lopez left her meeting with SAC Logan."

"One moment, Officer Hawk, I'll check."

Lee waited, and the longer the seconds went by, the more he was convinced that something was wrong. He sat up, ready to move, when the switchboard operator got back on the line. "Officer Hawk. Agent Lopez had no meeting with SAC Logan after the general conference early this morning. Isn't she with you?"

Lee cursed, hung up, and climbed down from the hogan. He was running down toward where he'd hidden his police unit when the cell phone vibrated against his chest.

He switched his rifle to his left hand, stopped, and

pulled the phone from his shirt pocket, looking around for signs of Muller, Diane, or anyone.

"Diane?"

"Yes, and her new best friends. It's good to talk to you again, Officer Nez. Or should I call you Officer Hawk now? After all these years, I thought you'd have made sergeant by now."

## CHAPTER 17

Lee tried hard not to show any fear in his voice. "You have the woman FBI agent, Major Muller? What are you hoping to do, use her as a hostage to buy your escape?"

"That, and perhaps another item or two. Come on, don't play stupid with me. You know what we were looking for near that Navajo hogan. And now you're going to give it to me, aren't you?"

"Even if I *can* locate that box again, it might be too dangerous for anyone to move or handle. The container has probably fallen apart by now. Do you know what the radiation would do to you if the container has broken open? Sunlight will kill you in minutes. Imagine what *this* form of radiation can do." Lee was trying to come up with an angle that might give him a way to save Diane.

"Probably nothing. I worked in a nuclear-power plant in East Germany during the seventies, and never experienced any problems, even once when there was an accident. I believe that only ultraviolet radiation will harm someone like us, but I'm willing to risk your life to be certain. You *do* want to save your woman partner, don't you? This way, you could make up for the one you got killed so long ago.

Where's the noble warrior I've always read about in those stories of the Old West?"

Lee tried to come up with some kind of miracle, an instant plan that would give him an opportunity to turn things around. He wasn't about to live with the blood of another innocent on his hands. He'd lost Annie, but he wouldn't lose Diane to his enemies as well. The death of the only person he'd ever really loved was already enough for him to carry through the decades, and he was beginning to care about Diane, probably too much.

"The woman isn't my partner, she's just an ambitious federal bureaucrat after the plutonium and your hide, in that order. Her career comes first, not the life of a fellow officer. If you doubt my words, consider her dead partner and her dead supervisor. All I want is to put you in your coffin for good. Kill her, and I'll just have one more excuse to hunt you down."

Lee kept talking. "But don't try to play games or push me. I can keep you from getting what you want and you know that or you wouldn't be trying to make a deal with me. I suppose a trade is what you're asking, isn't it, vampire?"

"Are you really willing to risk the life of this good-looking woman over a little overheated metal? What is the plutonium to you? It's just been sitting there for half a century, and nobody but you and I even remember it at all. Hell, even the spy who helped me set up the ambush is dead. I killed him myself just to keep it our little secret."

Muller was arrogant, but not quite sure what Lee's angle was, and that encouraged Lee.

"I'll tell you what, Muller. *If* you can get past the roadblocks, and the police and federal officers on patrol for three murdering terrorists, you can come and look for the plutonium with your pale-skinned friends. But I have a feeling that not even a vampire can get around this big state without a vehicle, and you can't carry the plutonium under your arm and run off, can you? You need me, and don't you forget that. If I discover or even suspect you've harmed another person in my state, Agent Lopez included, I'll have every armed man in New Mexico on your trail, and a hundred scientists arguing over who gets first look at this box of mine. Try me."

Lee disconnected the call before Muller could respond, and climbed into his unit. He'd just started the engine when the phone rang again. He let it buzz three times before answering.

"If you hang up on me again, she dies!" Muller yelled. "We do this my way!"

Lee hung up and held his breath. It seemed like an eternity had gone by before the phone rang again.

"Okay, we need to make a deal," Muller snarled. "Get the plutonium, bring it to me, and you get the FBI woman alive and still relatively uninjured. But, if anyone makes a move on us, if we suspect anyone but you is anywhere close to us at all, she'll be the first of many to die. You already know how difficult we are to kill. We could take dozens, maybe even hundreds, of lives."

"We're still assuming that the plutonium won't kill me when I go get it." Lee tried to sound unemotional, but he was elated that the plan he'd come up with off the cuff was starting to develop. "Prove to me that you haven't killed the FBI woman."

He waited on the line for a moment before Diane's voice came on. "Sorry to interfere with your little vendetta, Officer Hawk. I thought I had a meeting, but got hijacked on the way downtown. I shot one of them, the one who set me up with the phone call, but she's healed up again already. You know how they are. Just like you, but even bigger assholes." Her words were measured, and there was anger in her voice. Maybe she was furious at his apparent disregard for her life, or maybe she understood his strategy and was skillfully playing along. Hopefully, Diane would remain smart, and alive.

"Remember what I said about the body count going up if you try any more tricks," Muller said, taking over the phone again. "I'll be in touch. Once you have the merchandise, we can discuss where to meet."

Lee understood the significance now of Lewis's pockets being searched after he'd been killed. Ingrid had found Diane's and his phone numbers, probably in the SAC's notebook. Ingrid had posed as the new SAC's aide, and neither he nor Diane had known her voice.

He called the state police dispatcher and left word that the fugitives had picked up a hostage. He didn't mention Diane by name, afraid that some of the ill-trained auxiliaries manning roadblocks would make things worse, not better. But he had to tell the FBI about their agent, so he dialed again and let the Albuquerque Bureau know that Diane had apparently been lured into a trap, and was now held by Muller.

They should be observed and reported, but not approached without backup. Diane wouldn't have expected anything less. By then, he'd reached John Buck's home in his borrowed state police cruiser. Lee turned off the engine, and waited inside, behind the wheel. It was customary when approaching a Navajo dwelling to wait to be invited. If no one came to acknowledge his presence and wave him inside, it meant either no one was home, or he wasn't welcome, and should leave.

The medicine man wasn't in his medicine hogan. There was a flickering light through a house window that suggested a television set was on. A curtain had moved when Lee drove up, and soon the front door opened.

"Come inside, Officer," John said, just loud enough for Lee to hear, all the time watching the yard. His dog was by his side as he came in, and Lee noticed Buck's rifle just inside the door on a small wooden table.

Lee went inside quickly, thanking the medicine man for his hospitality and accepting the cup of coffee offered.

"You're alone tonight?"

Lee nodded. "And my partner, the woman who was with me, is in the hands of my enemies, the walkers of the night. We were forced to split up for a while, and that's when they lured her into a trap."

Buck nodded. "She's a brave woman. Is she still . . ."

"Alive? For now, but they intend to use her to force me into bringing them the box I hid the night I met your uncle. She's a hostage."

"And you need my help. What can I do?" The middle-aged Navajo man reached for his rifle.

"I would be grateful if you can do two things for me, but I must tell you that both could be very dangerous." Lee didn't want to put anyone else at risk, but too many had died already, or were in danger, for him to turn back now.

"Life is dangerous. None of us will get out of it alive. What is it you need, someone to watch your back?"

"Something much more important than that. I'm going to leave you a cell phone, and a unit to recharge the battery. I'll show you how to use it in a few minutes."

"I've used one before, but no need. There is a telephone farther down the highway at a neighbor's home. I can use that to call whoever you want me to."

"This phone will save you precious time, and I have another to use, so I won't do without. I'd like you to keep watch over your land, yet stay hidden as you did when you observed my visits. If the night walkers return, or anyone else comes to dig anywhere within a five-minute walk of the old hogan, here is a list of numbers I want you to call." Lee handed him a page from a small pocket notebook.

Buck looked down at the paper. "Police, FBI, state and federal government, fire departments, and the television stations in Albuquerque. What do you want me to tell them?"

Lee thought about that for a moment, then wrote three sentences down on the back of the paper.

The medicine man looked at the paper again. " 'The terrorists who killed the FBI agents are here. I think they're trying to dig up buried explosives. Office Hawk asked me to call for help.' Are explosives hidden there?" John asked.

"Worse than that. What's there may be radioactive. Tell whoever arrives in response to your calls that you heard they have plutonium out there. They should check for radiation before digging. And stay away from there yourself."

"My intentions exactly. You said there were two things you needed me to do?" John Buck placed the paper under a salt shaker on the table.

"I know it will be very distasteful for you even to talk about it, but I need to find out if you suspect anyone around here—Navajos—of walking the path of Navajo witches, the evil ones?" Lee was careful not to mention the word "skinwalkers" around the *hataalii*. Speaking about skinwalkers was said to summon any who were close, though he'd learned a long time ago that smelling like a night walker was a guarantee.

Buck quickly took a pinch of corn pollen from a medicine pouch and said a blessing for both of them before answering.

"There is a family, of sorts, that lives across the freeway up along a ridge, a few miles from here, just below one of the big power lines. They're Navajo, but they keep to themselves. Few speak to them, and nobody goes around there. Animals which wander onto that land seldom return, and some have been found mutilated, with perverted things done to their bodies. Some say wolves from there have been among their sheep, but not killed them, yet we all know the Mexican gray wolf no longer roams these hills. I keep my flint and protection against evil close by, and they haven't come for me. They fear my medicine, and my .30-30." He patted his rifle.

"You've already risked a lot, and I'm asking you to place yourself in danger for me despite the fact that I'm a stranger. Thank you and stay safe. I have to go now." Lee stood, and nodded to John Buck.

"Good luck to you, night walker. Bring back the woman safely. You need a woman like that one to share your secrets, not an old man like me."

Lee thought about Diane as he drove back toward the Interstate, taking his spare cell phone out of the glove compartment and turning it on. Then he put the images of her aside and proceeded beneath the underpass south onto the opposite slope of the valley.

He parked the patrol unit behind some trees halfway up the reverse slope, and moved quickly on foot uphill, stopping every few minutes to listen and catch his breath. Alone and with little fear of being observed, he could move quickly now, and silently, like the wind. He was searching for a dwelling in the forest.

He found two houses, but one was abandoned, and the other was unoccupied at the moment. Lee continued his search, covering several miles during the night, but found no animals or people at all. It was close to daybreak when he finally discovered a small clearing in the trees. Ten feet from the low flames of a small campfire were three young Navajo women and an old man, all naked, sweat beaded upon their bodies, on their knees around a half-dressed figure on the ground.

It was completely dark, a moonless night illuminated only by the stars, and although he could see perfectly well, the motionless figure was closer to the fire than the Navajo witches, so they could see it. There was a breeze blowing in his face, so he was in no danger of being detected by smell.

The Navajo words they were chanting sounded strange at first, then he realized it must be some skinwalker version of a Sing or blessing. The women were taking the clothes off the reclining figure, and it soon became apparent from the way they pulled and tugged at his arms and legs that the person, a middle-aged man, was either dead or unconscious.

They stripped off all his clothes, and the old man took the pants and boots, putting them in a pile beside him. The three women then removed his watch, and a wedding ring, arguing back and forth over who got which.

The smallest of the women, slender with a light streak in her waist-length black hair, and probably in her mid-twenties, at first appeared to have lost the argument. She sat back, licking her arms like a cat. Behind her, next to her well-formed backside, Lee could see a wallet that the young woman had concealed from the others.

Lee sat motionless as black fur began to form on her skin, and her head began to lengthen. Holding her arms out, her fingers began to contract, like the special effects of a horror movie, and her nails began to condense into claws. He had a feeling this would be a real-life catfight.

One of the other women, the oldest of the three females, looked at the shape-shifting and began to laugh, pointing toward the east, where the sky was starting to lighten.

The woman who'd started to assume the form of a cat snarled, then sat down, quickly assuming human form again. Then she stood, turning her back toward the others as she surreptitiously picked up the wallet. She kicked the reclining man, and Lee realized he was undoubtedly dead.

The two women who had taken the ring and watch stood, picked up a blanket from beyond the fire, and walked off together up the hill. The old man cackled, stood, and hurriedly put on the dead man's pants. Carrying the boots, he walked off after the two women.

The one left behind stood and looked around. Lee got a good look at her face. The woman was young and attractive, somehow familiar to him. He tried not to stare at her body, and felt uncomfortable knowing that he could see her but she had no idea he was there, in the dark, watching.

Convinced she was alone, the woman grabbed the dead man by the heels and pulled him over to a small arroyo. Using her bare feet, she rolled the body off the edge and into the wash.

Walking back to the fire, she picked up the remaining blanket, draped it over her shoulder, then walked down a narrow trail in the opposite direction from the one the two women and old man had taken.

Lee stood and circled around quickly, finding the path the young woman skinwalker had taken, but remaining downwind so he couldn't be detected. If she'd taken the form of a mountain lion or panther, it would have been much more difficult.

Within a minute, the woman came along, looking through the wallet and chuckling, oblivious to everything else around her and clearly unafraid. She had the blanket wrapped around her now, her long hair pushed to one side, dangling down in front over one shoulder. Her eyes shone like black pearls, and she smelled like smoke and piñon pitch.

Lee stepped out and grabbed her arm before she knew he was there, placing one hand over her mouth. "Police! Don't make a sound," he whispered harshly.

She tried to shout, but in a blur of motion, he shoved his handkerchief into her mouth, and she gagged, but couldn't scream.

He turned her around, holding her with one arm around her upper body like a vise, and held out his state police badge with the other so she could see it.

"I'm State Policeman Leo Hawk, and you and your witch friends just robbed and maybe even killed a man. You're under arrest."

He pocketed the badge, then maneuvered her around so she could get a good look at him and vice versa. His mouth dropped, and he realized why she looked familiar. The Navajo witch reminded him of Annie, so much so, she could have been her sister. The eyes were different, though, full of anger, not love.

The blanket fell, and she stood there naked and afraid. Then she picked up his vampire scent, and her fear was transformed into a seductive smile. She wanted him now, and not just his body. She wanted his blood.

Fighting the memories of Annie in his arms, Lee scooped the blanket up and held it against her. "Wrap this around yourself, and don't drop it again or I'll let you stay cold. You're coming with me to Grants, to the police station." She grabbed the blanket with one hand, tried to drape it over her shoulder, and it fell off.

She then began to cough, struggling against the gag in her mouth. He removed it. "Behave yourself, or it goes back in your mouth."

"I need both hands to wrap the blanket around myself," she said with a smile. "Or maybe you can just hold it against me while we walk? I like a man's touch."

Lee frowned. "Sorry. I'm definitely not in the mood." He let go of her other hand.

The second he did, she ducked away and ran up the trail, shouting at the top of her lungs. He chased her at less than half speed for a hundred yards, breathing as if he were an asthmatic low on inhaler, pretending to be struggling against the growing light. Then, he stopped, listened for a moment, and jogged back down the hill to his squad car.

"I hope she remembers I was going to Grants," he muttered as he started the unit and backed around. The freeway exit was about two miles away, and he knew where he was headed next.

As he roared up the ramp onto I-40, which in his Lee Nez days had been part of Route 66, he thought of Annie, then remembered it was Diane who was in trouble. It took a while to make the switch mentally, and he cursed whatever it was in his head that kept bringing back the memories. They were interfering with more important things now—the living, and Diane deserved better from him.

He concentrated all his thoughts toward the past twenty-four hours, then recalled everything Muller had said, and what he'd said back. Finally he was back on track. Logically, they had Diane in Grants, it was the only place nearby that was large enough to hide without sticking out as strangers.

Now, he was using himself as bait, but, hopefully, when the sharks came looking, they'd go for the big fish first.

Lee pulled up at a roadblock southeast of the Bluewater Lake turnoff just before dawn. It was bright heading into the sun like this, and he was grateful for the protection of the windshield and his own powerful sunglasses. He'd stopped a few miles back to put on extra sunblock, not knowing how long he'd be out of the unit in the oncoming sunlight.

Grants police officers, Cibola County deputies, and auxiliary volunteers armed with riot guns, hunting rifles, and an assortment of handguns nervously manned the post, and if he hadn't been in a squad car, he'd have had a fifteen-minute wait at least. A dozen or more eighteen-wheelers were lined up, their trailers being opened two or three at a time as the vehicles were thoroughly searched.

A Grants PD sergeant came up to his unit after he'd been motioned forward to the barrier, which was comprised of four department vehicles that blocked the center of the east-bound lanes. Vehicles, once cleared, were waved past on the right shoulder only.

"Good morning, Officer Hawk. Lose that fine-looking FBI partner of yours already?" The sergeant, a red-haired Hispanic Lee recognized as Isaac Jaramillo, pointed his finger at Lee, a gesture, unbeknownst to Isaac, that was considered threatening to Navajos.

Lee had long ago learned to ignore the cultural ignorance of basically decent people and look for their positive qualities. Also, today his mind was on other more important things than raising other people's political consciousness.

"Agent Lopez came through earlier with some other Bureau people, right? Coming into Grants from the east?"

"So I heard. I didn't see her myself, but there were three other agents in the vehicle. Takes three of them to equal you, right?"

"They're only FBI. I'm a full-blooded Indian." Lee shot back, remembering that expression from a favorite movie of his, one where the good Indians won and the bad FBI lost, more or less.

"What time was that, and was she still in that Bureau sedan?"

"Don't think so." Sergeant Jaramillo turned and yelled to another officer, who was waving an old man in a pickup through. "Dancroft, that good-looking FBI woman. When did she come through, and what kind of vehicle was she in?"

The officer looked at Jaramillo, then at Lee in his state patrol unit, and shrugged. "I'd just come on duty, maybe ten P.M., ten-thirty. I think the vehicle was a blue Ford SUV. One of the big new ones—an Expedition, Excursion, or something like that."

Jaramillo looked back at Lee. "Close enough?"

Lee nodded. As he'd suspected, the vampires had changed vehicles again, and passed through before he'd gotten Muller's call. "Yeah. If you run across her, let me know. I'd like to talk to her privately, not in front of the other agents, and especially not on the radio net."

"Yeah, wouldn't we all? Hey, you blew your chance." The sergeant winked.

"Isaac, one more thing, and I'd like you to pass this on to everyone at the roadblock, and arrange to have your replacements do the same, okay?"

"What's that, Hawk?"

"Every time you see four or more adult Navajos coming through here, no children aboard, give me a call on the radio, okay? Especially if one is a young woman with a light streak in her hair. If you can't get me on the radio, give me a call on a land line. Here's my cell number." Lee handed him a card with the number on the back, then described the others as best he could in case they decided to come in separate vehicles.

"Witnesses?"

"Could be. Let them through without saying anything, though, but get their plate numbers. They're nervous around cops, and I want to interview them away from this chaos." He waved at the line of traffic, getting longer as morning traffic increased.

"Okay. Just east-bound, right?"

"Right. Don't forget to brief everyone."

Lee waved, and drove past the cars stopped ahead, moving around on the right shoulder and back onto the Interstate. The sun was coming up, and the small city of Grants lay ahead, mostly to his left among the jagged remnants of a geologically recent lava flow.

Somewhere, nestled among the tongues of that ancient red-hot rock, long since crystallized, were four people hiding, one a prisoner of the most dangerous creatures to walk this land since the dinosaurs.

## CHAPTER 18

Lee stopped at a gas station beside a local fast-food restaurant, and gassed up the unit and bought a small foam cooler, a six-pack of sodas, and some ice. He'd need the sugar and fluids later on, he knew.

He suspected that the vampires had switched vehicles again since passing through the checkpoint, so he put in a call to the Grants PD dispatcher. Calls were coming in from all over the area, naturally, because of the current crisis, and every available officer was on duty now.

Without saying why, Lee asked that any calls concerning stolen or missing vehicles be relayed to him. He also wanted to know if any Ford SUVs matching the description of the vehicle Muller had used to get Diane and the others through the roadblock had turned up in the area.

The vampires would have to hole up for the day or continue driving whatever vehicle they had now, and the longer they drove around, the more likely they would be discovered. He was betting on their having found a hiding place while it was still dark.

Lee believed that they'd find a building in Grants or the immediate area and hole up. Most of the older houses didn't have garages, but there were enough in the area to hide the vehicle with a good chance of avoiding immediate discovery.

He waited, eating *huevos rancheros*, bacon, and drinking coffee, wishing he had a quart of good calves' blood for a quick pick-me-up instead of the sodas out in the cooler. Within the hour, his cell phone rang. "Yes?"

It was Muller. "You know who this is. Tell me you have the plutonium, and make it quick. I don't want any attempts to trace this call."

The Germans didn't know Lee had the ability to remain out in sunlight much longer than they did, so he used that fact to his advantage. "I could tell you I have the stuff, but it wouldn't be true. I need more time. I have a problem with sunlight too, remember? My skin starts to smoke when I'm working hard and sweating off the sunblock. I keep having to take a break and get back into my car. I'm putting on sunblock now, then I'll get back to the digging."

Lee looked around, hoping that he wasn't the unluckiest man in the world and Muller or his people could actually see him now, sitting in the back of a Grants restaurant.

"You have until tonight. That's how long your FBI agent will live unless you deliver the plutonium. And if we meet up with anyone in the meantime, like a police officer, she'll be the first one to die. Do you understand where I'm coming from, Officer Nez?"

"Exactly. But I can't call off the search. I don't have that kind of clout, especially concerning terrorists who've already killed law-enforcement officers. The best I could do was mention that you may have a hostage, and any officers shouldn't make any quick moves if you're spotted. If I were you, I'd start keeping my fingers crossed and hope that it's really cloudy this afternoon so I can have the box in my car by evening."

"Get it done."

"Yeah, yeah. Now let me talk to Agent Lopez."

"No. You have to trust me on this, Indian. She's still alive."

"Screw trust. How did you blow up the federal agents? A grenade? You know that wasn't necessary. They had no idea who you really are."

"That wasn't me, not that I wouldn't have done the same. Those men were following us. I had someone following them. But you've guessed that already. Enough chitchat. Get back to work. I assuming you're digging the material up from some hole in the ground."

"Possibly. Sorry, I'm not risking another blister until I hear from her personally. I can live without her, but if she dies, you won't. Did you know that the governor is thinking of calling out the National Guard, and mobilizing local army units? New Mexico won't be big enough to hide you then, Muller, and vampires will show up on aircraft thermal sensors. You can't hide forever, even in the dark."

There was a twenty-second pause, then Diane came on the line. "I'm alive, no thanks to you, Hawk. When are you going to give them what they want so I can walk?"

"Hey, you're a hostage, try to act like one. I'm doing the best I can." Lee hated having to take this tone when he didn't feel anything but fear for her safety, but if Muller knew he could have it all his way, she'd never get out alive.

Muller came back on the line. "Okay, cop. Now get back to work. Just pray that none of your police dogs stumble across us, wherever we are. I'll call you back later, but don't try to find us. We change locations every hour."

Lee knew that was a lie. The hazards of moving were too great. He knew the Bureau could get equipment in to get a relatively good fix on a call, but that would mean getting them directly involved, and that could result in getting a lot of people killed, including Diane.

Lee thought about renting a vehicle and driving around Grants, maybe getting lucky, but knew it would be just that if he spotted where Muller had Diane. He went to his unit and found a shaded spot to park, waiting for news that the plan he'd already set in motion was working. If the plan didn't work out, he'd have to try and locate the plutonium in the hope of saving Diane.

Less than an hour went by before he got a call on the cell phone from Sergeant Jaramillo, who was still working the Interstate roadblock west of Grants.

"I just waved through a group of four Indian adults in a pickup, Patrolman Hawk. They didn't have any youngsters with them. Is this what you had in mind?"

"Three women in their early twenties to thirties, at least one of them really attractive, and an old man, perhaps?"

"How did you know?"

"Superior brainpower. I'm not some local hick cop."

Jaramillo laughed. "You owe this hick cop a dinner at Sadie's, you know? Or better yet, tell that FBI lady what a good-looking man I am next time you run into her."

"I hope to do that," Lee replied. "But, for now, which way did the pickup with the Indians go?"

"I watched until they got out of sight. They exited just east of state road 605. Looks like they're heading into town. It's a green Ford, an F-150 about three or four years old." He gave Lee the tag number as well.

"Thanks again. Let me know if you see any other group of three young Indian women and an old man pass by. Okay?"

"*Bueno.* Catch you later."

Lee walked out to his unit and got inside quickly. The

sun was high in the sky now, and he was grateful for the sunscreen and tinted windows. He backed out of the parking slot easily, and headed away from the roadside business zone that lined most of the isolated communities in New Mexico and, to a certain extent, all of small-town America.

Five minutes later, he started driving down every residential street, systematically watching for that green pickup, hoping to see them before they saw him. Unless he missed his guess completely, they'd be searching for a holed-up Navajo vampire-cop, cruising around with their windows open, trying to pick up his scent.

He didn't have the ability, no full vampire did either, but he knew from grim experience that a skinwalker could detect a half vampire from quite a distance, and somewhere there were three full-blooded vampires holed up inside a house, shed, garage, or business. With the police looking for them, they'd avoid hotels or motels, where the desk clerk would have seen them coming in.

Lee intended to use the skinwalkers like bloodhounds to pick up Muller's trail. The skinwalkers would eventually find them if the vampires were here, and all he'd have to do was watch the watchers.

After an hour and a half, Lee finally located the green pickup, but only the old man was inside. It occurred to him that the women had split up, being dropped off in different neighborhoods to walk the streets. This would enable the skinwalkers to cover a larger area. The Navajo man was probably going to pick up the women once they finished searching their assigned neighborhoods.

He followed the driver, keeping his windows up so he wouldn't broadcast his scent. Lee's experience told him that the skinwalkers would work as a pack when they struck. If they were armed, they might attack in daytime in their human forms, but with all the extra police in the area, he expected them to avoid using guns and attracting unwanted attention.

Keeping his distance, he was able to guess the pattern the old man was following—a simple sequence, moving south to north whenever possible.

This went on for hours. Finally, near three P.M., when Lee had nearly run out of time, the old Navajo witch approached one of the women—not the pretty young one Lee had "met"—and she ran up to the truck, obviously very excited. Lee pulled to the curb around the corner and watched. The woman pointed down the street, then jumped into the vehicle, which hurried off. They were apparently going to pick up the other women.

Somewhere along that street in front of him, Lee knew, was the source of the skinwalker woman's excitement—Muller and the other two vampires—and hopefully, Diane, alive and pissed off as hell.

At least one of the vampires was sure to be keeping watch, so it would be dangerous for him to drive or walk down the street, especially in his marked state police vehicle. He'd have to keep his distance a while longer and see where the skinwalkers directed their efforts. At least his borrowed state police unit was one of those that didn't have the emergency lights on the top of the roof, which would have been a dead giveaway even at a distance.

Lee drove down a side street, then parked the unit at a convenience store. Quickly he changed his look from a denim jacket to a longer one of black leather. A lot of cops in New Mexico drove their units off-duty, but he didn't want to be recognized. Emptying the small cooler and placing the handheld police radio inside, he was set. He thought about affecting a limp, but knew that it was something he might forget about at the wrong time and give himself away.

Strolling along the side of the street slowly, cooler in hand, he hopefully looked like someone either coming home or heading for work. Reaching the spot where the woman skinwalker had flagged down the pickup, he sat down on the curb beneath the shade of an elm tree, as if he were waiting for a ride.

Ten minutes later, expecting the pickup to arrive any moment, Lee was surprised to see a Grants police car cruise slowly by, then stop a few houses down from where he was seated. An elderly Hispanic woman came out of an old, well-maintained adobe home, and waved at the officer.

The officer got out of the vehicle, and walked over to the lady, who pointed toward another house with a rental sign out on the dried-out, weed-filled lawn at the corner of the next block.

"Damn, lady. If they're in there, watching, they'll see what you're doing!" Lee muttered, standing up quickly. "Come on, Officer, keep your cool and don't do something stupid."

The officer motioned the woman back toward her house. As soon as the woman headed for her door, the officer walked quickly over to his unit and jumped inside.

Lee reached inside his "lunch box" for his handheld radio, but the officer was already on the radio, apparently. "Unit fourteen requesting immediate backup at 2115 South Acoma. Possible 10–27 suspects occupying rental house at this address. Dispatch please relay to all available units. Officer requests backup."

Lee thumbed the switch on his own transmit button, hoping Muller wasn't monitoring a police-band radio. "Unit fifty-one, this is State Police Officer Hawk. Remain in your current position. I have this site under observation and am approaching your unit from behind on foot. Repeat, hold your position."

The officer in unit fourteen stuck his head out the window and looked back at Lee, who was striding toward him, using the city unit to screen himself from view of the house.

The officer got out of his unit, holding his hand low and gesturing to Lee.

Suddenly a concussion wave struck Lee on the chest, and the right side of the rental house exploded into shattered glass and debris. Lee and the officer flattened.

Lee looked toward the blast just in time to see the garage doors of the rental burst open.

A silver delivery truck roared out of the gravel driveway, bounced onto the street, and slid around the next corner, tires squealing.

The police officer stood, and turned to Lee. "What the . . . ?"

"Those *are* the cop killers. Get in and follow them," Lee yelled, sprinting up to the front passenger side before the officer could even open his door.

"Damn, you're fast. How can you move like that?" The officer stared at Lee, who was knocking at the passenger door loudly. It was locked.

"Talk later. Let me in, then haul ass." Lee hooked up his seat belt and called for pursuit from the local police dispatcher on his radio.

The officer, named Antonio, according to a name tag on his uniform, burned rubber for fifty feet as he accelerated. The unit slid around the corner, the tires grabbed asphalt again, and they raced down the street. The van was three blocks ahead, heading northwest.

Officer Antonio switched on his emergency lights and

siren halfway down the block, taking a hand off the steering wheel only for a second.

"What happened with the old lady, the neighbor? What did she see?" Lee asked the officer.

"She was watching the house for the landlord. It's furnished, but was supposed to be unoccupied. When she came over to check, she heard the TV on inside, so she called the station, thinking it was squatters, or kids breaking in after ditching school."

The officer tried to keep pace with the van, which was headed north away from the direction of the Interstate. They were losing ground, which wasn't unexpected. Lee's reaction times and driving skills were lightning fast, and those of full vampires were probably better than his. At least, in daylight, Muller and the other two couldn't leave the van without seeking shelter from the sun.

A ridge ran diagonally from NE to SW at the western edge of Grants, so Lee knew that the fleeing van had to head north on state road 547, or reverse direction soon and head back south. Another ridge prevented an eastern escape.

"What direction can they go to avoid roadblocks?" Lee asked as they made a sharp left turn.

"Nowhere out of Grants. Every way in and out is covered. The Malpais, lava flow, really limits the back roads in this part of New Mexico," Officer Antonio yelled above the roar of the engine. They were headed southwest now, going twice the speed limit toward the freeway.

Just before reaching a roadblock of two police cars on the upcoming freeway ramp, the silver van made a hard left, bounced across the railroad tracks, and hurtled northwest, parallel to the freeway.

"Hang on. They're headed for Broadview Acres."

"What else is in that direction?" Lee tried to remember. He'd seldom gone farther than the eateries close to the freeway in Grants.

"The rodeo grounds, a housing area, and the airstrip. Highway 605, of course, but once past Ambrosia Lake or San Mateo, you reach a dead end."

The van disappeared from sight for a moment, then Lee saw it ahead, passing the rodeo grounds.

He listened to the radio calls. The McKinley County sheriff's department had already set up a roadblock by Ambrosia Lake, and was sending one of their units south to establish a barrier at the county line, about ten miles north of their current position.

Lee wished he had his own unit now, they were still losing ground.

"They'll probably head into the housing development and try to circle around and outflank the roadblock south of Bluewater. But there are units covering the old highway there. They'll stop them." Officer Antonio nodded.

"No, they're turning east, onto the airstrip. See the van?" Lee pointed ahead to his right.

Antonio chuckled. "We've got them then. No place to go, unless they plan to sprout wings."

"One of the fugitives is a pilot. Let's hope there's no plane sitting around."

A half mile away was a gravel road leading to the small airstrip, a lopsided T with the crossbar running roughly north and south.

"Hey, there's a news helicopter from Albuquerque. They must have come to Grants to follow the dragnet. I hope they take off before the van gets there." Antonio's voice changed tone.

"Can you get them on the radio?" Lee ordered sharply above the sound of the siren. He watched the van racing toward the chopper, which was idling at the apex of the runways. A white van was also moving toward the helicopter, but Muller would get there first.

Officer Antonio was arguing with the dispatcher, trying to get word to the helicopter pilot, who was on a different frequency. Lee knew that the newspeople had no idea what was going on, all they saw was an airmail delivery truck hurrying up. With the sound of their own helicopter's engine, they probably couldn't hear the police sirens.

As Officer Antonio finally reached the runway, the van slid to a stop less than fifty feet from the helicopter. Lee knew they were already too late to stop them.

Muller and his companions jumped out of the van, weapons drawn and pointed toward the helicopter. Muller himself was carrying Diane over his shoulder like a sack of flour. She was probably drugged or unconscious.

"Damn." Lee clinched his fist, watching a cameraman and another person, probably their reporter, being thrown onto the ground. One of Muller's companions stood by the pilot's side, pointing a pistol inside.

"They're hijacking the helicopter! How did they know it was there?" Officer Antonio growled.

"Maybe on TV. The news stations do live reports, especially on manhunts this big."

Officer Antonio hit the brakes, sliding the last twenty feet, struggling to keep the unit from skidding to left or right and rolling.

Lee didn't bother getting out. The helicopter was already off the ground, pulling away as it whipped into the air. If Muller found out Lee wasn't out by Fort Wingate, rushing to unearth the plutonium, Diane was as good as dead. With luck, the vampires wouldn't be rushing off to where they thought he was.

His cell phone rang fifteen seconds later, and Lee knew who it was even before he answered.

Officer Antonio was arguing with Dispatch and reporting what had happened at the same time, so Lee stepped out of the patrol unit to take the call, hurrying to get far away from background noise that might give him away.

"What the hell are you trying to pull, Indian? You want to see if your partner can fly?" Muller was angry and loud, and Lee could hear the sound of the helicopter in the background.

"Huh? What's going on, and where are you? A power plant?" Lee pushed it, playing dumb in the hope of avoiding making things worse, if such a thing was possible.

"Some nosy old lady called the cops. But don't worry, we got away thanks to a very informative television report. Nothing's changed. You still have to deliver the goods."

"Where, exactly? I still haven't been able to dig the thing out, working a few minutes at a time to avoid becoming toast. I buried the box twenty feet inside a cave," he lied, "then collapsed the entrance. There's a lot of rock to move. I may even need to get a backhoe out here. It might take all night otherwise."

"That's *your* problem. I'll call back in an hour for an update. Sunset is coming soon, and you'd better get that box to me tonight or the woman will never see another sunrise."

"She's still alive, right? Let me speak to her."

"Not possible. She's asleep right now. I had to tap her on the head when the police pulled up outside. She's alive, but this time you're going to have to take my word for it, Nez."

"I'll get you the box, but forget about delivery unless I get a chance to speak with her and make sure she's still alive." The connection started to fade, and Lee could barely hear.

"Keep digging. I'll let you know where to come."

Then the line went dead.

Lee pocketed the phone, and noticed the reporter, a leggy, bleach-blond, amber-eyed beauty, running up. The cameraman was sitting on the ground, messing with his camera and talking to the man in the rental van that had presumably come to pick them up at the airstrip.

"I'm Christine Sierra from Channel 6 in Albuquerque. Those were the suspects in the killing of those FBI agents, weren't they?" She held up a tape recorder while brushing her windblown hair out of her eyes. "How did they end up out here?"

Lee shook his head, and pointed to Officer Antonio. "He knows more about it than I do." He didn't want to be identified and was glad for the disguise he was wearing. If Diane's kidnappers learned he wasn't out digging for them . . .

"Wait. Was that woman with them a hostage, or part of their gang?"

"Ask Officer Antonio." Lee shrugged.

Hearing the sound of approaching sirens, Lee turned to watch. The reporter, seeing he wasn't going to say anything else, ran toward the police officer.

Lee walked over to the silver van. Maybe something in there would provide some clue to what they were up to. He had to have a run of luck come his way soon, or Diane, if she wasn't already dead, was going to be gone before morning. Muller was right on the edge, and Lee suspected that the vampire and those with him weren't going to be taken without a terrible fight.

The house Muller and his people had taken refuge in had pretty much burned to the ground by the time Lee got back to the location. The explosion had been the result of a hand grenade, probably, and although all of their food and water had been left in the van at the airport, that could be replaced.

The blue SUV they'd had when passing through the roadblock with Diane had been in the garage as well, with the courier who drove the silver van tied up inside, still alive. Officers on the scene had managed to push the SUV out of the garage in time.

FBI and county people were examining it now and questioning the delivery-truck driver, who'd been hijacked just before dawn, and forced to radio his dispatcher frequently to cover for his absence. Fingerprints would be found, but that wouldn't serve any useful purpose. The suspects had already been identified.

He, meanwhile, was already on his way to Albuquerque in his police cruiser. There were two or three agencies in the Grants area trying to find and debrief him, but once he'd learned that the Channel 6 helicopter had been found, abandoned in a park at Westgate Heights on the outskirts of Albuquerque, he knew where he had to be.

Lee went to Diane's apartment. He'd picked the lock in seconds, and holed up there to recharge the batteries for his cell phone, in case Muller called. The complex had bars on the windows, and Lee knew that no wolves would be crashing through the windows while he was taking a quick shower and putting on the uniform he'd managed to borrow.

•

An hour later, after finding some leftovers to eat in Diane's kitchen, including some liver he had to thaw out, he drove to the Albuquerque state police office. If they didn't hear from him soon, he'd be considered missing, and if there was one thing he didn't want, it was to get on a search list along with Muller and his people, and Diane. Every law-enforcement agency and their auxiliaries were on the lookout for them now. Even members of the German Air Force unit at Holloman had volunteered to help, but been politely turned down, according to newscasters. They'd just add to the confusion, Lee knew.

Christine Sierra of Channel 6 was a news story herself, and appeared on several stations other than her own, who also aired the remote broadcast made just before their helicopter was hijacked. Use of the video probably cost those stations a bit of pride and some cash. Lee knew that the woman was destined for stardom, and maybe an anchor spot on weekdays. If not, she'd have other offers coming in soon enough.

Nobody had apparently realized that the live broadcast made just before the hijacking had informed Muller that a helicopter would soon be at his disposal at the Grants airport.

Fortunately, the most recent story didn't mention Lee, though there was an audio interview with Grants Police Officer Antonio and some video from a borrowed camera.

But when Lee had seen the newswoman's image, he'd thought of Diane, hoping that she was still alive and well enough to curse him. She had to know he wouldn't give up trying to get her back, but she also knew he could never give in to Muller's demands. The helicopter pilot, now a hostage too, apparently, would make any rescue attempt even more complicated.

Pulling up into the parking lot of the local office, he straightened his uniform, which was a size too large, checked the polish on his boots, then walked through the doors. He hoped, when he left, he'd still be with the department, though he knew his future as a cop here was nearly at an end no matter what happened in the next twenty-four hours.

## CHAPTER 19

Where in the hell have you been, Officer Hawk?" A sergeant Lee recognized as a desk jockey from Santa Fe was behind the counter where a lieutenant would normally be, talking on the phone.

Sergeant Edmonds put the caller on hold. "Half the damn officers in the state are looking for you, including the F'ing Bee Eye.

"Get on this line right now and talk to Lieutenant Richmond, who's in Grants. Explain it to him, not me." Edmonds handed him the phone, then sat back in the chair to watch Lee squirm.

Lee yes-sirred and no-sirred for about five minutes, and once Richmond had gotten it out of his system, they could talk.

"You got some lucky breaks," Richmond admitted reluctantly. "APD and the country have officers looking over that helicopter now. It touched down just after dark."

"Any sign of the occupants?" Albuquerque was a big place to hide, and there were a lot of houses and businesses in the fastest-growing part of the city, the west side.

"Not even the pilot. APD has officers knocking on doors.

They'll turn up somewhere. Roadblocks are at every bridge up and down the valley, and they have aircraft and helicopters checking the streets and parks." Richmond was calming down now, speaking rationally again.

"Then one more officer out there isn't going to make much difference, is it? My guess is that they're holed up inside somebody's residence, or a business. Maybe the house-to-house will pay off." Lee knew that he had to use his head and reason this out.

"SAC Logan needs to talk to you," Richmond ordered. "He wants to know everything about what happened to Agent Lopez."

"All I know is that Lopez left her apartment to meet with her bosses down at the FBI building after she got a call. We were supposed to meet later, and she never showed up. Next time I heard about her, she was apparently with Muller's people in Grants. I deduced from a conversation with a local officer that Muller had used her to get them through the roadblocks, posing as fellow agents. Later, I was closing in on them when they escaped from that house in Grants. A neighbor lady got curious and called the cops before I could intervene. It looked to me like they had drugged Lopez. Muller carried her into the helicopter over his shoulder." Lee left out the details he knew would only get him into trouble.

"I wonder what they're doing, or trying to do. Terrorists always have an agenda. Is it just to generate fear by killing those people who are supposed to protect the country? Muller and the Plummers are leaving a trail of victims, all law-enforcement personnel," Richmond said.

"This all started out over something to do with that Navajo group that attacked me, and I still don't know enough about them to even hazard a guess on their motivation," Lee lied.

"Has anybody heard of any demands they're making for Agent Lopez's release?" Lee added, knowing full well that he couldn't suggest what they were actually after without ruining his chances of getting Diane back alive. "If it wasn't for the Navajo connection, my guess would be some kind of assassination. Haven't the FBI or the CIA been able to get us more on this group?"

"Not according to the local Bureau. Logan says the CIA has been keeping their heads in a dark place, if you know what that means. Whatever it is, Officer Hawk, I want you to get over to the FBI building and spill your guts. Give them everything you've given me, and answer their questions. Then give me a call."

"Yes sir, Lieutenant." Lee hung up, and handed the phone back to Edmonds, who'd been listening to every word, obviously trying to guess what Richmond was saying as well.

"Butt in a sling, right?"

Lee shrugged. "Not really. I just want to catch those guys before anyone else gets hurt. Give me a call on the radio if you get any updates on the hostage or Muller."

"I don't work for you, Hawk."

"You don't work for anything but your career, I know that, Sergeant. But I'm the only one in this room who has a chance of saving Agent Lopez's life, and the helicopter pilot's as well. You'd better not keep a word of news from me, understand?"

Lee leaned over the desk until he was right in Edmonds's face. Edmonds held his ground, but was turning redder by the second. "I'm your superior, Patrolman Hawk. Don't forget that."

Lee stood and walked to the door. "You outrank me, Sergeant Edmonds. You're not, by any stretch of your admittedly limited imagination, my superior."

It was dark by now. Lee was back in his unit, still trying to put Edmonds out of his mind, when his cell phone rang.

"Who is this?" Medicine man John Buck was whispering, but Lee was able to recognize his voice instantly.

"Your late uncle's patient," Lee responded, figuring his own voice would convince the *hataalii* he was speaking to the right person.

"I have some bad news. One of those walkers of the night has returned with a tall, light-haired woman, and there is another person they're keeping tied up, maybe your partner. I could tell the captive was a woman, and she had dark hair. I saw them drive by in an old van."

"Did they see you?"

"I don't think so. I was in a tree, and they never looked up." Buck sounded calm, despite the danger.

"Did they go to the hogan, the killed one they were at before?"

"Yes. And they have shovels. The man was looking around, though, not digging, while the woman guarded their prisoner with a pistol. I don't think they know where you hid whatever it was. They keep looking at maps."

Lee thought about it. Muller or his crewman didn't have the radiation detectors now, so they were working blind, though they had the area narrowed down, and were looking for places where a hole could have been quickly dug and refilled. Lee had to get back there, and get there fast, before something really bad happened to Diane.

"Leave the area, *hataalii*, very quietly. Take your dog and walk down the highway or to a neighbor's, and get as far away as possible. They might remember you from the other night, and think you might know something they don't, like where to dig. The tall woman is also a walker of the night, and she is very dangerous. She's killed two FBI agents already. Take your rifle, but go now, and remember they can see you in the dark, and they can move as fast as deer. They are hard to kill. Only fire or beheading will work unless you can somehow destroy their heart completely. Don't try to fight them unless you have no other choice."

"Are you coming?"

"I'm on my way now. Now go before they come searching for you."

Lee disconnected the call.

He headed immediately for the Interstate. He had to get to Bowlegs's old hogan, but it looked like he also needed a new plan. He knew the woman was Ingrid Plummer, but was the man with her Muller or Kurt Plummer? If Diane was the hostage, where was the pilot and the other vampire?

Lee drove west down the Interstate as fast as he could push the police cruiser, using his emergency lights to clear the way ahead. Driving on automatic, using his excellent vision and reflexes, he tried to determine how the two Germans had evaded all the roadblocks and arrived back at Bowlegs's hogan so quickly.

Then he had the answer. Muller probably did know how to fly the helicopter. The vampires could have dumped the pilot once they were away from Grants, then Muller had flown to an isolated home, stealing the van and neutralizing the residents.

Two of the vampires had taken Diane and holed up in the van until dark, while the third, Muller, had flown to Albuquerque, landed, and ditched the helicopter. This would mislead law-enforcement authorities, and they would waste their time searching in the state's largest city. By then, of course, Diane could be dead. If they dug in the right place and found the plutonium, she'd no longer be needed alive as a hostage against him. And it wouldn't take them long in any case to realize he was not where he was supposed to be, digging up the box for them.

Lee had no problem getting through the roadblocks, but he had to slow down, be identified, and waved on each time. At least the drive to Grants took less than an hour at the speed he was traveling.

The radio had been crackling with calls from officers checking out suspect vehicles and individuals, and Lee only half listened, but finally he had a call come through for him.

"Hawk, this is Sergeant Edmonds. I have some information that you might find useful."

"Go ahead, Sergeant." Lee needed to know what happened to Muller or whoever had piloted the helicopter to Albuquerque. He now seriously doubted the pilot had been on the helicopter for long, and it would have been tricky getting rid of a body once they landed.

"The house-to-house check hasn't turned up any suspects, but a vehicle was stolen from a neighborhood home just after the chopper landed. That vehicle has now been found, and you won't believe where." Edmonds chuckled.

"Okay, you got me, Sergeant. Where was the stolen vehicle?"

"A block from Agent Lopez's apartment. Think that's a coincidence?"

"If you believe in them. Any news on the car thief?"

"A man walking his dog saw a tall, fit-looking blond man exiting the car, but the man disappeared very quickly into an alley. The witness thinks it could have been Muller."

Lee wondered if Muller had been coming to Diane's

apartment, looking for him. If this was the case, then Muller may have just missed finding him. Maybe Lee's luck was better than he thought.

"I recommend that the area be searched as well. It sounds like something Muller would do. He'd have Agent Lopez's address, from her car or wallet, or from whatever was taken from Agent Lewis's pockets after he was killed."

"A search is already under way. The pilot of the news chopper is still missing, any idea where he could be?"

"If he's lucky, he's still alive, somewhere on the ground in the middle of nowhere. I suspect Muller flew the chopper back to Albuquerque, not the pilot, so the German could have just thrown him out of the cockpit. Kurt Plummer and his wife were probably set down somewhere else entirely, with their hostage. They won't be in Albuquerque."

"Why are you so sure?"

"Instinct. Muller is smarter than most people. He'd think of misdirecting everyone by splitting up."

"Doesn't sound too smart. Now he's in Albuquerque, completely on his own, then. What's your twenty, by the way? The connection is fading."

"Heading to Grants. I have a meeting to attend." Lee hung up the mike before Edmonds could respond.

Lee tried to puzzle out where Muller could be, but soon realized he just didn't have enough information. He gave up to concentrate instead on a plan to rescue Diane. He still had to find a way to get her away from two vampires, one a woman who was willing to kill apparently just as easily as Muller did. And that woman must have already known that Diane was the one who had shot her husband before, and her too, when Diane was carjacked. No love would be lost between the two, but Ingrid held all the cards.

The first thing Lee had to do was find Muller's people and Diane without being spotted. Then he'd decide what to do.

Lee drove past the turnoff that led to the killed hogan and John Buck's home, and parked on the shoulder a mile down the Interstate. Despite the fact that it was close to midnight, he used skinblock to cover his face and hands, then replaced his state police uniform hat with a baseball-style field cap discovered under the seat.

Slipping out of the patrol unit, he ran down the side of the road embankment, hurtled the four-foot-high fence, then raced across the open meadow toward the trees a quarter mile farther up the slope. He always enjoyed running at full speed, not holding back for fear someone would notice his inhuman pace. Right now, he didn't care if anyone saw him or not. It was nighttime, and at this hour, almost anything could be explained away as an illusion of darkness.

Knowing that someone would be keeping watch, Lee decided to approach from uphill, which meant he'd be forced to travel an additional half mile or so, rather than running directly to the killed hogan.

He passed within a quarter mile of Buck's medicine hogan and home. The television was on, apparently. Lee could hear music and laughter. Hopefully, Buck had done that to make the night walkers think he was still around.

Lee stopped behind a tree and watched carefully for signs of movement, but all he could hear was the low ripple of water in the small stream and the rustle of leaves among some of the nonconiferous plants along the hillside.

The color shift of his enhanced night vision made the sky appear gray rather than blue, and all but the brightest colors were washed out slightly by the darkness, but if somebody was out there, watching for him, he couldn't spot them.

Running uphill again, Lee crossed the twenty-foot-wide streambed in a long stride, landing on the opposite bank with barely a sound. Recalling with an almost photographic memory the route he and Diane had taken across that slope a few days ago, Lee moved uphill at a different angle this time, staying within the trees and reaching the top of the forested ridge about a quarter mile above the hogan.

Looking across the valley, he could see a faint glimmer of firelight on the opposite slope. He wondered if it was the skinwalkers he'd tricked into searching for the vampires in Grants. If he somehow succeeded in killing Muller and his companions, Lee knew it was his responsibility to go after the skinwalkers next.

He remembered the young woman with the streak in her hair, and how she'd reminded him of Annie. She was smart and resourceful, and that, combined with her shape-shifting ability, would make her especially dangerous. Hopefully, he'd remember the basic evil within skinwalkers, despite her disarming charisma, and not hesitate when he confronted her again. She'd certainly made his pulse race before.

Catching his breath, Lee tried to follow the line of the Interstate west with his eyes and spot his patrol unit, but as he'd intended, it was hidden by a lower ridge. He located Buck's home about halfway to the Interstate, standing in a clearing that looked much smaller from here. He couldn't make out any lights now, but that might have just been because of the angle.

Checking his pistol, Lee started downhill, one careful step at a time. First, he'd head for the area where the plutonium had been buried and ensure that no one else had been digging there. Then he'd try to move in on Muller's partners.

Diane had become important to him, of course, and he'd do everything he could to save her. But stopping Muller had always been his primary goal, and he knew that any relationship with the FBI woman, even if they managed to both come out of this alive, had no future. She'd been his partner for a while. He'd enjoyed her company and wished her well, but that was all he could afford to remember. He knew now that no matter how much he'd grown to care for Diane, his heart still belonged to Annie, and he thought it probably always would.

Even if Diane cared for him as well, her career was the focus of her life, and she would never turn her back on that to join his half-assed crusade against the shape-shifters.

A hundred yards and ten stealthy minutes later, Lee heard the thud of a shovel against the earth, then another. Two people were digging, apparently. He inched closer, taking his steps in time with the thud of the shovels as much as he could, stopping occasionally to watch for motion among the piñons and junipers ahead, and to listen.

Lee could hear his own heartbeat, he was moving so quietly. But he knew that taking his time now might make all the difference in getting Diane free, and walking away from all this before morning.

Five minutes later, he looked out at the small ridge that wound itself around the hillside, trying to recall the exact spot under the overhang where he'd buried the box. Over the decades since he'd buried the material, he'd seen nature slowly reshape the entire area. No trace of his work had remained for long.

Taking a step, he heard or felt movement behind him. Suddenly his pistol was jerked out of his hand, and he was struck in the middle of the back. Tumbling downslope, Lee groped for his backup pistol, but a rush of wind told him he'd been too slow.

"Don't think about trying it, Nez. I have your service weapon, and I can pull the trigger even faster than you can think about it. You're fast, but I'm faster. Maybe Navajos are just slow-motion vampires. You think?"

Lee turned his head and saw Muller smiling down at him from ten feet away. He was dusty and dirty, and carried a Glock semiauto pistol in his belt. Muller couldn't know what the *hataalii* had done to protect Lee from becoming a full vampire. Maybe that knowledge could be used against him somehow.

"Is this where you hid the plutonium, Indian?

"Come on up. *Mach Schnell!*" Muller added loudly.

Lee heard footsteps, and saw Diane first, her hair disheveled and her face dusty and damp from perspiration.

A tall, slender woman with short, severely styled straw-colored hair was with her. Ingrid Plummer, no doubt. She followed Diane by a half-dozen feet, aiming a Glock at her back.

Diane was carrying a shovel. She almost smiled when she saw Lee, but covered for it quickly.

Despite the dirt and sweat, she looked in good condition. Just seeing her alive was enough. But he was careful to hide any expression.

"Your rescue attempt, I presume, Officer Hawk," Diane said wearily. "Did you bring three wooden stakes?"

Kurt Plummer moved up swiftly from Lee's left, his movements graceful, like those of a tiger bounding uphill. The dark-haired vampire had light eyes, nearly colorless, and like Muller, he had on a long-sleeved knit shirt with a high crew collar.

Kurt had a Glock identical to the ones carried by his wife and Muller, and Diane's pistol was stuck in his belt as well.

"How did you manage to get back here so quickly?" Kurt smiled. "I thought you were going to steal a motorcycle and go cross-country."

"Our Navajo friend decided to give me a ride."

Lee nodded. "Damn. You were in the trunk of my car, right? That's why you went to Agent Lopez's address. You suspected I'd be going there eventually."

"See, Kurt. I told you he wasn't completely stupid—for a cop."

Diane raised her eyebrows at him questioningly. She obviously thought he had a plan. He shrugged.

"Run out of ideas, you two?" Muller laughed. "It's about time. I haven't had so much trouble, in what, fifty years or so?"

"He came alone?" Ingrid asked, looking around curiously. "I thought you said he wasn't completely stupid."

"I heard most of what he said on the radio, but didn't risk getting out of the trunk when he stopped somewhere along the way. Where was that, Officer? It didn't smell like a restaurant or a gasoline station."

"That was the state police district office. They wanted to know what was going on. I didn't tell them you were vampires, of course, they'd have put me on parking-meter duty. But the FBI did send a few cars to follow me, and they can locate my unit using a global-positioning device under the front seat." Lee tried to sound as matter-of-fact as possible. Part of what he said *was* true.

"Good. I wonder what these light-fearing people will do when the evil sun comes up and they have no place to hide.

That van gets pretty small after eight hours inside." Diane tried to sound sarcastic, and it was working.

"Well, what do you think?" Kurt asked.

Muller looked at his watch. "We have a bit of time before it gets too light to stay outside. We can assume he's lying, otherwise he'd have a hard time explaining his obsession to kill and mangle our bodies. He came alone. My guess is that most of the officers in New Mexico are still searching in the Albuquerque area."

"We can take the time to finish blocking off the hogan. It'll be better than that old van, and the Navajos won't come around, not to a place where someone has died. Right, Nez?" Kurt waved his gun at Lee.

"Unless they follow the Anglo way, like me. There are several Navajo police officers in the area now. They'd search a hogan, even a killed one. It's their job."

"He's lying. Let me convince him to tell the truth." Ingrid aimed her pistol at Diane's leg.

"Don't fire your weapon. Everyone within miles of here will hear that, and sooner or later, cops will be checking his patrol unit out on the Interstate." Muller snarled at Ingrid. "We don't want any more attention drawn to us.

"But you can use your knife," he added with a smile.

Ingrid nodded slowly, and her eyes went cold.

## CHAPTER 20

Stop!" Lee knew he needed to stall them for a while. Soon, they'd be forced to wait until tomorrow night if they wanted to avoid being easily spotted by law-enforcement officers on the few roads in the area. "I lied about there being anyone following me." For once, he hoped he *had* been followed. "I have a secret of my own to protect too, remember.

"And there's no location device in my patrol unit," he continued, having successfully diverted their attention from injuring Diane. "Think the state would put up that kind of money just to find a cop car? We're not supposed to get lost in the first place."

"Quit stalling and show us where to dig, or I'll start carving on your friend here." Ingrid touched the side of Diane's neck with the blade, and Diane froze, careful not to react and provoke her.

"It's right around here somewhere, I think. But the ground has eroded a lot since 1945, and I can't be sure. It was dark and I was half dead when I buried it, and that was a long time ago. It may take hours of making test holes before I locate the spot. Why don't you use the radiation detectors you had before?" Lee looked back and forth along the embankment. He really couldn't remember *exactly* where to dig, of course, but knew a shallow trench along the edge of the overhang would probably locate the spot easily enough.

"They had to leave them at the house they blew up with the grenade, Hawk," Diane said, disgusted with him. "You'd think someone as old as you would have developed *some* intelligence. Just show them where to dig."

"Oh, we're not going to be the ones digging, you and your extremely lucky partner will be doing that," Muller said, looking at Kurt and Ingrid and laughing. "Now, if you want to live to see the sunlight, Agent Lopez, use that shovel."

"Where? He never showed *me* the spot. All I know is that it's somewhere on this hillside. Unless he lied to me too."

Ingrid pressed the knife blade a little deeper.

"Okay." Lee nodded. "I'll start digging, but not until you promise to let her go once you have what you want. Tie her up somewhere if you want so she won't get free until you're long gone. You can use me as a hostage for your getaway. I'm more durable," Lee offered.

"I'll consider it, depending upon how quickly you prove you can locate the box."

"We have two shovels. You can both dig," Plummer said with a harsh laugh. "How about it, Ingrid?"

Muller nodded, and the woman vampire stepped back, placing her knife in a sheath and her pistol in her belt before she walked back down the hill to retrieve the tool.

"We probably won't uncover the box before daylight, but we can put a dent in the digging," Lee said with a shrug, walking to a spot about five feet away where the ground looked relatively soft, then stabbing his shovel into the earth.

If he was going to dig, he wanted to find an easy place to start.

After a few hours passed, they still hadn't found the box, and the sun was nearly up. Muller was hurrying Lee and Diane toward the hogan. The vampires had found a rope outside John Buck's hogan and used it to connect Lee and Diane by their ankles. Neither could run or move quickly without yanking the other off their feet.

Ingrid had also stolen blankets and food from Buck's house, and the vampires had pulled their vehicle right up beside the front entrance of the hogan, under the trees. They managed to block out light leaks, and the windows in the vehicle screened out the harmful rays. Ingrid and her husband were putting the final touches on sealing up things and were fifty feet away.

Lee caught Diane's eye, nodded imperceptibly, then stumbled slightly, enough to alert Muller, who'd been turning back to look at the horizon every few seconds.

"Clumsy ass. Watch your step," Muller growled, "or I'll kill the woman right now." He swung his pistol around at Diane.

Lee raised his shovel, threatening Muller. "I've had about enough of your Nazi mentality."

Instead of swinging the shovel at Muller, however, Lee jammed it down with all his superhuman strength. He severed the rope with a stab of the sharp edge, then dove at Muller's midsection.

The vampire was fast, but Lee's unexpected tactics had taken Muller by surprise. Lee managed to get a grip on his enemy's gun hand, pulling it around toward the hogan. The pistol went off with a loud pop, and Ingrid and Kurt dove to the ground, scrambling for their own weapons.

Diane was gone in a flash, heading right toward the rising sun at full speed. Lee tried to spin Muller around, holding on to the gun with both hands, but the vampire was more powerful, angling his pistol toward Diana despite Lee's efforts.

Lee kicked Muller right in the groin, doubling him up, then tackled him. "Get this bastard off of me," Muller yelled, "but don't kill him. Then get the woman. No shooting."

Lee knew it was coming, and moved in close as Kurt and Ingrid ran up, pummeling him with fists and feet. He looked back toward the sun, which was almost up.

He felt the impact of a knife in his back, but hung on tight to Muller to keep him from following Diane. But he couldn't fight long, and slowly sank into blackness as the cold pain continued. Then he passed out.

Lee regained consciousness sometime later. He was lying on the ground and something hard was poking him in the back, but at least it wasn't a knife. The musky scent and absence of light upon his closed eyelids told him he was inside the hogan.

He'd fake unconsciousness as long as possible, trying to gather information before they realized that he'd recovered.

The sound of crinkling paper and the crunch of teeth reminded him of granola bars, and he worried about his stomach growling. Coming back from near-death always gave him an appetite.

He wasn't worried that they might be speaking in German. That was one of several languages besides Spanish he'd learned in his long life. Being alone nearly every moment of those years had given him time to study, and though he'd learned to play dumb around some people, like Muller and his fellow criminals, he held college degrees, honestly earned, in three of his identities.

He felt a gentle hand on his shoulder, and realized that it must be Diane. She hadn't gotten away after all, but at least she was still alive.

"Has he healed yet?" Muller's voice was distinctive, and in English.

"No, but his heart is beating. You nearly killed him, you pigs." Diane's voice rose slightly, but she was in control.

"He's probably used to that after all these years. You should be grateful we brought him inside instead of letting him burn up in the sun," Ingrid said coldly.

"That's just because he's the only one who has any idea where to dig for whatever he hid. We didn't find it last night, did we? Why are you so sure there was plutonium in that box anyway? There was never any report of any turning up missing that I know of, and everything from that era has been declassified by now." Diane was trying logic.

"Not everything. Governments lie, it's part of their nature in order to survive, just like a wolf killing a lamb. And when the military is involved, it's almost a guarantee the entire truth will remain hidden. Of course we'd stacked the deck. One of our spies was in a position of power within the military and knew it had never been found or reported missing, officially. But we flew aerial surveys, and got a strong, very localized image somewhere within a hundred meters of this location, even with the crude instrumentation we were able to rent. It's here, all right," Kurt added.

"So why are you after the plutonium now? You're terrorists, I know that, and so does every law-enforcement officer in the country," Diane asked Muller.

"If we tell you, we'll have to kill you. Still want to know?" Ingrid laughed.

Lee knew from their meeting in Albuquerque that Interpol suspected Muller's group was trying to find a way to free one of their comrades who'd been captured during a foiled assassination attempt. Diane was obviously hoping for confirmation. Sometimes people with a conscience had the need to explain their actions. But such a concept was lost on these animals. He knew they'd be killed anyway. Like Muller, Ingrid was deeply disturbed, and Lee had heard that women made the best terrorists.

"You think we're really going to tell you our plans?" Muller sneered. "Ingrid's right. You don't want to destroy your only chance of getting out of this alive."

"We're going to die anyway. What does it matter?" Diane continued.

"Forget it. You'll see for yourself what's coming."

"Or maybe you won't," Ingrid whispered.

The conversation ended, but Diane stayed by his side, he could hear her breathing. She slipped her hand down upon his, and held it for a while. He took a quick look and saw the concern in her eyes, though she wasn't looking at him at the moment. Finally, realizing that soon they'd know he was awake, he gave her hand a squeeze, and opened his eyes.

Kurt saw the movement, and raised the pistol he had in his hand. "Resurrection time."

Muller, who'd been keeping watch from a narrow gap between two logs, turned around to look. Then he checked his watch. "An hour. We'd have healed completely in half that time. He's a weakling."

"Must have been that German blood that turned me. Half beer, no doubt." Lee had been feeling fine as of more than fifteen minutes ago, but he was just as happy to have them underestimate him.

Diane was scowling at him now. "Sorry, I hoped to buy more time for you, Agent Lopez," Lee said. "The sun was coming up, and I thought . . ."

"Ingrid, that vampire bitch, is pretty fast. But I still nearly made it into the clearing before she tackled me."

"I should have cut your puny throat yesterday, or thrown you out of the helicopter with the pilot. Bet you would have bounced higher than he did, with all that baby fat." Ingrid took out her knife.

"You sound like a man, and you're built like one too, you skinny slut," Diane replied.

"Ladies, ladies, no catfights, please. We have hours to go before dark, and I hate bickering." Muller laughed. "What do you say, Ingrid?"

"She was a wildcat even before I turned her, Wolfgang. Right, *Liebchen*?" Kurt reached over and pulled his wife roughly to him for a kiss. Ingrid responded passionately, then he yelped, ended the kiss, and laughed, rubbing his lip.

"That's why you love me, Kurt. I bite like a vampire."

"You not only bite, you suck," Diane grumbled.

Lee laughed, and sat up. "Well, now that we're all friends again, when is lunch? I'm hungry."

"You think we're going to feed you, cop? Forget about it. You eat once we get the plutonium," Kurt sneered, and Ingrid laughed.

"Feeling weak after all that energy burn? Healing costs calories," Ingrid added.

"Feed him before he starts cracking those lame jokes of his," Diane added. "I'm hungry too, and I still haven't died yet today."

"We can fix that," Ingrid said, reaching for her knife.

"*Liebchen*, you can kill her *after* we get the plutonium. For now, give them both a candy bar and some water. If they can't dig tonight, *we'll* have to do it," Kurt answered.

"Save the peanut-butter cups for me, though. Give them the yogurt clusters. They suck," Ingrid sneered.

Diane started to speak.

"Don't say it, *mortal*," Ingrid said, pointing her finger at Diane.

"Go for a walk and cool off," Lee said to Ingrid with a smile, gesturing toward the door.

Diane smiled, but said nothing. Muller and Kurt groaned at the same time.

"God, I can't wait until both of you are dead," Ingrid sighed.

"You first, sunshine." Diane smiled, then ducked as Ingrid faked a jab at her.

"This is going to be a hell of a long day." Muller shook his head slowly.


Time passed slowly and the hogan began to heat up as midday approached. The vampires took turns watching the area from the inside of the van and through a few chinks they'd discovered between the log sides, making sure to avoid direct sunlight. But it was relatively quiet except for the occasional buzzing of a fly. While one of the three kept watch and another guarded them, the third slept. They'd been on the run nearly as long as Diane and Lee, and Muller knew they were running down as well, despite their phenomenal constitutions.

Lee indicated to Diane that they should both rest, knowing that they'd be forced to dig that evening. He slept fitfully, but Diane seemed to be asleep, at least part of the time. It was hard for either of them to think of sleeping through so much of their remaining short lives, but little else could be done, at least until they were outside where there was room to maneuver. Up close, they were hopelessly outclassed, not only on strength, but with reaction times as well.

On several occasions Lee moved to a new position, or tried to stand, and that instantly got all their attention. Ingrid was the jumpiest of them all, and definitely the most volatile. Lee noted that she carried a grenade in her jacket pocket.

He was dozing, around four in the afternoon, when he heard the roar of heavy machinery somewhere close, and was instantly awake.

"What the hell is that? Sounds like a tank." Muller, who'd been sleeping, rushed to one of the chinks between the logs to look out. Ingrid stepped aside, and Kurt, who was guarding them, looked anxiously toward the doorway.

"Listen. The sound has changed, like it's in gear." Kurt's voice went up a note higher than usual.

"Maybe it's that Navajo man who lives across the stream, down there in the house beside that other hogan. You said he was there the night you tried to find Nez and this woman." Ingrid grabbed Muller by the sleeve. "Did he have a tractor? I didn't see any fields, not big enough to plow, at least."

Lee looked at Diane, who shrugged. Like him, she was subtly stretching, getting ready to move quickly.

"Stay where you are," Kurt said, motioning toward her with his pistol. "You're not moving unless we move."

Lee listened, and thought he recognized the sound, having been around a lot of highway construction sites while on patrol. He nodded to Diane. "Sounds like good news to me."

"It's some kind of tracked machine! Listen to that clank.

Those are treads." Kurt's voice went up another level, and Muller nodded.

The German pilot turned to Lee. "That Navajo who lives near here. What does he do?"

"Some kind of medicine man, I think. But maybe he has a part-time job working for the highway department. Perhaps someone is grading the road."

Muller shook his head. "He knows about us, doesn't he? What did you tell him?"

"Oh, that a couple of vampires—three, I guess with the Amazon here—were out to get us. He believed that right away."

The sound of the machine was getting closer, and picking up speed. Muller looked at Kurt, then Ingrid. "Get them into the van, and watch them closely. If either one moves, shoot her in the stomach. That's particularly painful, I've learned."

The ground started shaking, and Ingrid looked back at Muller. "Come on you two, move now, or I'll shoot her."

Diane stood as slowly as she dared, and stepped forward. Ingrid pushed her toward the entrance. On the other side of the blanket was the open sliding door of the van. Diane stopped there, and Ingrid pushed her so hard, she fell onto the seat. "You next, cop."

Lee stepped forward, took Diane's arm, and led her to the backseat. It was a minivan designed for a large family with three bench seats. "Not all the way back, in the middle seat." Muller looked over, then motioned to Kurt.

"Get the shovels, the maps and blankets loaded up, quickly. We're going to have to get out of here," Muller yelled.

The ground was moving even more now, and dust was shaking down from the ceiling of the hogan. The covered hole, where Bowlegs's body had apparently been removed years earlier, was starting to change shape slightly. The logs on that wall had been cut open, and they weren't resting very securely anymore.

Kurt grabbed the remaining food and a blanket from the earthen floor. He moved past Muller, and sat down in the driver's position. Lee could see something large, lumbering, and yellow coming up the dirt track. It was definitely a bull-dozer, and he wagered that if the driver wasn't John Buck, he was still responsible for it.

Muller yanked the last blanket off the van, hopped in, closed the door, and turned to watch Lee and Diane. She was smiling. "I wish that was me on that bulldozer right now," she said.

A loud crunch was followed by a pine tree toppling like a fuzzy domino, and a massive, shining steel blade appeared just fifty feet away, lumbering toward them.

"Get moving. If he hits us with that blade, he'll open this van like a can of sardines," Muller yelled.

Kurt put the van into gear, and inched forward, running through waist-high brush that scratched noisily at the un-dercarriage. The vehicle rattled and rocked as he turned sharply to the left. The roar of the bulldozer was over-powering now, and Lee looked over his shoulder. The ma-chine sloughed to its left, and now was aimed directly to intercept the van.

"Faster. He's going to ram us!" Ingrid shouted, taking her eyes off Diane and Lee to stare, open-eyed, at the shiny blade and clanking treads that were approaching. Black smoke rose up from the tip of the exhaust stack, but the driver was out of view.

## CHAPTER 21

The van fishtailed, hopped over a rock in its way, and shot past the heavy caterpillar treads, quickly reaching the trail the machine had just made.

They bounced up and down like ripples across a pond on the hard earth formed into two corduroy tracks as Kurt tried to put some distance between them and the bulldozer. Lee's teeth rattled, but he managed to hang on and turn back to look at the dozer, which had already spun around and was coming in their direction again.

Ingrid was looking back too, and he thought of trying to grab her pistol. "Don't try it, Nez! Ingrid, pay attention! That slow machine will never catch us now," Muller yelled.

"Watch Nez. I've got an idea," Ingrid shouted back. "Let the dozer get closer, Kurt." She reached into her pocket and took out the grenade, then slid open the window about four inches, keeping her hand back from the opening and the direct rays of the sun. She pulled the ring, and held the grenade beside the window, watching the dozer rumble closer.

Lee couldn't reach Ingrid without jumping over the back of the seat, and Muller could stop him before he could do that. And if the grenade fell inside the vehicle, it would probably explode before anybody could pick it up and throw it outside. Diane would certainly be killed, and if there was a fire, they might all die.

"Slower, just a little closer," Ingrid teased.

Diane looked at Lee, then Ingrid. "Come on, raise that blade some more," she urged, noting that whoever was operating the dozer had raised the blade slightly to compensate for the uneven ground, not wanting to strike the surface at that speed and get thrown out of the operator's seat.

"Now!" Muller yelled, and Ingrid raised her hand and dropped the grenade from the window. Lee looked up and saw it bouncing along the ground just in front of the dozer. He reached over and pushed Diane down below the seat, covering her with his body just as the explosive device went off.

There was a muffled roar, the ground shook, and several small objects whistled by the van.

The bulldozer's engine noise dropped suddenly, and Lee looked back over the seat. Ingrid was watching out the back window, laughing. The big machine had thrown a track, and careened to the side before coming to a halt. "Got you, you sorry bastard."

Kurt drove down the trail toward the Interstate at a more leisurely pace now, avoiding the churned-up ground, and Lee looked anxiously for any other vehicles that might be around, possibly containing police officers, or even the FBI.

All he could see was a dump truck with a large trailer hooked up behind it parked on the trail. It belonged to one of the local highway department contractors. John Buck, or whoever was operating the dozer, had apparently come alone.

Suddenly there was a muffled gunshot and the right rear

tire of the van exploded. The van fishtailed, Kurt nearly losing control. Lee hung on, keeping one arm on Diane to steady her while turning to look for the source of the gunfire.

Beneath the trailer he caught a quick glimpse of a .30-30 poking out, and right away he knew where John Buck was. The vampires couldn't leave the vehicle now to fix the tire or run away, not with the sun at its brightest, and John was going to make sure they couldn't use the van to get very far either. He had a feeling John knew they were in the van too, and that's why he wasn't peppering the sides of the vehicle with bullets.

"That sounded like a shot. Where did it come from?" Muller looked around, trying to find the source.

Another shot rang out, and the van lurched again. "The other rear tire, it's gone too!" Ingrid looked around outside frantically, then spotted the rifle barrel under the semi.

"Back there, somebody with a rifle! Under the truck!"

"Keep moving! We're sitting ducks right now, and we can't leave the van. We'll fry in five minutes," Muller yelled.

Ingrid poked the barrel of her pistol out a small opening in the window.

"Don't! You'll never hit him from that angle, and our ears will be ringing for the next hour!"

"Damn." Ingrid shut the window and turned her pistol back toward Lee.

Kurt kept the van rolling on the tire rims, moving less than five miles an hour, down the dirt track toward the Interstate.

"What'll we do?" Kurt asked. "We can't go out on the highway like this, and we can't fix two tires. There's only one spare."

Muller looked ahead at the Interstate, constructed on a built-up ridge several feet above the floor of the valley.

"There." He pointed with his pistol. "Go through the underpass. There's an arroyo on the other side, and a small wooden bridge. I think there's a house up there somewhere, I remember seeing the lights last night. If we can get up there under the trees, we can pull into some shade and be able to get out of the van to fire down at the dozer if he fixes the track again and comes after us."

"We can also keep the rifleman at a distance," Kurt added.

"Once it's dark, we'll have the advantage. Be patient," Muller added. "It looks like this was the work of some of the locals, not the police, who are still wasting their time farther east. It's probably the man from that house closest to the hogan, the medicine man. Another friend of yours, Officer Nez?" Muller asked rhetorically.

At the speed the van was moving, it took ten minutes to reach the tree line on the upper slope of the valley. They nearly got stuck once when Kurt got off the tire ruts serving as a road. But Muller was worried about being stranded out in the open under sunlight, and insisted that Kurt keep moving forward.

Once they were under the shade of a tall pine, about fifty feet into the woods, Muller called for a halt. "Now we wait for sundown. Just keep watch for the man with the rifle. If he tries to come across the valley floor, we can catch him in the open."

"He'd have to be crazy to try that," Kurt said.

"The scales will tip in our favor soon. Once it's dark, we can track him down and take him out. Then we'll make one more attempt to get that buried box." Muller nodded. "Others are counting on us, and time is running out."

"I know just the way to convince our warrior cop to quit

stalling. I'll start by cutting off the pretty girl's fingers. Every time fifteen minutes go by that we don't have the box, she loses another. By the time an hour goes by, she'll probably have bled to death, though. How fast can you dig, cop?" Ingrid waved her blade around like a sword, making cutting noises until her husband started staring.

"There's a house around here somewhere, didn't you say?" Ingrid asked, quickly changing the subject.

"It must be farther up in the trees," Muller said with a shrug. "We'll have to keep watch until dark in case whoever is living there stumbles upon us. I doubt we'll have any problems, though. Of course, in the shade, we can always open the windows and shoot anyone who gets too close. If somebody gets curious and walks up, you two just start making out, and I'll say we came up here for a picnic. If they get too close, we'll shoot them, especially if Nez and the woman don't play along. Okay with you two?" Muller smiled at Lee and Diane.

"You think the driver of the dozer was injured?" Diane asked Lee, trying to ignore the vampires for a moment.

"I think the blade and the heavy segments of the track would have shielded him from the shrapnel. Hopefully, there are tools on the truck and trailer that brought it here, and he can make some repairs. If and when we go back over there after dark, I wouldn't be surprised to see it coming at us again." Lee didn't know how true that was, but he figured that anything to create doubt for the vampires was a useful strategy.

He was glad that Muller had decided to come up this particular slope seeking cover and protection. If anybody was in the area, the vampires would have a greeting party soon after dark, one they'd be surprised to see coming. He and Diane would be the ones knowing what was going on for a change. And this time, all the windows were already open.

After a while, with nothing to do but wait for dubious allies to make their move, he decided to try and warn Diane of what was to come. "Sitting here with you, looking out the window and breathing the fresh air, reminds me of the last time we were in my apartment in Los Cruces. We had dinner first, remember, Agent Lopez? Diane."

"Oh, no, not some romantic b.s. I thought you two didn't like each other." Ingrid chuckled. "Now I find out you've been spending time together in *his* apartment."

"I remember quite a bit about that evening." Diane's eyebrows rose, wondering what he was getting at. Then her eyes gleamed. "I've never been pawed so much in my life."

"Tonight I promise things will be different." Lee smiled as he realized Diane had understood something was up. "Smell the fresh air coming in?" Muller had rolled down one of the windows at the front of the van, which was in the deepest shade, and the breeze was blowing everyone's scent uphill, the right direction.

"You two shut up. Save your breath for digging. It won't be long until we can get moving again."

"Notice that the bulldozer hasn't moved? It looks like you two are going to be on your own again." Kurt had been guarding them, and turned to look across the valley. "With any kind of luck, this will be our last night here."

"That's what I'm hoping too." Diane looked up, flashing Ingrid a taunting grin. "Your last time anywhere, as a matter of fact."

"Shut up," Ingrid and Kurt said at the same time. Lee reached over and gave Diane's arm a gentle squeeze of encouragement. She caught his eye after the gesture, and he nodded subtly.

Nearly a half hour went by, and it was dark in the van, by ordinary human standards, which meant that only Diane's vision would be limited by the low light. The fact that they were parked among an unfamiliar stand of trees at the edge of a forest didn't bother the vampires much, Lee was glad to notice. Cockiness could be the weak spot of the strongest foe.

He was the only one who knew there was a skinwalker trail less than fifty feet from where the van was parked. If they'd made it back from Grants, the three Navajo women and the old man might have noticed his patrol car off the road not too far up the Interstate, and been watching for him all day. Now that the scent of three full-blooded vampires, plus himself, was nearly at their front door, he had a feeling the shape-shifters would be paying them a visit.

"Let me go try and see if there's a vehicle around here we can steal—maybe at that house around here. It would save us some time," Ingrid suggested.

Lee had been keeping watch, listening and looking for any signs of the skinwalkers. If they were around here at all, they were being extremely careful. He thought he'd seen an animal moving through the brush once, but it could have been just a shadow. If they'd caught his scent already, that would explain their caution, knowing that he knew they were around.

"I'm going with you," Kurt said. "We'll watch each other's backs."

Ingrid and Kurt stepped out of the partially open door of the van, and walked uphill, disappearing into the woods within a minute.

Trying to appear disinterested, and knowing Muller was watching him, he reached over and touched Diane on the arm. She smiled. "Hungry?"

"I could eat a horse, or even a wolf, if it would stand still long enough."

He heard the sound of someone crashing through the brush, and watched as Ingrid ran up to the van, an anxious look in her eyes. Kurt was right behind her, his pistol out.

"What's wrong?" Muller said, instantly alert for danger, trying to look past them into the trees.

"I heard something big moving through the brush, and it didn't sound like a man," Ingrid said, jumping quickly into the van and pulling out her pistol. Kurt stood just outside by the door, searching the shadows.

"Probably a cow." Lee shrugged. "The forest service leases grazing rights all over the area. Or could it be a Navajo vampire?"

"I bet it's your friend with the rifle, or a few local cops planning to ambush us once it got dark. Talk about a dumb move." Muller climbed out of the van and checked his pistol.

"You could be right, but if it was the guy with the rifle, and he knows what we are, he would have insisted on a daylight attack. Or maybe it's just whoever lives in that house up the hill. Either way, I think it's time we gave them a courtesy call, but with Ingrid here guarding our prisoners." Kurt nodded. "Shall we go hunting?"

"Why do I have to stay here and baby-sit these weaklings?" Ingrid had her courage back, apparently.

"We have more tactical training and combat experience, Ingrid, and you're finally out of grenades. But you have my permission to slap the woman around if they cause any trouble. Just don't injure her too much, unless you want to do her share of the digging," Muller instructed.

"What's a little digging?" Ingrid winked at Diane, who rolled her eyes.

The male vampires slipped away quickly, working their way uphill about fifteen feet apart from each other, advancing like combat veterans. They had their pistols ready, and were supremely confident. Something moved in the brush farther up the hill, and they quickened their pace, moving farther apart to outflank whatever it was.

Leaves rustled and Ingrid turned just as a golden blur of muscle and teeth leaped into the van through the open window, slamming her across the interior and into the passenger door. Her pistol went flying. The cougar ripped at her throat as Ingrid screamed, trying to hold the animal off with one hand while she groped blindly for her knife with the other.

Lee leaped forward and grabbed Ingrid's knife off the floor, whirling around just as an enormous gray wolf leaped into the van through the open door. The blade caught the beast on an outstretched leg, and the animal howled, twisting around to snap at Lee's arm. Lee dove out the door. Diane was already scrambling out the window, and he slammed the door shut and turned to grab her arms and pull. She flew out, knocking him down as she landed on top of him.

"Under the van!" He pushed her beneath and handed her the bloody knife he was holding, then ducked down as the wolf leaped out the window, slashing at his back with razor-sharp canines as it passed over him. Ingrid screamed hysterically inside the van as the cougar continued to maul her. She tried to climb out the passenger window, her bloody hands slipping against the metal, but was pulled back inside.

The wolf, limping badly but full of fight, crept uphill toward the sound of gunshots, ignoring Lee and Diane.

"There are two more skinwalkers. Stay under there, and stab anyone who isn't me that comes close."

Lee grabbed a dead limb from a pine and broke it off. Holding the jagged edge forward like a spear, he moved uphill in the direction the vampires had taken, keeping a sharp eye out for the wolf.

He heard shouts ahead, and gunfire. Trying to decide who was more dangerous, he crouched behind a rock and waited, watching. Ingrid's screams had stopped, and the cougar stepped back outside the van, blood on its muzzle. Lee noticed a light-colored streak on the side of its head, and knew it was the young Navajo woman who looked like Annie.

She stood and watched Lee for a second, then stuck her head beneath the van and growled. With a cry of pain, the cougar jumped back, licking a slash under her eye. The animal slipped off into the forest on the other side of the van.

Lee ran back to the van and opened the door, holding the jagged branch out to stab, if necessary. Ingrid fell out onto the ground, unconscious and bloody from a torn throat and shredded upper arms.

He grabbed Ingrid's pistol from the slippery, blood-soaked floor of the vehicle, and spotting another weapon and spare magazine under the seat, took those as well. "Diane," he whispered. "Out this side. Hurry!"

She scrambled out on her belly, watching all around for the wolf. Gunshots and shouting continued up the hill, and somebody yelled out in pain. An animal howled.

Lee turned to shoot Ingrid in the heart, then heard voices approaching.

"She's down for now," Diane whispered harshly, grabbing his arm. "It's payback time for Muller and Kurt."

"Hide behind the van by the front tire," Lee whispered. He handed her one of the pistols. She immediately checked to make sure there was a shell in the chamber, then moved away.

Lee ducked behind a tree, pistol in one hand and make-shift spear in the other, and noted that Diane had disappeared around the side of the van.

Muller staggered down the hill, dragging Kurt, whom he held under the arm. Both were covered in blood, and it was obvious that Kurt had suffered a bad head wound.

Muller looked dazed, and he'd been raked badly across the face. One eye was a mass of blood. His pistol was dangling from his bleeding hand.

Before Lee could fire at the man, the cougar with the knife wound on her face leaped from a pine tree and caught Muller in the upper back. The German vampire's pistol fired into the ground as he fell. Without Muller's support, Kurt collapsed like a sack of potatoes, facedown.

The cougar grabbed Muller by the neck and shook him like a rag doll, then began to drag him off toward a thicket.

"Finish off Kurt!" Lee yelled, then ran after the cougar hauling away Muller.

The mountain lion, hearing Lee, fled. Muller lay motionless on the ground, alone, just on the other side of the brush.

Lee shot him in the heart three times at point-blank range, then turned around, searching for Diane. He heard two shots. "Diane, where are you?" He ran back down the hill quickly.

"I'm here." She stood beside Kurt, who had Lee's make-shift spear impaled in his chest. When she saw Lee approaching, she waved.

A black panther leaped from behind a rock and struck Diane from behind, driving her to the ground.

"No!" Lee ran frantically toward her, hearing shots and not knowing if they were from his pistol or hers. He was there in a few seconds, tackling the big cat and yanking the animal off her with all the strength he could muster. He twisted the panther's head around, ignoring the teeth sinking into his arm, until the animal's neck popped. The creature yelped, then sagged lifelessly to the ground.

On his knees, he turned and found Diane lying there on her back, her collar ripped open and blood pouring from her shoulder and neck onto the ground.

"Not as fast as you," she whispered. "Did we get the vampires?"

Lee nodded. "Don't talk, don't move. I can stop the bleeding." He looked around frantically for something to use as a bandage.

"Never happen." Diane smiled weakly. Bubbles formed at the wound on her throat, and she coughed. "Is this what dying feels like?"

Lee took her hand, trying to think of a way to save Diane. The van would barely move, and the highway was more than a mile away. Any medical help was a half hour or more down the road. What could he do?

"Never told me about Annie. Guess you're off the hook." She had started to drift now, he could see it in her eyes.

"I'll miss you, night walker."

Lee held her hand, watching Diane slip away. With Annie, she'd been cold, dead for an hour or more when he found her body. If only he'd been there in time . . .

Lee ran clumsily around to the other side of the van

where Ingrid lay sprawled out, unconscious, but healing. The German woman was still alive. Diane had finished Kurt, but not Ingrid. Her blood still might save Diane.

Scooping up the injured vampire, he carried Ingrid around to the other side of the van, and lay her down next to Diane. He sat down his pistol and reached into his boot, looking for his knife, then remembered Kurt had taken it hours ago.

Lee felt a hand touch his shoulder, and his heart nearly stopped. He'd been so worried about Diane, he'd forgotten about Ingrid!

Turning, he met her gaze, and the hate inside her was terrible to see. He reached for his pistol, but it was gone, already in her hand.

"Your turn to die!" she screamed, pointing straight at his heart from two feet away.

There was an explosion, and a hole appeared in Ingrid's chest, spraying blood everywhere. Lee jerked away in shock.

Ingrid dropped the pistol and flopped down on her back, thrashing about like a fish out of water.

Lee turned and saw John Buck standing there, his .30-30 aimed at the woman vampire, who was wounded horribly but still not dead. John was pale, something you don't see often with a Navajo.

"What does it take to kill a creature like that?" the medicine man asked, his mouth open. He fired again, and the woman trembled as another hole appeared right above her heart. Finally she stopped moving.

"Thank you isn't enough," Lee mumbled, looking up at the medicine man, who kept looking back and forth between the dead panther, Ingrid, and blood-soaked Diane.

"Maybe I shouldn't have shot that night walker again, though. Can you save your friend with your own blood?"

He knew he had to try. He was only a half vampire, but perhaps he could keep her alive long enough to get some help.

Looking around, he found the knife on the ground, and quickly slashed his wrist. He felt cold as the blood oozed out, but knew he had to hurry.

Taking Diane's wrist, he made another cut, hoping she was still alive and pumping blood. As the precious fluid emerged, he pressed his seeping wound firmly against Diane's, praying that the blood would mingle, as it had so many years ago with him.

He sat there, holding their wounds together as one, looking for signs of life and healing in Diane's body.

Minutes went by, and Lee began to hear sounds in the forest around him, like the soft pad of footsteps. John turned around slowly, peering into the dark, his rifle up and ready. Neither spoke, not wanting to draw any more attention.

Keeping their wrists in contact, Lee turned as much as he could, checking from time to time for signs of an animal approaching. His night vision was a blessing, but it wouldn't let him see past the van to whatever was on the other side, and he couldn't see through the thick brush in several places.

Finally he noticed that the blood on Diane's neck wound had stopped seeping out. Was she dead? He reached over with his free hand and felt at her neck for her pulse, his hand shaking. Her heart was still beating, and if anything, was stronger than before. The gash at her throat was closing.

"Yes!" he yelled out loud, not caring if a pack of wolves was steps away. Lee took his wrist away from hers, and noted that both their cuts were healing.

"Give me a heart attack, will you? So she's alive?" The

medicine man gestured toward Diane. "I kind of like her, don't you?"

"Yes. You could say that." Lee took off his jacket, rolled it up, then slipped it under Diane's head as gently as he could. He picked up his pistol again now that both hands were free.

"What about the other night walkers? And the Navajo witches?" Buck looked around as he fed fresh rounds into his rifle. "I shot a wolf uphill from here. He was limping badly. Any others around?"

"A mountain lion—cougar. She was cut under her eye, and has a light-colored streak on her coat. I think it was the youngest woman, but wouldn't swear to it. Everyone else is dead, finally. At least I hope. Did you see the vampires over there?" He gestured with a cock of his head.

The *hataalii* nodded. "They looked really dead to me before. I'm not going any closer, though."

"Friend, did your uncle ever teach you the Sing needed to treat the vampire sickness?" Lee recalled how Bowlegs had treated him that night with special herbs and songs, helping to reduce the change in him, making him less than a full vampire, and able to withstand more sunlight.

"I know the Sing, but have never been asked to conduct it." Buck shrugged.

"She isn't Navajo. Will the ceremony work for her, *hataalii*? Maybe limit her affliction, as your uncle did for me?"

"We can try, but we need to get her to my medicine hogan soon. Can you carry her that far?" John looked around, wary of the skinwalker cougar still out there somewhere.

"To Albuquerque, if need be. Let's go now." Lee stuck his and Diane's pistol in his belt, then picked her up gently. She opened her eyes.

"Feel so strange, like in a dream. What's happening to me?" she whispered.

"No time to talk about it. We're going for help. Hang on to my neck." Lee started straight downhill ahead of the medicine man, who followed closely, his rifle ready.

Lee moved quickly, forcing the *hataalii* to jog to keep up, knowing that unless the medicine man could provide Diane with the powerful medicine necessary, she'd be a walker of the night like him. If not, at least she'd still be alive.

The cougar screamed loudly somewhere farther up the mountain, and the sound chilled Lee to his bones. He quickened his pace, and the medicine man did too.

"A black panther attacked me," Diane whispered in his ear. Her grip on him was now strong and steady, and he knew she was healed, at least physically.

"I should be dead, but I feel strong, Lee. Set me down, and I can walk." Diane patted him on the arm, and he stopped, easing her to the grass in front of him.

The *hataalii* caught up to them. "We must hurry if I'm going to be able to do anything to stop the changes." He looked at Diane, his eyes wide.

"You mixed my blood with theirs, didn't you?" Diane looked at the *hataalii*. "It's like daytime outside for me now, but the colors have all faded a bit, and the sky is gray. I'm a vampire now, aren't I? A night walker."

"It was me, not the *hataalii*, and it was my blood." Lee reached out and took her shoulders, turning her to face him. "I alone made that decision. It was the only way to save your life. You may hate me for it later, but for now we need to see if anything can be done to stop or slow the process. This man's uncle helped me, maybe the *hataalii* can do the same for you."

"Wait." John Buck held up his hand, then reached into his pocket and took out a flashlight. He aimed it down toward the underpass, and turned it on and off three times.

The roar of a diesel truck engine down below reached up the side of the valley to them, and headlights came on. "The bulldozer operator is waiting for my signal. He'll come to give us a ride to my medicine hogan."

Ten minutes later, the *hataalii* led Diane into his medicine hogan. Lee was standing outside beside the truck driver, who was looking at him strangely. It was understandable, considering the amount of dried blood that he and Diane had on their bodies and clothes, and the fact that they both looked perfectly healthy.

John appeared at the entrance, pushing aside the blanket. "Come inside, friend of my uncle. My patient wants you to be with her during the cure."

Lee stepped inside. Diane was seated on a sheepskin, and she looked up anxiously as he entered. "I don't blame you for this, Lee. I would have done the same for you, whether you liked it or not. I wanted you to know that before the medicine man begins."

Lee nodded. He still felt guilty, not for trying to save Diane no matter what the cost, but for doing it for selfish reasons. He'd grown attached to the woman, and would have done anything to save her. Now, unless the Navajo medicine worked on her more effectively than it did on him, she'd have to pay a price. Immortality meant some sorrows never ended, and she'd face an eternity in shadows—like him.

John Buck brought out his talisman against evil, blessed the three of them with corn pollen, and then produced an old-looking medicine pouch. He took two smaller pouches from the leather bag, then mixed the contents in a small pottery bowl. He added a liquid squeezed from an herb, then mixed the medicine and blessed it with a short song. Pouring hot water into the bowl from a container on the fire pit, he blessed the contents, then gave it to Diane.

She drank the liquid down, grimacing, as he sang a curing song. Then the medicine man began another preparation, and the process continued, for hours.

Finally, just before dawn, Diane went to sleep, exhausted from the ritual and all she had endured before it. Lee went outside with the *hataalii*. His friend, the bulldozer operator, had already left in the truck.

Lee wanted to ask about the process, and Diane's prognosis, but didn't want to seem to question the medicine man's skill. John Buck had already done so much for them, keeping them alive with his friend's help, then saving them from Ingrid.

"I know the questions in your mind. You want to know if the cure helped her or not. All I can tell you is that we'll know when she wakes up, after the sun comes out. You are only half vampire, so perhaps the cure will work on her. But be careful and don't let her injure herself finding out. If my medicine only works on the *Dineh*, then stay with her until she has a chance to adapt and accept what she has become. When it is dark again, you can go back and do whatever is needed to the remains of those you fought and defeated. I know you have other secrets to keep."

Buck continued. "Many times yesterday I thought about calling all those people on the paper you gave me, needing their help. But I finally decided they would have gotten you two killed in the process. They had no idea what was really going on. And I knew that you realized there were Navajo witches on that mountainside that would seek out the night walkers."

"And your friend, the bulldozer operator? He can be trusted?" Lee wondered how the man was accepting all he'd seen.

"He's my brother. He'll say nothing. I'm sure you'll have a good story to tell the state police and FBI when the time is right. Your enemies will be blamed for damaging the bull-dozer, I trust."

"I'll see to it personally. Thank you for everything. But remain vigilant. A mountain lion escaped last night, one with a human memory. She's an attractive young woman, but now may have a scar on her face, unless it heals when she changes form again. You will know her from a light streak in her hair."

"I'm not worried. Like wolves, when a witch pack is dec-imated, the survivors usually move on to new hunting grounds. I still have my rifle, and my dog is safe at my brother's home. He'll be back with me tomorrow."

The *hataalii* walked away slowly, rifle still in hand, and Lee watched until he'd reached his house. Then Lee went back into the hogan.

The sun would be up soon, and Diane would know if he'd doomed her to the loneliness of a night walker.

## CHAPTER 22

Lee sat down on the floor of the medicine hogan, watching Diane sleep, wondering if she was dreaming.

She looked small and vulnerable, and had thrown off most of the thin wool blanket that he'd covered her with earlier this morning.

But he knew Diane was strong inside, smart, and a woman of integrity. He'd gotten to know her as well as he'd known any woman, except for Annie, and he'd liked what he'd seen in her heart. She represented good, not evil, and he was certain she would never use her new abilities against others, as had Muller and his people.

Lee recalled what he'd felt and done when he'd discovered he'd been turned, and had become a walker of the night. He'd learned as a Navajo the importance of balance in nature, and in an individual's life. His thrill over immortality was tempered by his condemnation to life in the shadows and constant fear of discovery.

Vampires were one of humanity's biggest secrets, and the legends of old that had become grist for Hollywood movies and horror novels provided a distorted view of the reality one faced as a night walker. Some of the stories, such as the legendary avoidance of sunlight, were essentially true, while the blood feeding was quite wide of the mark. Blood was very nourishing for his kind, and it was the vector for the ailment. He supposed that was how the story began.

One truth in all the stories—movies, books, and reality alike—was the inherent loneliness most vampires faced unless they had another of their kind as a companion. Even then, they had to keep their lives a secret for fear of discovery.

The world just wasn't ready for a revelation like this, and perhaps it never would be, though he wondered if vampirism had been the basis for the promise of immortality certain religions gave as a reward for their followers.

"It wasn't just a dream, was it, Lee?" Diane said, and he turned to look down into her sleepy eyes.

He shook his head, and she sat up, pushing the blanket aside. "Do you think the *hataa* . . . medicine man, was able to help reduce the condition . . . of me being a vampire?" She started to stand, and he took her hand.

She rose easily, obviously strong and refreshed, and let go of his hand, checking her shoulder and moving her arm around tentatively. She then put her hand up to her blood-crusted throat. "I really need a bath, don't I?"

"We both do. But the wounds are healed. Notice how strong you feel, charged with energy?"

"Like I was a kid again. How long does the feeling last?" Diane looked at her hands, stretching out her fingers, then her arms in an enormous yawn. "Excuse me." She smiled.

"Glad to see that smile again. We haven't had much reason for that over the past several days, have we?" Lee reached for two cups sitting on a small shelf against the wall, and brought them over. "I have instant coffee already in these. Care for a cup?"

"I'd love one. Is there any sugar around?" She touched the pot Buck used to heat water, and noticed it was hot. "I'll pour."

A few minutes later, they were sipping their coffee, looking around the hogan, avoiding the obvious topic.

Finally Diane brought it up. "How will I know . . . if it worked?"

"Well, we know you can heal yourself, and your sight, even in the dim light here, is nearly perfect. Correct?"

"Still kind of dark, but I can see enough to get around. Certainly not perfect—not like last night. Maybe because you're half vampire, I'm only one quarter?" Diane said, then looked up at the blue sky that was visible through the smoke hole of the hogan. "What about that?"

"Unfortunately, the only way to find out is by sticking your finger into the sun's fire and seeing if you get burned," Lee said.

She looked at him skeptically. "You mean that, literally. Would I burst into flames, or something?"

"Not unless you're a full vampire. I've seen how they are affected by the sun, though, and I experience the same sensations, only more slowly and with much less intensity. The first thing that happens is that you immediately feel heat on the skin. In a few seconds more, the skin starts to darken, and within five minutes or less, a full vampire would be burning up, literally, as you said. After a few hours, you'd need dental records to be identified. It's disgusting, actually."

"And the reason Muller, Ingrid, and Kurt survived in New Mexico is by staying out of the sun, wearing gallons of sunblock, and covering their bodies completely. If I'm part vampire now, I'm going to need something besides my FBI standard-issue bad-ass shades."

"Exactly. But if your vision doesn't seem as good as it was last night, maybe you got a full cure, or at least more than I did. But before we start thinking about applying the lotion, we need to know."

She looked up again at the blue sky that was visible through the smoke hole, then shrugged. "Well, the sun's up now. Let's put it to the test." Diane stepped toward the blanket serving as a door.

"Let's take it slowly. You don't want to burn your eyes, then have to walk around blind until you heal. Just stick a finger out into the direct sunlight."

Diane reached out, moving her finger slowly toward a beam of light from the sun. Dust motes floated in the beam like tiny insects, and she hesitated. "I'll know if I'm like you, or them?"

"You'll know."

She stuck her finger out an inch farther, and held it there for a few seconds. "Can't feel a thing. I'll leave it out a while."

"Maybe you're completely cured. Be careful."

She stood there for about five minutes, then pulled her finger back. "The *hataalii*'s ceremony and herbs worked! I'm normal—well, for me."

"Yes, so it appears." He grabbed her hand and squeezed it, and she squeezed back, not letting go as she looked into his eyes.

"I don't have to cut myself, do I, just to make sure?"

"No. If the sun didn't get you, I wouldn't count on a quick heal either. You've got your life back now."

"I don't know if I should be happy or depressed about it though. Being a half vampire would have made me a kick-ass FBI agent." She grinned.

"You do pretty well just like you are, Diane. And you

have a lot more freedom than a night walker will ever have," Lee reminded. "You can still kick ass."

"True." She let go of his hand finally, and stepped back, her smile fading. "And that brings us back to some unfinished business. We'll hunt tonight as a team. How many shape-shifters got away?"

"There were four in that particular pack. At least two were killed last night, maybe a third one by Kurt and Muller before they were brought down."

"You are immune to their bites, right? I mean you won't turn into a skinwalker?"

"No, but you will. So be very careful."

"Always. Now tell me, did the mountain lion that I cut with the knife get away?"

"Yes. She's a young woman with a light streak in her hair. She and I have met before, and she's a crafty creature. She's . . ." Lee couldn't help but remember her face . . . Annie's face.

"She's what? Lee?"

"She reminds me of someone else I used to know, that's all. No big deal."

Diane looked at him closely, then either understood, or had the good sense not to pursue it further. "Okay, we'll catch them tonight. That's when they shape-shift?"

"Yes," Lee said, wondering if Diane would be depressed later once she realized she'd lost her chance at immortality. But right now, she seemed just happy to be alive. Near-death experiences had a tendency to do that, he'd discovered more than once.

"I think I'm going to enjoy this hunt, partner."

Lee nodded. They had become a real team the past few days, and Diane had discovered another world, and probably even more about herself and her own values and beliefs.

Soon their reasons for working together would end. How would she cope with the knowledge she had about him and that other, usually hidden world out there? He wanted them to stay close, though he knew that Annie's memory prevented anything deeper than friendship, at least for now.

He wondered how Diane felt about him, and what she was thinking right now. Then Lee wondered why that was so important to him, despite memories of Annie. "How about another cup of coffee?"

That night neither had much to say, except for some needed strategy discussions, though Diane seemed to appreciate his company. Lee drove down the dirt path past the derelict bulldozer in his police cruiser, which had apparently escaped close scrutiny from any passing authorities. Diane was in the passenger seat. They'd cleaned up, and were wearing clothes that were intact, thanks to loans from John Buck. They were also armed to the hilt now with nine-millimeter pistols and the department shotgun, which had been in the squad car instead of the optional AR-15 semi-auto assault rifle.

Lee had turned on his police radio and periodically heard calls asking for him, though it was apparent the dragnet for Muller's group was continuing full strength in Albuquerque, more than ninety miles away. But he'd only listened, not responding. They still had work to do that nobody else needed to know about before they could report Muller's demise.

"According to John's brother, nobody has come around looking for us, and no strangers have been by either, though several police cars have been through via the Interstate. I'm glad he was able to retrieve the squad car for us, and am frankly surprised that nobody had it towed away yesterday."

"Now that I've got some practical experience dealing with skinwalkers, and with your night vision, we should be able to track down this woman skinwalker before sunup. If she's still around, of course." Diane kept watch out her window as Lee drove beneath the underpass. The scars in the pavement left by the rims of the van yesterday were still obvious.

"We're past where the truck was waiting for us, and I think there are vehicle tracks over those." Lee looked ahead. He didn't have the headlights on, they weren't needed, and he was moving slowly so they wouldn't generate much vehicle noise.

He stopped and looked over the hood. "There's only one set, so they either came this way, or left, not both."

"You said earlier that the old Navajo man skinwalker had a pickup?"

"Right. Let's get out and walk from here," Lee suggested, stopping the slow-moving car. "Remember that the mountain lion was cut, but when she changed back into human form, she might have healed. So if the skinwalker, the young woman, shape-shifted back into an animal tonight, she's healed up and healthy."

Lee slipped out the driver's side, locked the door behind him, and joined Diane in front of the unit. She had the shotgun, and a pistol in her belt.

They moved uphill, not taking the path but moving wide to the left, intending to circle around from above, then eventually reach the van from the opposite side, the direction the black panther had come when it had attacked Diane. The wind was coming from the east, their right, so their scent wouldn't precede them into the area.

Lee and Diane moved swiftly now that they'd both had

the chance to eat and rest up from their ordeal. Diane's brief possession of vampire powers had resulted in the healing of all her minor cuts and muscle strains, and though no longer a walker of the night, she had bounce in her step again.

Eventually they reached a well-traveled path leading east and west, and Lee pointed out large wolf and cat tracks going in both directions. Diane had a flashlight, but didn't want to use it.

Taking the path west, they discovered it turned uphill, and soon Lee stopped and pointed to the roof of a small house built into the hillside.

There was a strong lock on the door, but it was simple in design, and Lee had it open in seconds while Diane kept watch. There were no lights on inside, but Diane had her flashlight.

"Whew! Sure smells like animals live here," Diane whispered. The house had two rooms, one a multipurpose living room-kitchen with a small color TV, an inexpensive wooden table with four chairs, and a small stove and refrigerator. The place was filthy, with dirty dishes in the sink and animal prints all over the worn vinyl floor. Cockroaches scattered from the sink, and flies hovered around a trail of dark splotches on the floor where a cougar had walked through drops of blood. There was a light fixture overhead in the center of the ceiling, but they kept the room dark.

Lee looked into the bedroom, and Diane joined him. There was one large bed, dirty sheets, and a large comforter. Mostly women's clothes were hanging from a metal rack or tossed over a small dressing table.

"Where did they all sleep?" she asked.

"Together. Navajo witches don't have the same taboos as the rest of us." He shrugged, then walked back into the living room.

Once it was clear the place was unoccupied, they left and continued east, staying just below the trail in the forest, moving side by side but fifteen feet apart. Lee kept checking the trees, and Diane, realizing he was looking for mountain lions, kept from walking beneath any trees big enough to hide such predators.

Lee stopped, and pointed ahead to a mound on the ground. Moving closer, Diane saw that it was a wolf, dead of multiple wounds, including a cut on the leg. Whoever this was had died in animal form, and would become fodder for scavengers. A second, older-looking wolf was also dead nearby, probably the one that had attacked Muller and Kurt first.

It took fifteen minutes to move around the location where the van had been parked. Something slipped through the brush just ahead, and both Lee and Diane raised their weapons quickly.

"It's a coyote. Much too small to be a skinwalker. Let it go," Lee whispered, then stepped forward.

They moved closer to the van, and saw the scavenged carcass of the long, jet-black panther.

Diane crouched down low and slipped around the side of the van, using her flashlight sparingly. The beam began shaking when she found the first vampire remains. "Ugh. Ingrid's burned to a crisp, but her clothes are still intact."

Lee came around from the front of the van and joined her. "It's a different kind of burning, oxidation still, but not the kind that causes forest fires, fortunately. That's what happens to the bodies when they're out in the sun, dead or alive. Remember what it looks like, and you'll know when a walker of the night has met his or her deadliest enemy."

Lee walked over to check on the other vampires, and his

heart began to beat faster. What if they weren't there, and hadn't really died last night like Ingrid?

He stopped and looked down, and he sighed audibly, finding Kurt's ashes. The branch Diane had jammed into his heart still stood there, pinning his shirt to the ground. Climbing up to the thicket, he also found Muller's body—at least what he'd become after death. Both bodies had been disturbed, and not by animals.

He went back down to Diane, who was sitting on the step of the van, still searching around Ingrid's body with her flashlight, her earlier attack of nerves replaced by cool analysis. "Somebody robbed her. Ingrid's watch and jewelry are gone, so's her money. Her purse has been searched as well. A human did this."

Lee nodded. "I noticed the outturned pockets and absence of watches on the men. This isn't the kind of thing a Navajo would normally do, hang around the dead. I expect it was the work of the surviving skinwalker, who came back after daylight in human form. If it was her, she must have left in the pickup with everything she could take from the bodies and the van. She probably has the weapons we left behind too, including our knives. I doubt we're going to find her around here. Like John Buck said, the survivor of the pack has moved on."

"You're certainly right about it being a woman." Diane set the shotgun down across her knees, still searching around with the flashlight.

"What did you see?"

Diane aimed her light at the purse. "Ingrid's makeup is missing too."

"So we'll watch for the young woman with the streak in her hair, okay? But I doubt she'll ever be coming back here." Lee wondered what he'd do if he encountered the skinwalker in her human form again. Could he kill someone who looked so much like Annie?

"Well, we've already discussed what to do next. Do we go ahead with that plan now?" Diane looked up at him.

"It'll be the only way to bring New Mexico back to normal. And some law-enforcement officers will finally get some sleep." Lee nodded.

"And the military and State Department, as well as the German government, will be the ones with sleepless nights for a while. But that's where it all started, I suppose."

Together, they walked quickly back to his patrol unit, and five minutes later, half of New Mexico was on the way to the foothills east of Fort Wingate.

Diane ran with Lee to her apartment door. "I wonder what the neighbor will think. I've never brought a man home. Well, I didn't till I met you." She sighed.

"Is that a good sigh, or a bad one?"

"How about an honest one? I can't say any more than that at the moment. I know I'm not the only woman in your life." She took off her jacket and started to sit down on the sofa, then caught herself and stood. "I'm too dirty to sit down, aren't I?"

Standing in the middle of the floor, she slipped off one of her shoes, then the other. Walking to the entrance to the short hallway, she turned to Lee. "I get the shower first!"

Lee looked down at his own dusty, dirty clothes, then shrugged. "It's your apartment. Just don't use all the hot water, okay?"

He sat down in the middle of the floor, eased down into a reclining position on the carpet, and went to sleep, his pistol by his side.

Lee woke up a half hour later. Diane, barefooted and wearing a T-shirt and blue jeans, was staring down at him pensively. "You could have used the couch, or the bed. Everything around here can be cleaned, you know."

"Don't know your rules—yet. Thanks anyway. I slept on the floor a lot when I was a kid."

"You ought to know by now I break a lot of rules. At least I have since I met you. Now go ahead and take a shower. I'll fix us some breakfast, and maybe even lunch. You have a hell of an appetite." She started for the kitchen area.

"I'll have to go back out to the car and bring in the shotgun and that uniform I borrowed." He put on his cap and sunglasses, then his leather driving gloves. "I also have the rest of that bottle of sunblock."

She picked up his pistol from the carpet. "Don't leave home without this either. We still have an enemy or two out there looking for us."

He nodded, taking the pistol and sticking it into his pocket. "Keep yours handy too."

"Right."

He hurried out to the car. With the sunblock on, he would be safe probably for an hour or more, but it never paid to take his time outside, he'd learned.

Five minutes later, he was back up in the apartment and in the shower, and fifteen minutes after that, they were together in the kitchen area, fixing breakfast and listening and half watching the television, which was across the room on a stand.

Every local television station and the cable news networks as well were talking about the unfolding story, which had interrupted regular programming.

Lee leaned back in his chair, shaking his head after listening for a full ten minutes. "So Wolfgang Muller and his companions were terrorists after a shipment of 'enriched uranium' that had been stolen in transit during World War II. I guess this is as close as they're ever going to get to the truth. What happened to rookie Benny Mondragon and all those soldiers will never reach the light of day. I doubt any records survived without being censored or maybe even doctored by the spy Nazi Germany had in place. I wonder if any of the men who took out the bodies and cleaned up the ambush site back in '45 are still alive?"

"Maybe somebody will finally come forward, though I doubt they knew about the plutonium," Diane said.

"The whole incident never made the newspapers back then except as a vaguely worded vehicle accident. No one in the military or scientific community ever said a word or wrote anything down officially about the theft, and I searched all the records I could find when they became declassified. When the atomic bomb was finally tested and successful, what some of the observers called the second sunrise, all attention was focused on ending the war."

"Well, the feds and state officials still had to give a reason for sealing off the area. If the feds had said plutonium this morning, it would have definitely caused a panic." Diane took a sip of coffee.

"At least John Buck will be given a fair shake. He's a hero now, along with his brother, for discovering the terrorists with the uranium and arranging for what some out-of-the-loop reporters are calling Navajo Justice. The land the feds are giving him in exchange is more than fair, along with all that financial compensation." Lee pushed his cup away, having finished a second cup, and knowing even that wouldn't keep him awake today.

"The press is still tiptoeing around the news that Navajos

were involved, and used wolf hybrids and a trained black panther to attack Muller and the Plummer couple. Then the hogwash that the Navajos burned the bodies. The dead wolves are being treated like heroes for stopping foreign terrorists. Maybe the wolf-reintroduction program will finally get some respect in New Mexico."

"Well, we're off the case now, officially, though we probably haven't heard the last of it." Lee walked over to the window and made sure the curtain was tightly drawn.

Diane shrugged. "I'm glad, at least, that we're not part of the team looking for the three Navajo women and the old man who lived in that house. Dead skinwalkers will be hard to find, and we're the only ones who can close that case. Well, and John Buck. But I think he and his brother will keep their mouths shut."

"Well, he and we know there's one other Navajo out there, that woman, who knows some of the truth, and we don't want to attract her attention," Lee continued. "But I'm going to track her down, you know. I have to. She knows what I am."

"And we still have to find the other skinwalker, the woman who killed my partner. That's how I got into all this with you in the first place." Diane nodded. "Count me in on the hunt."